A WOMAN ON THE RUN . . .

Suddenly she heard feet coming her way. Ahead of her she saw the two figures of her interrogators, the doctor and the cab driver. They were running now, and she heard the crunch of glass under their feet. Quickly she pushed the hand truck toward them. It collided with the cab driver, who fell into the broken glass. Sunny heard him scream and saw the figure of the doctor bending over him. The cab driver looked up at her. Blood was streaming down his face, and he held his palms up incredulously, examining the stigmata there. In the dim light, a shard of light glistened from his cheek.

"Get her," he said to his companion, his voice losing control. Sunny took off down another dark box-lined passage. "Get her," she heard again . . .

K.K.Beck

WITHOUT A TRACE

JOVE BOOKS, NEW YORK

WITHOUT A TRACE

A Jove Book/published by arrangement with
the author

PRINTING HISTORY
Jove edition/September 1988

ISBN: 0-515-09700-4

Jove Books are published by The Berkley Publishing Group,
200 Madison Avenue, New York, New York 10016.
The name "JOVE" and the "J" logo
are trademarks belonging to Jove Publications, Inc.

PRINTED IN THE UNITED STATES OF AMERICA

10 9 8 7 6 5 4 3 2 1

For Cousin Mosse,
formerly of the OSS

Tusen Takk

Prologue

THE BLOND MAN could see the cabin now, nestled against the forest at the edge of a glade. It was little more than a hut made of heavy logs. There were plenty of these cabins in Norway, summer places and abandoned homesteads that often served as informal shelters for groups of young skiers. The resistance groups had used them at the beginning of the war, during the short time they tried to fight the Germans openly, and now, in the underground war. The cabin looked like a glittery Christmas card, hunched under a bulbous mound of snow. In the summer, he knew, grass and wildflowers grew on the sod roof. He'd even seen goats grazing on top of a cabin like this one.

He stopped for a moment to rest against a fir. Skiing cross-country was hard work. He jammed his poles into a snowbank and slipped off his gray canvas knapsack. He was a young man, barely twenty-four, but he was tired. His face was sunburned and weathered, and his pale blue eyes, framed by squint lines, were older than twenty-four.

He thought about the cylindrical brass Primus stove in his knapsack and considered making some tea, but he didn't want to hang around any longer than he had to. He was a cautious man. His comrades sometimes thought he was too cautious. Because they were Norwegians, fighting defensively, fighting back against an occupier, their spirit was different from his. He was a German, an exile who had left his own country because of the National Socialists and then found himself fighting his own countrymen. His struggle lacked some of the reckless gaiety that occasionally cropped up among the Norwegians. Sometimes they reminded him of schoolchildren playing tricks on the teacher.

His caution had paid off. He was still alive, and now the war was almost over. From his knapsack he took a sandwich of dark rye bread spread with some lardlike imitation butter. He ate it rather meticulously and watched the wet snow slide from the branches around him and crash into the drifts. At every spring thaw he had wondered if the end of the war was coming soon. Now it really was coming. He smiled, thinking of a cache he'd saved for the day the Nazis were defeated. He'd wrapped several bundles of parachute silk from Allied drops and buried them under a large stone at the place near here. He knew what a superb present the meters of red and blue silk would make for some girl. It would probably be a German girl, because soon he would be going home. He'd be going home the victor. He presumed his mother was still alive.

Sometimes, when he was tired, he wished the struggle would end with the war, but he knew that the struggle to determine the nature of the peace would continue. It was already well underway, a dark undercurrent that sometimes flared into violence, in the resistance movements all over Europe. Here in Norway it had been comparatively peaceful, but he knew it might be different in Germany. Fascism must be rooted out completely, even if it meant more struggle.

He brushed a few crumbs of rye bread from his thick sweater, a Norwegian sweater with little V-shaped flecks across a field of blue, slipped back into his knapsack straps, and pushed off into the sloppy snow.

Who knows? Maybe this little errand has something to

do with the struggle to come. The thought intrigued him, but he checked it. It didn't do to speculate. Yet the order had come in an irregular way, not that there was any doubt about its authenticity.

He approached the cabin with firm strokes of his short wooden skis. No use acting hesitant. If you're walking into a trap, or skiing into one, it makes it all the worse if you look frightened.

The moss-covered door of rough planks swung slowly open. A tall man with dark hair stood there. He could only be an American, because he was smiling broadly in that silly way Americans seemed to do, and he had those American teeth, a straight white row that looked like it could crack walnuts. He certainly hadn't expected an American.

The stranger spoke. "It is a perfect day for taking a ski tour." He spoke in Norwegian, but being foreign himself, the blond man wasn't sure about his accent. It didn't sound particularly American. The characteristic singsong rhythm of authentic Norwegian was there, making a statement sound like a question.

"Yes" was the reply, which was absurd of course, because the snow was wet and slow. "I wish I had more time, but I must go back to Oslo. I am a student there."

"Do you study geology?"

"No, I study engineering."

This ritual over, the American or whatever he was smiled even more broadly. "Come in," he said hospitably, still speaking Norwegian. "I have some hot tea."

Hot tea sounded good, but unnecessary. He hesitated, then said: "Let us just transact our business. I have no time."

The American shrugged. "I'll bring you some." He went into the cabin and came back out immediately with a glass of tea. The blond man had never known Americans to drink tea from a glass in the Russian fashion, and it amused him. He took the glass and, although the tea was too hot, drank. Over the rim of the glass, he saw into the warm-looking interior of the cabin and smelled wood smoke and the close smell of human habitation. Inside, wrapped in blankets in a built-in bunk bed, was what appeared to be a sleeping man.

He didn't like the feel of it. These fellows should have been on skis, too, and taken off as soon as they turned the thing over. It was foolish to hole up anywhere. Concern must have shown on his face, because the smiling, dark-haired American now said: "We'll be getting on our way soon. My buddy here had a bad spill. Ankle's swollen. We're waiting for it to heal up." He reached inside his loose canvas jacket and handed over an oilskin packet.

The blond man finished his tea and gave back the glass. Should he offer to help in some way? "Perhaps I can send someone," he began.

"No" came a husky, weak voice from within the cabin. In English it said: "Tell him to take the packet and go." Was it American or British English? His ear wasn't keen enough to detect the difference.

The blond man was relieved. He hated any departure from the plan. Nodding curtly, he pushed off. As he skied back to the small railway station, mostly pleasantly down-hill, he thought about Americans. They seemed so foreign to him, so unlike Europeans. He had never understood them at all. He felt it might be important now to learn to understand them.

1

SUNNY SINCLAIR STOOD in the shade of the ramada, at the end of the turquoise pool, watching her daughter Audrey swim. Audrey swam in a sure, practiced fashion and in her white swimsuit looked young and strong with long tanned arms and legs. The two of them both had those long Scandinavian bones and looked remarkably alike, although Audrey's body lacked the tautness of her mother's.

It was a pity, thought Sunny as she collected empty glasses and plates from a low table in the shade of the ramada, that they hadn't given Audrey a Scandinavian name. Sunny had wanted to name her Solveig, which means Sunny, but Gordon had balked. Audrey sounded so English and respectable, and they'd just seen *Roman Holiday* with Audrey Hepburn, whom Gordon found enchanting, so Sunny had given in. Their son, Erik, had the Scandinavian name, and he didn't look it at all, with a shorter, stockier body type and American eyes, a mixture of everything, but mostly green and amber.

Audrey would do a few more laps. She always did. Sunny took the tray into the kitchen, dark in contrast to the bleached-out light of the patio, partly to escape the heat and partly to escape Audrey.

She wanted to tell her daughter about finding Billy St. Clair again, yet something stopped her. She wasn't sure what. Mother and daughter usually confided fully in each other. Perhaps it was a habit older than the habit of confidences; the habit of keeping secrets.

She put the dishes in the dishwasher, the lemonade in the refrigerator, the tray in its accustomed place on the sideboard, and sponged off the Mexican-tiled counter. The tiles were cobalt blue with flowers of bright orange, very festive, she had always thought, and nice and irregular because they were handmade. After twenty years she knew every bump in the surface.

Imagine seeing Billy St. Clair again, after all these years and at the Arizona Inn, too. Of course, it was a natural spot for Billy: elegant. The Duke and Duchess of Windsor had stayed there. There was some old saw about a café. If you sat there long enough, everyone in the world would pass by eventually. Was it in Paris? Wherever it was, she was sure Billy St. Clair had a regular table. Billy's job had been to find people. He'd found Sunny a long time ago, and now he had found her again.

What would Billy possibly want with her now? She was a respectable widow—a respectable, comfortably well-off widow, with two grown children, a sprawling adobe house that was much too grand for one person, especially a rather ascetic person, and a brief but exciting career a long time ago that she hadn't been able to discuss. Now, although the oath had expired, she still never discussed it.

"Mom?" Audrey padded into the kitchen. Water dripped from her swimsuit, and her fair hair, darkened by wetness, was slicked back. There were beads of water on her thick lashes.

"Why do you always come into the house wet?" said Sunny with a frown. After a swim she always rubbed herself dry with a nice rough towel.

"Why not? It all evaporates anyway. Why'd you take the

lemonade in?'' Opening the refrigerator, Audrey pulled out the green glass jug of lemonade. "Thank God,'' she said with feeling, "you have a pool. The whole time I was growing up I took it for granted. I love to come here now and get away from that damn apartment. Oh, did I tell you? The air-conditioning there is acting weird again. Makes that rackety noise.''

"I'm glad you come and see me," said Sunny. "I like you rummaging around in the refrigerator and leaving the cupboard doors hanging open. I like finding you've borrowed my clothes and thrown your laundry in with mine and left it for me to sort. Makes me feel wanted.''

Audrey laughed. "How can I take care of you in your old age when you still bring out the child in me? It's true, as soon as I walk in the door, I revert. Suddenly everything's easy again and you're here to take care of everything in that calm way of yours.''

Sunny kissed her daughter on the cheek. "Don't worry, as soon as I have some grandchildren I'll turn my attention to them and let you grow up.''

Audrey poured two glasses of lemonade, handed one to her mother, and set the other on the counter. "Carl and I talked about it again last night.'' She gnawed on her cuticle and looked deeply into Sunny's eyes.

Sunny resisted the temptation to yank her daughter's hand away from her mouth. "And?'' she said, trying to sound casual.

"He says we're still too young to take on the responsibility.''

"That's ridiculous. You're twenty-seven, Audrey.'' Sunny turned to the window above the sink and inspected the row of cacti in painted Mexican pots along the sill. Why keep cacti on the windowsill when there was a desertful right outside? Why grow them anyway? They were squat, ugly things. They didn't seem to need food or water, just an occasional dusting off.

"I know," said Audrey. "But he does want them eventually. He just doesn't want them now. There are so many things we still need."

"I'm sorry, darling. I don't mean to be a nag about this." She'd throw the depressing row of cacti out. Or plant them outside. Not that they'd care. "I know it's none of my business, but I'm worried you'll never get around to it. And you'll miss something. And I'll miss something." She sat down at the kitchen table, a delicate, glass-topped table of white wrought iron, frivolous and un-tablelike. "You see, I feel sort of between things. I'm not a mother anymore, really. Or a wife. Or anything. I'm marking time until I can be a grandmother. Can you understand that?"

Audrey sat down beside her and took her hand. "Mom! I had no idea you felt so strongly about it."

"You know what Betty Lacy told me the other day? Her first grandchild is about eighteen months now. She said it's as if she were watching a play, and the action slows down. Then, in the second act, a new character appears and everything takes on new interest."

"Mom, you can't expect us to have a child just so you can be a grandmother!"

Sunny did expect that, but she said: "Of course not. I don't want to be a pushy mother. Or one of those women who exist simply through their children. I always felt like that about Mama. We were her whole life, and whatever happened to us happened to her.

"You know, Audrey, when I moved to Arizona, after I was first married, I hated it here. It seemed alien and dry and ugly. But I felt a certain exhilaration at being away from Mama. I hope you and Erik never feel that way about me. I'm really ashamed of myself, carrying on about this grandchild business."

"You should have had a career, Mom."

Sunny laughed. "I suppose so. Been one of those hard-looking women who sold real estate in the fifties and made a fortune. Really, darling, I think it's wonderful how different things are for women today, but I wonder if jobs are really the answer to everything. One reason so many men are boring at parties is because they never had anything but their tedious careers.''

''You don't mean that about Daddy, do you?''

Sunny laughed. She felt in control again and relaxed against the back of her chair. ''No, I was never bored by your father. Exasperated once in a while, but never bored.''

''Are you bored now, Mom?''

''I guess I am.'' Sunny smiled. Thank God she was having dinner with Billy tonight. He really couldn't have come at a better time, whatever it was he wanted. And she felt sure he wanted something. Why else would he have said, although their meeting was supposedly a chance meeting, ''Thank goodness, Sunny, you don't have one of those leathery Arizona complexions. I was afraid I'd find you looking like an old, tanned hide.''

Later Sunny found herself preparing for dinner with Billy St. Clair with unaccustomed excitement. She gave a last, wide-eyed, checking-her-makeup look at herself in the sweep of mirror in the dressing room. Then, chiding herself for her vanity, she turned out the light on herself. The impression of her own face looking back at her became imprinted on her eyelids for a few seconds. It was a pleasant impression; a soft pair of blond waves, like bird's wings, shot through with silver, framing a squarish, delicately boned face. Her eyes were dark blue in an expanse of lightly tanned skin. Her mouth was intelligent but generous, and painted a shiny pink.

She wore a gray chiffon dress. It was too dressy for Tucson, but somehow Billy St. Clair brought out one's old high standards. Besides, it was a very flattering dress, and Billy hadn't seen her since she was a girl. She had never felt any attraction to Billy, though he had always charmed her, but she had her pride. While she couldn't look twenty again, she could still look pretty at fifty-seven. It was amazing to think that the war had ended thirty-five years ago this year.

When she saw Billy she was glad she'd chosen the gray chiffon. He looked very formal and elegant in a navy blue suit with a muted stripe. There was a linen handkerchief in his breast pocket, with three crisp points to it. He was already at their table, and while she was being seated by the maître d', Billy bobbed up and down nervously, brandishing a napkin and a smoldering cigarette. But when she smiled, he smiled back and he looked like his old self. It was a beautiful smile, which creased his round, pink face into a disconcerting network of wrinkles. His smile hadn't changed. Neither had his hair, which had always looked as if it were going to recede. It had apparently stopped a few distinguished inches into his temples.

"Ah, Miss Isdahl," he said in his Long Island drawl. He pronounced the name *Izzdle* instead of *Eece-doll,* making it sound like a WASP name. He fiddled with a martini glass.

"I'm Mrs. Sinclair now." She arranged the folds of her dress in her lap.

"Sinclair. Hate the name. People always think my name is Sinclair. '*Saint* Clair,' I say. Like St. Louis, Missouri." He glanced at her left hand, without the ring. "Divorced?" he said cheerfully.

"Widowed. And the ring was my grandmother's, so I gave it to my daughter when she got married."

"Ah." He favored her with another marvelous smile. "Still smoke?" Out came a black enamel case and a gold Dunhill lighter.

"No, but you've made it look so elegant, I think I'll have one." She felt a dizzy rush as he lit her cigarette, but the second puff tasted delicious. She made a mental note not to smoke another. She was enjoying this one too much.

"I'm married to number four now," said Billy.

"Sounds expensive."

"You may joke, but it's just 'cause I'm so old-fashioned. I

keep thinking I should make honest women of them." He reached inside his coat and flipped out a wallet. "Here's a picture of Kikuko." For a second Sunny thought he might have pictures of all his wives. Kikuko looked about Audrey's age, an attractive Japanese woman with dramatic makeup. Sunny thought it out of character for Billy to show family photographs. She imagined he was proud of Kikuko's youth. She had always found the practice of rich men taking on a series of youthful wives, despite their own advancing age, vulgar.

The waiter arrived. Sunny ordered a margarita. Billy eyed his empty martini glass, still sporting its olive. "I see you've gone completely native. Think I'll join you. Bring us two margaritas, please. But only if this lady promises to eat the salt from mine." He giggled.

"What have you been up to besides getting married and divorced?" said Sunny.

"Same old stuff. After the war I just kept at it. Never good for anything else. My father ran the family business into the ground, so I never got a chance. To run it into the ground myself, that is. Ha."

She thought Billy looked too old to be a spy. It was a silly thought, really, because he was about her age, and she never felt too old for anything, but Billy looked tired, and despite his good humor, he looked unhappy.

"Retired?"

He looked peevish. "Not taken out and shot yet, but out to pasture. One never really retires from our business completely."

"I did."

He brushed that aside. "They've got me semiretired. I'm writing my memoirs for the company library. We've got a library full of memoirs that no one outside the agency ever sees. We paw through yellowing old files and natter away to typists. Curious, isn't it? I suppose it's got to be done, for the future. But it's really a make-work project to keep old spies out of mischief. I doubt anyone will ever read it. They've got a lot of us old fossils cranking this stuff out.''

Sunny wished she could read Billy's memoirs. She envied him. He'd stayed close to it all. She wanted to know all about his career, but the old professional etiquette restrained her. If she was to learn anything, she'd have to sit and wait.

They each had another margarita. Billy asked Sunny all about her years with Gordon, her children, her life now. She never remembered Billy taking such an interest in another person's life. Perhaps he was less preoccupied with himself now. She rejected that idea. She decided she was being tested in some way.

''All sounds very nice,'' he said at the end of her sketchy biography. ''Life has treated you well. And you know, Sunny, you look absolutely marvelous. Tan, but not too tan. Rich. Thin. And still as attractive as ever.''

''Words to gladden an old widow's heart.''

''I would have recognized you anywhere.''

''Oh, come now. I was barely twenty. Surely you must have wondered if I was that same person.''

''Barely twenty.'' Billy's face took on a sentimental cast. ''My, we were all so young then, weren't we?''

''We didn't think so then.''

''Sunny, you wouldn't believe what the OSS turned into. Seeing you after all these years brings back the old days. We were great. The OSS was great. It was different then. Better. The young people who are running the CIA aren't like we were. Sometimes I'm ashamed for our country. To see something so noble and true veer off course . . .''

He reached over, took her hand and squeezed it, and drained his glass. Sunny thought they'd better get some food soon or Billy would be crying. Not that she wasn't somehow moved by his outburst.

Billy brandished cigarette case and lighter again. Sunny took her second cigarette. ''You know, Sunny, when I think about these bastards that are running things now, and get myself all worked up, I stop and think about us when we were it. The whole goddamned outfit. You know. what we had that these young kids don't?'' He paused theatrically. ''We had heart.''

''Are you sure you're not romanticizing?'' she said gently. ''We were just a lot of wholesome young Americans who were charged with saving the world. Thank God we were so young, or we might have been taken aback at the enormity of the task.''

Billy ignored her. ''Heart. We had heart. Remember? Say, remember Alex Markoff? Now, there was a guy with heart. I never see any young guys coming up in the agency like Alex.''

She drew in her breath. ''Alex! Billy, what happened to Alex? He died in the war, didn't he?''

''Alex? No.'' Billy's brows shot up in surprise. ''Is that what you thought?''

With a nearly imperceptible gesture of his hand, Billy flagged the waiter. Not one but two handsome young Latin waiters came to his side. Sunny was envious. Besides carrying a handbag and suitcases simultaneously, hailing waiters was the only task she had never been able to do well now that she was widowed.

From an inside pocket, Billy extracted a pair of horn-rimmed half-moon spectacles, the kind State Department spokesmen always seemed to wear at Congressional hearings on TV. He examined first the wine list, then the menu, then the two side by side. ''Tell me, Sunny, do you think seafood this far from the ocean is wise?'' He made his mouth into a prissy, contemplative rosebud.

''We're not that far from the ocean. Guaymas, in Mexico, is just a few hours away.'' Sunny really had no idea whether they imported fish from Mexico. One of the waiters assured Billy the fish was not frozen.

"The sole looks interesting," Billy said.

"The sole is fine." She had never cared much about food. She wanted to finish ordering so she could hear about Alex.

"And to begin?" Billy peered over the spectacles and the menu, looking like Alice's Cheshire cat.

"You decide," said Sunny impatiently.

"Fine, fine." He looked relieved. It was obvious he relished the idea of selecting a meal without the irritating interference of a second party.

"I chose the sole," he explained to the wine steward, "because of the 1971 Montrachet."

"Excellent choice, sir."

"Yes, yes. Of course. Now, while we're waiting, bring us a bottle of this." He poked at the list.

"Aren't you ashamed of yourself?" said Sunny. "Being a wine connoisseur and starting out with cocktails. Bad for the palate, isn't it?"

Billy laughed. "I just like to drink, period. Now, what were we talking about? Heart. That was it."

"Alex Markoff," she corrected.

A split of champagne arrived. Billy waved the waiter away and began twisting off the wire himself. Was this an old spy's habit, sending away the waiter so he could go on with his recruitment pitch or whatever it was Billy had talked about in restaurants for the last thirty-odd years? The cork pushed gently against his palm with a little hiss. He poured out the glasses. "Now, that'll wash away those nasty cocktails and clear our palates for the Montrachet. Not a bad list for out in the middle of the damned desert.

"To heart," he toasted.

Sunny was always a little embarrassed by toasting. Her childhood had been filled with the interminable Norwegian *skøls*. As a teenager she'd been taught the proper technique. At some point during the meal you must establish eye contact with everyone at the table. The eyes must meet, you must drink (or pretend to if your glass was empty), and your eyes must meet again. Mama and Papa had even toasted regular Americans like that, and the guests were invariably confused. At weddings and funerals came the long, mawkish toasts.

"Heart. *Skøl*," she said brusquely. "Now, please tell me about Alex."

"Did what I did. Joined up for the Cold War. Handy fellow for the times. White Russian family, you know. Spoke the language fluently."

"Is he one of the old fossils writing their memoirs?" She couldn't imagine this, but it made sense.

Billy looked uncomfortable. "Hardly. Accident. Or suicide. Took his little sailboat out on San Francisco Bay. It drifted back to shore without Alex."

"I can't believe it." She set her glass down firmly. "When?"

"About ten years ago. Surprised you didn't read about it. The papers picked it up because of his company connections. He'd resigned. Had a bad patch in Southeast Asia." He frowned. "Should have been riding a desk. Too old for the field."

Sunny's eyes filled with tears. She blinked them back, thinking protectively of her mascara.

"My goodness, dear girl. You look positively ashen. Have a little champagne," he said kindly. "I didn't know you were so close."

Sunny took a sip. "It was a long time ago."

"And he was the first one, wasn't he?" said Billy simply. "And you loved him. How delightful for you both.

"Now, my first one was Frau Schultz, our German tutor. Or tutoress, I suppose I should say. I didn't love Frau Schultz. As a matter of fact, I was terrified of her. She was a hearty, stout thing. Physical culture enthusiast. I guess that's why she needed a wiry fifteen-year-old boy."

Sunny laughed.

"There," he said. "That's better."

"Billy, he was so young when I knew him. He loved life. He never had a bad patch. He'd never been disappointed. But it can't have been suicide. Surely it must have been an accident."

"There was a note. Maybe it was better. He knew where a lot of bodies were buried. Besides," he added, "there wasn't any place for him anymore. He had heart."

"So did you, Billy."

"Mine got lost along the way. But you know, Sunny, I think it's still here somewhere." He tapped his chest. "Who knows, it might come in handy again."

She frowned. All this talk about heart embarrassed her.

"And so might yours," he said. "Be needed again. It's such a rare thing these days. Ah, here comes our first course."

After dinner, Billy St. Clair congratulated himself on inserting the key on the first try. See, he told himself as he surveyed the interior of his little bungalow, you're not actually drunk. You just had a fine meal at the Arizona Inn, and you walked back perfectly through the lobby and out to your casita.

But Billy knew that he was drunk. God, during the war he'd been able to consume vast amounts of booze. Good stuff, too. Those were the glory days, they really were. Nice clean fight against a loathsome enemy. And England. London! It was a wonderful time to be young. The most gallant men from all over Europe and America were there. Kings and queens, too. And beautiful girls. There were lots of beautiful girls and they all knew a fellow might die tomorrow, so it would only be the decent thing to do to let him die happy.

He'd been able to profit from the girls' generous impulses with vast amounts of booze in him, and if necessary, in the girls. He couldn't do that anymore. And of course, having his Mayfair flat had helped, too. It had given him an enormous edge, and not just sexually. The flat, lent out to other guys by the night, meant favors. Good whiskey. Good introductions. Even the odd secret. The flat had been a gold mine. After all, in those days a man couldn't take a respectable-looking girl to a hotel, where all your pals would find out. Especially not a nice, respectable-looking girl like Sunny Isdahl.

Billy had been raised by an honest-to-God British nanny, so, even though he was more than a little drunk, he managed to remove his clothes, fold them neatly on his chair, give his shoes a quick brushing and brush off the shoulders of his coat, too. He did start to attack the coat with the shoe brush, but stopped himself in time.

Billy had also been brought up to take care with valuables in hotels, so he put his small gold cufflinks in a little leather pouch, and, after removing a pair of white silk pajamas and laying them out on the bed, he locked the pouch in his suitcase. When Billy stepped into the shower, he washed his pink, pear-shaped body with a cake of hard-milled Dunhill soap. He always traveled with his own soap. Hotel soap always smelled to him like sordid liaisons. He rubbed himself dry, placed his wallet and a Browning automatic under his pillow, got into his pajamas, poured himself a few fingers of Scotch in a toothbrush glass, and slipped into bed.

They wouldn't like it in Washington that he traveled with the Browning, especially inside the country. There'd been a big flap when he'd set off a hijack device in Honolulu once. It had been careless, but it was hard to break a lifelong habit. Now he always packed it in his suitcase. They were nothing but a bunch of damn college boys in Washington, whispering in the corridors that old St. Clair actually knew Wild Bill Donovan back at the dawn of time. How dare they tell him not to travel with the gun? Mother had always traveled with a gun, a pretty little ladies' gun. Only used it once that he knew of, when she winged that little Belgian in her hotel room.

Later Billy's brother, Edgar, had blamed Billy for the incident. "You know how she is when she drinks," he'd said. "These Europeans think American women are loose, especially when they travel alone as she does. You should have stayed closer to her, and this fellow wouldn't have misinterpreted her vivaciousness. He wouldn't have tried to force his way into her room in the first place."

Billy hadn't told Edgar that Mother had invited the fellow in. The gunplay took place an hour later. Billy had bought off the police and the Belgian. Was Mother the least bit grateful? Ha! "Edgar is right, Billy," she'd said, forgetting the real events as she did so often and so conveniently.

Edgar, good old Edgar, with the face of the Arrow Shirt man, and the guilelessness of a Henry James American hero, never knew Mother lied, or even that she believed her own lies. Easy to do, really, believe your own lies. An asset actually in Billy's line. He took a sip of Scotch.

He wondered if Edgar ever would have discovered the truth about Mother. He had half-heartedly hoped that someday he would, but Billy himself joined in the conspiracy, a conspiracy of the whole world almost, to keep Edgar pure. Even at Cambridge, surrounded by all kinds of decadent British aristocrats, a lot of them queers and degenerates and Moral Re-Armers and Communists and God knows what all, Edgar was always a blue-eyed innocent.

Any hope that he'd change someday was dashed the day he stepped on a land mine in North Africa that the French had claimed wasn't there at all. It was better that way maybe. Edgar never had to grow up. He was inspiring as a young dead hero. As an old man he would have been ridiculous.

Of course, Billy was becoming a little ridiculous as an old man, too. Girls didn't tell him he looked like William Powell anymore. They didn't know who William Powell was. But whatever anyone thought, Billy was still in there, pitching. The young punks back at Langley didn't know it, but he was in the game for one last inning. It might be the most important thing he'd ever done. For himself anyway.

He thought he had her. Sunny Isdahl. One more talk and she'd agree to help him. She'd certainly aged gracefully. All the better. If anyone could smoke him out, she could. She was still sexy and smart. She'd done a good job as a field agent back during the war. Just that one mission, of course, but she'd handled it well. And, more important, she liked the work.

When he'd recruited her before, back in 'forty-two, he hadn't been as shrewd as he was now. Since then, he'd recruited hundreds of agents, and he knew all the buttons to push, all the weaknesses to exploit. There were as many ways to recruit an agent as there were to skin a cat, but when you got someone like Sunny, you got them for life.

People like Sunny had a certain look. There was a little quiver of excitement about them when you skirted around secrets or danger. Some people just thrived on that excitement, on the idea that violence or the threat of violence lay underneath it all. Sunny Isdahl had that quality. Billy could be sure of it.

Had he sensed that about her back in 'forty-two? She had been a pretty girl, he remembered that, kind of soft and blond and cool. Funny, now that she was older she was much sexier. The softness was gone; now the essence was laid bare in her face and body, a kind of tension. All he remembered from back then was that he wanted to lay her when he got her to London. But he didn't remember the quiver of excitement, the look of the spy, in her then. Maybe he couldn't spot it then.

He never did lay her. No one did, as far as he knew, except of course Alex Markoff, and Billy didn't find that out until later. The first time Billy saw her he'd thought how hard to get she'd be. She was kind of spoiled-looking. There was a touch of sullenness about the mouth. She was certainly much more sophisticated than any little Norwegian girl from Seattle had the right to be at nineteen.

She'd just come in from tennis, and she threw her racket next to him on the sofa where he'd been waiting. She walked over to a low table with a sherry decanter and small, cut glasses, wearing her tennis dress, perfectly unaware that her long pale legs looked shockingly naked in the old-fashioned parlor. She poured them a sherry. The whole room smelled of sherry, and was hung, he recalled now, with brownish, highly varnished paintings.

"How would you like," he began as he always did and had ever since, "to do something for your country?"

"Which one," she said with a little frown.

"Which one?"

"Well, I'm an American of course," she'd said easily, "but I'm a Norwegian-American, and I've just come back from Norway. I'm doing Norwegian relief work now. Isn't that why you're here? Mama said you had something to do with the Norwegian relief effort."

"You can do something for both your countries, Miss Isdahl." All he'd had to go on were some clippings from the Seattle *Times*. They were feature stories about her lectures to women's groups. She also seemed to be organizing legions of knitters. There was a photograph of her in front of a mound of donated knitting wool. He hadn't expected her to be so poised, so grown-up, so attractive.

He'd wanted her for Washington, but now he decided she belonged in London. He'd manage to get her there. He wanted to surround himself with attractive young people, people to add to his circle of Edgar's old friends. She was a refreshingly different type.

"Your Norwegian, it's fluent?" he asked now.

"It's my first language. Can you use that?"

"We certainly can. The home front is important of course, but I think you can do much more valuable work than you're doing here."

Her face took on a nice animation. The sullenness vanished. He knew then that he had her.

Billy looked thoughtfully now at the last sip of Scotch. If only he'd be as successful with her the second time out. It had certainly been easy to find her. Maybe that was a good sign. He'd checked into the Arizona Inn and set about arranging a way for their paths to cross. Instead, she'd wandered into the bar with a group of friends. Billy almost laughed out loud when he saw her, because she was carrying a tennis racket this time, too. Instead of a tennis dress, though, she wore a masculine-looking white polo shirt and a pair of tailored white shorts. Her thighs hadn't changed a bit.

He'd thought getting her to help was a long shot. It really was a desperate situation, a situation that called for long shots. As soon as he saw her, though, he thought it wasn't such a crazy plan after all.

Sunny was born at home. Her mother, Anna Magdalena Isdahl, had an easy delivery (it was her second child) and felt sufficiently strong a few hours after the birth to bicker with her husband about the baby's name.

Mrs. Isdahl maintained that Sonja was too ordinary a name. She had something more elaborate in mind. Ottinius Isdahl, who had long felt the burden of a too-distinguished name, having been born the eighth child during a period in Norway when Latin-sounding names were popular, pointed out that here in America Sonja was not a common name.

Sonja had been the name of his nurse back in the old country, now well into her eighties and the recipient of a small stipend from her old charge. Sonja sent thick *lusekofter* sweaters she knit herself every Christmas, and she wrote letters on thin blue airmail paper, reminding Ottinius to take his daily jot of *tran*, or cod-liver oil, the universal Norwegian health tonic.

Finally Anna Magdalena collapsed back against the pillows. She agreed that the baby could be named after the old nurse, but that Sonja must be spelt Sonia, so her daughter wouldn't have to spend a lifetime correcting the spelling. Ottinius, gracious in victory as always, kissed his wife's forehead and suggested little Sonia share her middle name.

A few weeks later the baby was christened Sonia Magdalena in Seattle's largest Norwegian church. Pastor Hansen officiated. A hard-eyed man whose sermons about eternal damnation hadn't transplanted too well to a milder land where life was easier, Pastor Hansen drove more than a few well-heeled Norwegian families away from Lutheranism to the Espicopal church.

Little Sonia learned Norwegian and English simultaneously. In school her name became further anglicized to Sunny. The nickname stuck, and it seemed to fit her. She had a corona of red-gold hair and a friendly manner. At Queen Anne High School, Sunny was popular with boys, and with girls, too, some of whom felt that being her friend would make them more popular with boys. When she was sixteen, Ottinius gave her a baby-blue Ford, which she drove too fast and which made her life perfect.

New acquaintances always told Sunny that her nickname described her perfectly, but the impact of her youth and vitality obscured the fact that her eyes were a cool blue-gray with a shrewd light in them. Her last name, Isdahl, meant "valley of ice." No one noticed that it, too, caught some of her essential nature.

When Sunny was seventeen, her mother's sister Ragnhild took her to Norway. An adolescent trip to the old country was customary for families like the Isdahls. She went with her aunt because her mother didn't want to travel without her husband, and Ottinius had no desire to return home, even for a visit.

Sunny's father had left Norway after an obstreperous youth. His family had all but given up on him. When strings were pulled, and he sailed out as a young officer in the merchant marine, the family sighed a collective sigh of relief. They hoped he wouldn't jump ship in the tropics somewhere and lead a dissolute life—but if he did he would be unembarrassingly far from Kristiana, as Oslo was then called.

Instead, he jumped ship in Seattle. Actually, he resigned his commission in the proper manner. He met a girl, married her, started a ship's chandelry, and prospered.

His bride, Anna Magdalena Larsen, had come to America as a baby. There was already a thriving Norwegian colony in Seattle, whose members got along somewhat uneasily with the Danes, Finns, and Swedes. Her family formed part of a small circle of quasi-bohemians who thought of themselves as the intelligentsia of the Norwegian community.

Guardians of cultural life in Seattle as a whole didn't know the rather odd little group existed. They saw Norwegians principally as a valuable pool of scrupulously clean and God-fearing domestic servants. The hardworking fishermen and carpenters in Ballard, the Scandinavian neighborhood, ignored them, too.

So they got up their poetry readings and musicales and amateur theatricals strictly for their own benefit. It was in a Norwegian-language production of Ibsen's *A Doll's House* that Ottinius first saw Anna Magdalena. He thought her performance uninspired, but he decided he wanted to marry her.

Sunny hadn't wanted to take the trip. She sulked as her mother packed her trunk. All this carrying on about the old country embarrassed her. Besides, from everything she had heard, Norway looked exactly like home, with the same rocky coves, deep salt-water inlets, and fir-covered mountains. She had a very nice new boyfriend, whose family belonged to the Seattle Tennis Club, and she was planning to spend a good deal of time on her game.

In August of 1939, she wrote her parents:

"Dear Mama and Papa,

"I'm really sorry I was so ungrateful about the trip. Now

I'm glad I came. It's wonderful, too, to see Tante Regnhild so happy. I know she's grateful, Papa.

"Yesterday at breakfast, Uncle Eivind and Aunt Gudrun did just what you do, Mama. After they ate their boiled eggs, they poked a hole in the bottom of the shell with their spoon. I always thought it was your own crazy little habit. They explained that when you do it, you save a soul at sea!

"Mama, I bought some long earrings, the traditional *solje* kind with little dingle dangles all over them. I think they will look terrific with a simple black evening dress. I want one as soon as I come back. I know you've said not until I'm twenty, but I really think you're wrong.

"In your last letter you worried about the political situation, Papa. Don't worry. Nothing will happen. Why should the Germans invade? Uncle Eivind says the rest of Europe forgets about us up here and goes on with their wars on their own. If anything does happen we'll come straight home. They can't detain us, we're both Americans. But, as I said before, I can't imagine it happening. This is such a small, peaceful country, and now that it's summer the nights are deliciously long and we spend afternoons in our bathing suits lying on warm rocks above the fjord outside the summer place. I'm beginning to feel very much at home here. Love to everyone, Sonia."

2

THE MORNING AFTER dinner with Billy, Sunny was cross with herself. Her mouth felt like cotton-wool, her head ached. She fumbled at the side of the bed for the television remote control and turned on the *Today Show*. She'd give herself another twenty minutes, until nine, and then she'd go for her swim as usual.

She seldom drank too much, and even more seldom did she smoke, which made it all worse. Especially the inside of her mouth. She noticed with repugnance her gray chiffon dress sprawled on a small chair, and beneath it her shoes, one standing upright on its teetering heel, the other on its side.

Really, it was almost as if Billy had plied her with liquor. They'd had cocktails, champagne, white burgundy, sauterne, and then Cointreau. Of course, it was a sentimental sort of evening. Wincing, she decided that made it even more embarrassing. Billy had been mawkish about the old days, about London and Alex and Sunny and Wild Bill Donovan, for God's sake. And she'd gone along with it. They were like a couple of old drunks at the Veteran's Hall, weeping into their beer about what fun they'd had.

War was not supposed to be fun. Sure, they had both pretended it was the gallantry of it all that had been so moving. And she'd been one of the guys in a man's war. She'd liked that.

Billy had talked about "heart" over and over again. But she knew now, cold sober, that it wasn't "heart" that had motivated them. It was the sheer thrill of it all.

Thank God it wasn't hereditary. She'd been so relieved when her son, Erik, had done everything he could to get out of Vietnam. He'd succeeded finally, by getting a low number in the lottery.

She got out of bed and into her bathing suit. Better to shower after her swim and get the chlorine out of her hair. Chlorine yellowed gray hair. In the kitchen she fixed herself a drink of protein powder and raw egg in the blender. She may as well start detoxifying herself right away. Hangovers were a ghastly confirmation of human weakness.

As she sat at the kitchen table, drinking her protein drink and looking out at the desert, she wondered if she wasn't being too harsh with herself and with Billy. Maybe they had become the way they were, unhealthily thrilled by war, because they had been so young when it all started, when they'd been thrust into the thick of it. She'd been nineteen. Alex was a year older. Billy was just a little older than they had been, but he had seemed practically middle-aged then, partly because of the distinguished recession of hair at the temples, but also because he seemed sophisticated and world-weary.

Her own children at nineteen or twenty had been so sweet and amorphous. Audrey was still a plump adolescent, calling home from college, and later from her first apartment, collect. Erik had been gawky and stringy, working laboriously on his conscientious objector application as if it had been a school theme. Thank God they weren't poisoned by their war. Not directly anyway.

Her head had begun to clear by the time she dived into the deep end of the pool and started her laps. The freshness of the water finished the job. She always kept her pool a few degrees cooler than anyone else. She was tired as she neared the last of the twenty laps, but she pushed on. By the time she crawled out, she felt immensely better.

But she gave a suppressed scream as she headed toward the chair where she had draped her towel. A man was sitting there. Smiling like an apparition and dressed rather nattily in a beige tropical-weight suit, sat Billy. He handed her the towel.

"What are you doing here?" she snapped.

"Business."

"Don't tell me you're recruiting me again?" She made it sound like a joke.

"That's right," he said easily.

Sunny began to rub herself vigorously with the towel. "Don't be ridiculous. I had a delightful evening last night, Billy, but it's daylight now and I'm a respectable middle-aged lady and not about to get myself involved in any cloak and dagger stuff. And you shouldn't be, either. Aren't you supposed to be working on your memoirs?"

"That's right, but there's one last field assignment. A job I have to do. Unfinished business. My last bow. And I need you to help me."

Sunny sat opposite him in a white wicker chair. "What do you need?"

"I need you to find Alex."

"You told me he's dead."

"Everyone thought so. I don't think so anymore." Billy looked nervous. "How about offering me something?"

"I'll make some coffee."

"How about a nice Bloody Mary? I drank too much last night. Hair of the dog and all that."

Sunny frowned. "Worst thing for a hangover." But she led him into the living room and indicated the liquor cabinet. "I don't think there's any tomato juice. How about a screwdriver?" She went into the bedroom and put on her terry cloth robe, and into the kitchen in search of ice and orange juice.

When she came back into the living room with a tray, Billy was on the sofa with a small attaché case in front of him on the coffee table. He looked alarmingly like an insurance salesman, except for the vodka bottle in his hand.

Sunny knelt at the coffee table and mixed his drink, making it weak. He was an alcoholic, she decided, and she shouldn't be giving him this, but after all, it wasn't really her problem.

Billy sipped his drink. "Alex Markoff engineered his own disappearance," he said solemnly. "He had knowledge of agency activities in Southeast Asia that would have been more than embarrassing for our government. He was afraid for his life."

"But you were so sure last night that he killed himself."

He shrugged. "I wondered what your opinion was."

"My opinion? I haven't seen the man in years. I don't have an opinion. But if he was afraid for his life, why would he kill himself to save it?"

"Precisely," said Billy.

"Afraid for his life sounds a little dramatic anyway." Sunny frowned.

Billy waved his hand impatiently. "Or he was afraid he'd have to give embarrassing testimony. I don't know. Anyway, we think we've spotted him alive. Recently."

"Where?"

"That's not important yet. Listen to the rest. He was afraid he'd have to testify and jeopardize his agents in Southeast Asia. Who knows? The point is, they looked for him then and they couldn't find him. They gave up. I mean it wasn't as if he were publishing the names of active agents like *some* of our ex-employees. Besides, pretty soon no one cared about Vietnam anymore.

"The important fact is this." Billy leaned forward. "Something's come up recently. Something with which Alex was involved. And now the company wants him again. They really want him. He knows something terribly important, something he may not know the value of. When they find him they will probably kill him.''

"After ten years of not looking?"

"They wanted him for a different reason ten years ago. Something else has surfaced."

"Can you tell me what?"

"I don't know. I don't know as much as I used to. But I know more than I should. I've been able to keep track of things in the agency. And I'm afraid these smart-ass kids want to kill Alex."

"In the movies," said Sunny, "you people don't say 'kill.' You say 'terminate with extreme prejudice.' ''

"Those punk kids might. I don't. I say kill. As in 'Thou Shalt Not.' ''

Sunny wondered whether Billy were crazy or drunk or both. She suspected the latter. Whatever he·was, he was a security risk. She wondered if they kept an eye on him when he wasn't working on his memoirs. Or if he was working on his memoirs so they could keep an eye on him.

"So what do you want me to do?"

"I think you can find Alex."

"Why should I be able to if the CIA can't? If you can't?"

"Because you were lovers a long time ago. And he cared about you. And he might trust you. I want you to find him and warn him."

"Billy, this makes no sense. I'm supposed to find him where everyone else has failed, that is, *if* he's alive, and then tell him to continue to do what he's doing. If he's hiding he doesn't need someone to tell him to go into hiding."

Billy looked annoyed. "He needs all the information he can get. Say he knows something they don't want told. If he goes public, they can't kill him, and there wouldn't be reason to. Or say he thinks the other thing has cooled down, and he can come home again. He needs to know what's waiting for him."

Billy rattled the ice cubes in his glass.

"Billy," said Sunny gently, "this is silly. I don't want you to tell me any more about this. Alex is probably dead. And if he isn't, well, there's really nothing I can do to find him."

"You were a damn good agent," said Billy.

"Don't be ridiculous," said Sunny. "I was a translator. I had one field assignment."

"And you acquitted yourself well. You got a medal from the Norwegian government."

Sunny laughed. "It's a small country. Everyone in the unit got one."

Billy opened the attaché case and came up with a manila file folder. "This is part of Alex's file. I guess you'd call it the salient points." Beneath the manila folder lay packets of cash bound with red rubber bands.

"Billy, you shouldn't even have that file," she said, trying to ignore the cash.

"Goddamnit, why the hell shouldn't I?" His face reddened. "I worked with the guy. I cared about him. I still do. Sunny, I was his best friend in the world. You cared about him, too. I think he deserves a break from his old friends. God knows he's not going to get one from anyone else. Come here. Take a look."

Gingerly Sunny joined Billy on the sofa. He had an outline, just places and dates, in front of him.

"Alex Markoff left London before VE Day. Went into Norway." Sunny felt a stab of hatred. If he'd been alive, why hadn't he tried to find her? They'd talked about being together after the war.

"Went to the Russian-Norwegian border. Had himself repatriated as a Russian soldier. Alex was an American agent in Russia at the beginning of the Cold War. By the time Churchill and Stalin and Truman were at Potsdam, Alex was setting up a network inside Russia. We knew that would be the next one, and we were ready."

"So he couldn't say good-bye." Sunny remembered the

last time they'd been together. Now she understood a little better.

"They needed him. He came from a White Russian family. He spoke fluent Russian." He cleared his throat and took another sip. "Finally he came home. Via Iran. He married in 'forty-nine. I was best man. Nice woman. I knew her. High-strung blonde. They had a couple of kids. But his wife wasn't suited to the life. When she married him, she thought he'd be spending the rest of his career at Langley.

"He didn't. In the fifties he ended up in Tibet. Remember the Dalai Lama, all that? He was there then, working with the Tibetans. It was a lost cause, and like some of our other guys there, Alex identified strongly with the Tibetans. When he came back, when it was all over, he wasn't the same. I knew him then, Sunny. He had a Tibetan prayer wheel, I swear to God, and he was saying Tibetan prayers for the return of the Dalai Lama and the victory of the Tibetan troops.

"That kind of scared the agency. He was kind of Zenny, I guess you'd call it. I don't think his wife liked it much, either. Here she was, in the Junior League, and tied up with this guy mumbling Tibetan prayers to himself. It was a rough time. I think maybe she was relieved when he'd pulled himself together enough to get himself back into the field.

"This time he took Gloria with him. He worked with diplomatic cover in various spots around the world. Nothing really on the cutting edge, because they didn't really trust him not to flip back into his mystical stuff. His wife liked the embassy life. They were posted in Ankara, Brussels, Johannesburg, and London. The kids went to American schools; Gloria was active in the American women's clubs.

"By the mid-sixties his diplomatic cover had worn pretty thin. It didn't really matter, I suppose. In a sense, they were just parking him.

"But somehow he managed to get himself into Southeast Asia. I don't know much about that. No one does. It was high-powered stuff. Maybe one of the reasons he got the job was that he'd been away from the central action for so long. He was a good man for a very covert mission. And he'd proved himself setting up reliable networks.''

Billy stopped for breath and gave Sunny a long hard look.

"Maybe I'll join you," she said. She got a glass from the liquor cabinet and made herself a screwdriver with the melting ice cubes.

"Sunny, will you do it? Will you help Alex?" His voice was low, almost a whisper. The cheap seductiveness of his voice annoyed her. She set down her drink, deciding not to have it. She noticed his glass was empty. With the inbred instincts of a hostess, she handed her own, fresh drink to him. His shamefaced acceptance of the drink, his hand out in a snakelike gesture, made her pity him, but her pity was edged with contempt.

Did Billy care this much about Alex? Or did he just want to get back in the game?

"Of course not. It's absurd." She looked down at the gaping attaché case. "And what are you doing lugging all that money around?"

Billy smiled. "I made a little trip to Las Vegas. I got you some freshly laundered old money. You'll need funds. The assignment might take you far afield."

"It's absurd, Billy." The bundles of gray-green bills in red rubber bands looked like something from a film. "And besides, how am I supposed to find him?"

"If I knew that"—he sighed—"I could have done it myself. The strongest lead is the daughter. Marina." From another manila file folder he produced a glossy photograph of a woman. She looked about twenty-five or so, with dark hair and level, intelligent dark eyes. She was smiling, but there was something sad about the face.

"Marina lives in Burlingame, California. She's married now. Marina Markoff Cooper. She's right in the phone book. No attempt to hide, but won't cooperate. She denies her father's alive. The agency has worked very hard to find out if she believes differently. If they're in communication. She's very paranoid about the agency. As well she should be. I think she knows they may be out to kill her father.

"I've made less conventional approaches myself. But she doesn't trust me any more than she trusts the CIA."

"Well, you are the CIA," said Sunny.

"Maybe someone from outside the agency . . ."

Sunny picked up the photograph and looked at it carefully. "Looks like her father," she said.

"Want to look at a few more family snaps?" said Billy pleasantly, handing her the file.

Sunny wondered how often spies let people take their picture. She half-expected grainy shots, taken from parked vans of an aging Alex huddled over a drink at a foreign café, trenchcoat collar turned up. Instead she saw the usual collection any family had. A wedding picture, Alex in a morning coat smiling eagerly into the camera, his bride turned up toward him, showing a neat profile, a broad forehead, carefully waved blonde hair topped by a cascade of wedding veil. The lipstick of the era photographed black, in the black and white picture.

A family group on some suburban lawn. Two children, Alex, a little thicker than when she had known him, in a crazy Hawaiian shirt, grinning again. She had always thought of him as kind of brooding. In these pictures he looked like a happy family man.

Billy pointed to a little boy in one of the shots. "The son here, Ivan, died later. Vietnam."

"Oh, there's Pamela," said Sunny. "I knew her during the war. My flat mate. Remember? And Lars!"

"I remember," said Billy, reached into his jacket for his cigarette case.

Alex and his wife and Pamela and Lars were sitting around a nightclub table. There was a clutter of glasses and ashtrays on the table. The women wore evening hats. Sunny had

almost forgotten the day when cocktails meant a black velvet
bow on a bit of veil. That's what Pamela was wearing. Alex's
wife, Gloria, had a very chic creation of white feathers,
though perhaps they were pink or pale blue—she couldn't
tell from the black and white photograph. Sunny had had a
hat like that, almost a cage of stiff veiling and a few floaty
feathers on top. She couldn't imagine Audrey wearing
anything so silly, although Sunny had been about the same
age.

She pushed the pictures back into the file. "There's really
no point in thinking about this, Billy," she began.

"Well, think about it a little bit," said Billy, leaning back
and blowing rings of smoke toward the ceiling.

"I can't," she said. "I can't do it. And right now I have a
luncheon appointment. I have to get ready." She stood up.

He downed his drink in several gulps. "I'll be in touch."
He made his way out of the living room and she followed
him. "Don't see me out," he said. A few minutes later she
heard a car pull up, stop, and leave.

Later, as she walked back into the living room, dressed to
go out, clipping on an earring, she realized he'd left the
attaché case behind. The folders, however, with Alex's
résumé and family photographs, were gone.

"Damn," she thought, surveying the attaché case and
admiring its workmanship, lovely large cowhide stitches
outlining its oblong shape, "what will I do with that?"
Finally she put it between the mattress and the box springs in
the spare bedroom and set off for her lunch date.

Sunny had a standing lunch date once a month with two
women she'd known for years. They'd met when they'd all
come to the Southwest as brides through their husbands'
business connections. At first they had enjoyed complaining
about Tucson. Betty and Caroline were both from the East.
They longed for a change of seasons, for gardens (which were
nearly impossible to maintain in Southern Arizona, other
than dry-looking gardens of native cacti and succulents, with

the billow of a mesquite tree for contrast). At first, they had worn hats and gloves to lunch, but, as the years went by, they complained about Tucson less and less and their dress relaxed. Now white pants and canvas espadrilles and cotton knit tops in bright colors or vivid Pucci blouses had replaced the Grace Kelly powder-blue suits. As their children grew, native Arizonians, and as they learned to take a slower Latin pace, they settled into the rhythm of the Southwest. Now, instead of complaining about Arizona, they were apt to complain about the influx of Easterners, or Midwesterners, who had the tacky temerity to try and plant Eastern-style gardens when native plants were so obviously suitable, both aesthetically and ecologically. They all enjoyed *Sunset Magazine* and built ramadas and went shopping for antiques in Nogales. Today, as they sat at their favorite table going over the menus with a kind of feminine, giggly camaraderie, Sunny felt a new emotion. Much as she loved Betty and Caroline, she felt a small jot of smug superiority.

She bet that neither of them had been the subject of recruitment that morning. Even if Billy St. Clair were a rummy, washed-up old spy, he had tried to recruit her. And he'd tried to recruit her to find an old lover. Did Betty or Caroline even have old lovers?

It was only at dessert, always an occasion of good-natured banter about diets, that Caroline leaned over to Sunny and said:

"You know, my dear, a young man has been watching you throughout the meal." Betty giggled.

"You're joking," said Sunny, touching her throat in a self-conscious gesture.

"You can turn now," said Caroline, a sleek, dark woman who wore earrings of large single pearls.

Sunny turned. She half expected to find an old friend of her son's. Instead she saw herself looking at a young clean-cut man with gray eyes and the fair complexion of someone from out of Tucson. Their eyes met for a moment, and because she was too old to be coy, he lowered his gaze first. Something about the brief exchange made her wonder if he was somehow connected with Billy St. Clair.

But later she dismissed the thought. She was prepared to forget about Billy altogether, until she found a hand-delivered postcard from him in her mailbox.

She assumed it was hand-delivered. There was certainly no postmark. It was a garish color postcard of Mission San Xavier, and it said, in a loopy aristocratic hand, in fountain pen ink, "See you here at noon tomorrow. B. St.C."

Sunny was vexed. She was supposed to meet Billy at the mission? Well, it would be an opportunity to hand over the attaché case full of cash. God knows she had wondered what to do with that. She was still annoyed that she had to make a meeting at all to deliver it to him. She felt importuned by the whole incident. Billy had no right to come to her, play on her thirty-five-year-old feelings for Alex and then try and talk her into what she assumed could only be the crazy scheme of an alcoholic, probably psychotic, spy. There was an aura of seediness about it all. Yet, it never occurred to her not to make the meeting.

3

SUNNY HAD BEEN to Mission San Xavier many times before. It was a standard stopping point on her tours for out-of-town guests, first friends from Seattle, and later Gordon's business acquaintances and their wives. South of Tucson, halfway to the Mexican border, it was called "the White Dove of the Desert," and first-time visitors invariably remarked on the whiteness of the structure against the dark blue of the sky. It almost hurt your eyes.

Sunny pulled into the parking lot in front. It was hard to believe the mission was over two hundred years old. The dazzling white and the baroque detail gave it a youthful, almost festive appearance. Twin towers, one of them unfinished, flanked massive wooden arches, with intricate carvings. Behind the edifice, Sunny knew, were galleries and gardens, kitchens and dormitories for the fathers who had come to convert the Papago Indians. Now, the Indians well converted and the fathers mostly gone, it had a serene air about it, especially in the shady walled gardens, protected from the sun and the desert.

There were only a few cars in the parking lot. Mostly with Arizona or Mexican plates. There were a few California licenses, too. She wondered if any of them were Billy's.

Should she leave the attaché case in the car? Taking it

with her would be conspicuous, but handing it over in the parking lot would be, too, although there wasn't anyone in sight. She felt odd leaving a ton of cash in the car, so she took the case with her. In her rather prim skirt and blouse, high-heeled sandals on bare legs, she could be a route saleswoman who'd pulled off the road to see the mission. But why would the saleswoman take the attaché case with her? She changed her mind, opened the trunk, and threw the case in on top of her tennis racket. After locking the trunk, she went to the massive portals.

There was no sign of Billy. She decided against wandering around the sprawling complex. She would stay in the church itself. Hadn't her mother always told her, when they'd gone into a department store at Christmastime, "Now, if you get lost, don't move. Just stay in one place and you'll be easier to find"?

She slipped into the church, gaudily decorated with a massive gold altar and carvings of Indian cherubs. Some grim-looking European oils hung about, too, and the interior of the chapel was cool and smelled of incense.

A few large Papago women knelt at prayer, and Sunny stayed at the back. From outside she heard a young priest telling visitors in Spanish and English about the carvings.

"Here, on this side, we see a mouse. Now look, opposite him, on the other side of the door, we see a cat. There is an Indian legend about these carvings."

Sunny knew the legend. When the cat, who was poised to pounce on the mouse, finally did, the world would end. Or, more correctly perhaps, Jesus would come back to earth and judge the quick and the dead. Sunny wondered if the Indians believed the part about Judgment Day. Maybe the fathers had added that. Maybe the Indians were like the old Norwegians, who believed that some day it would all end, and the gods themselves would die.

Looking around, at the alien church, at its gold and rather frightening-looking statues, Sunny wondered how Christianity could have shaken the old Norse from their belief that the universe was winding itself down and all would end with a twilight of the gods. Sunny checked her watch. Billy should have found her by now.

Really, she thought, trying not to think about Billy or the attaché case at her feet, the Norwegians had been converted so late, only about a thousand years ago, they probably still believed in the old gods, and the Lutheran church was probably just a thin veneer over paganism. Now that she thought about it, she herself thought a twilight of the gods theologically sound.

Sunny waited an hour. Then, ignoring her mother's advice in department stores, she wandered through the grounds, stopped in the gift shop, looking at cheap religious medals and the plain Papago baskets for sale, and went to her car.

There was a curious sense of letdown about the whole expedition. All she had wanted to do was to give Billy back his attaché case and tell him she wanted nothing to do with finding Alex. But she wondered, too, if she wasn't disappointed not just because the business remained unfinished, but because she'd wanted a taste, just a little tiny taste, of the old excitement.

Before getting behind the wheel, she went to the trunk lid and unlocked it. The case lay where she had left it. Suddenly she felt a shadow behind her. She turned and saw a young man. He was a bookish-looking young man, with a shock of lanky dark hair hanging from a crooked part. He wore a khaki suit over a white shirt, open at the collar. His throat, delicately boned, was badly sunburned. If the suit hadn't told her he was from out of town, the patch of sunburn on the throat did.

She slammed the trunk lid down, nearly smashing his hand, for he'd put his arm on her car, encircling her.

"Excuse me," he said softly. "I wonder if I could borrow your jack?"

"Sorry," she said sharply. "You should belong to Triple A."

"Why did you slam down the trunk lid like that?" he said.

"Aren't you going to take anything out? I hope I didn't startle you."

"Yes, you did, and I was just checking to make sure my tennis racket was here."

"It was," he said. "Along with a briefcase and a jack."

"I'm sorry," she said firmly, her eyes scanning the deserted parking lot. The dusty collection of cars looked as if they'd been abandoned for years. She wondered for a second if Billy wouldn't suddenly appear, or if this young man was a friend of Billy. If he was, it made no difference. The rule had always been not to deviate from the plan. "I'm in a hurry. I'm sure someone else here can help you."

She sidled away from him and got behind the wheel, locking the driver's side. She reached for the button that controlled the other door locks. Without the key in the ignition, they didn't work. She twisted the key jerkily in the ignition, but now the young man was leaning in the passenger-side window. "I'm sorry I startled you," he said. "I didn't mean to."

She smiled an unfriendly smile and flicked the button that raised the windows. The electronic sound of their rising seemed excruciatingly slow. She yanked the car in gear and lurched forward.

As she left the parking lot and the young man, she glanced around for a car with a flat tire. There weren't any she could see.

At home Sunny collapsed into a kitchen chair. And she realized she was scared. "Why have I let myself get so distraught?" she said to herself. She busied herself, locking all the doors, a complex process, for there were sliding glass doors from all the bedrooms and from the living room that led to the walled courtyard with its cooling fountain. Another set of sliding glass doors led to the pool and the ramada on the other side of the house.

This done, she busied herself with hiding Billy's attaché case. It would make more sense to hide the case and its contents separately. That way, if someone found the case empty, they'd think the contents were somewhere other than in the house.

She put the cash and the documents in a large grocery bag. She hadn't really examined the things before. It would have seemed as though she were accepting Billy's task, and she had promised herself to stay out of it. But now, against her will, she felt involved. After all, Billy hadn't showed up and the man in khaki had been interested in the attaché case. She put it back between the mattresses and box springs in the spare bedroom. It had been Erik's bedroom once, and although she'd replaced all the horrible relics of his adolescence—old road signs and a black-light machine and sports pennants—with delicate Indian baskets and old Navajo rugs, it still seemed like Erik's old room. Audrey's room was a study now, and was completely transformed.

She went back to the kitchen and examined the paper bag. She began to count the money, which looked old, soft, fuzzy at the edges, rather like the pages of library books. There were twenty packets, in thick red rubber bands. She counted two of the packets. Each of them had a thousand dollars: ten twenties, ten fifties, and three one hundreds. She assumed the rest of the packets were identical. Billy was so methodical. She flipped open a passport. It was a U.S. passport in the name of Harriet Grey. Sunny rather liked the name. Harriet's picture was Sunny's driver's license picture, blown up and retouched. Sunny had always hated the picture. She looked so severe. It didn't look to her like a real passport picture, anyway. Driver's license pictures are always taken in ordinary clothes. People are more likely to wear pearls for their passport picture and worry about their hair. Sunny was wearing a T-shirt and looking rushed.

Harriet Grey, Sunny discovered by flipping through the passport, had traveled to Europe. There were stamps from Heathrow and Charles de Gaulle airports, dated last year. Harriet had been born in San Francisco five years after

Sunny. Well, that was flattering. Billy had figured she could pass for a woman five years younger, maybe after he'd seen her driver's license photo. And of course, those five years would have kept her out of the war.

Harriet also had an American Express card, an I. Magnin card, and Visa. And a California driver's license. This picture, Sunny noticed with admiration, was her last driver's license picture, so it didn't match the passport picture. She wished they'd switched the pictures. The last driver's license picture was much more flattering. Harriet was divorced. Her signature was still blank. Sunny squinted at the driver's license signature. That would be easy enough. It looked remarkably like her own handwriting. Not the handwriting on her signature, which was a little more abstract than her regular hand, but the way she normally wrote, a slightly sketchy version of the Palmer method they'd learned in school. People had sometimes told Sunny she wrote like a teacher, but really the letters weren't connected and the flourishes had been stripped away over the years. Her hand was really an efficient imitation of the laborious handwriting they'd learned at school.

Sunny felt like getting a pen and signing the passport and credit cards, but that would be admitting she planned to launch Billy's search for Alex. She couldn't do that. Still, the incident with the man in seersucker had been disturbing. And Billy had said the agency was desperate enough to kill Alex. What if she wanted to leave the area quickly? She chose three different ballpoint pens from a mug in her study and practiced on a sheet of paper. Harriet Grey's signature was easy to forge. She took a deep breath and wrote the name five more times, quickly. The results looked very natural. H. M. Grey would be even easier. She filled in the strips on the credit cards and on the passport. Really, she was beginning to feel rather fond of Harriet. She wondered idly why Harriet had been divorced. Had her husband left her for a younger woman? It depended on when she'd been divorced. If it was recently, that might make sense. But maybe it had happened years ago. But then Harriet surely would have remarried by now. After all, even though there was a glut of women her age, she was certainly attractive. Sunny laughed at her own conceit and put the documents in with the cash.

Perhaps the case would be safe in the guesthouse. Of course, the guesthouse had already been broken into. But with the new lock installed, it was much more secure. And besides, she planned to hide the case well.

The guesthouse was about twenty-five yards from the house, at the far edge of the property. If Sunny had built it now, she would have put it closer to the house. It was too isolated to be completely secure. It was well above the flood line, but it overlooked a picturesque arroyo, a deep fissure in the desert full of smooth rocks and bits of gray-green scrub. An old mesquite tree gave the small adobe structure some shade, and Sunny had hung two long necklaces of ceramic shapes in red clay in the trees, giant wind chimes made by a potter friend.

Sunny and Gordon had built the guesthouse together, and Sunny had insisted on a cedar-lined closet. Moths weren't unknown here, and out-of-town guests often came from colder places and brought wool clothing.

She took the screwdriver she'd brought with her and pried open two cedar boards at the back of the closet. She remembered when she had tapped the finishing nails in herself, and she remembered the size of the space between the adobe and the closet wall. A four-by-four's width. Sunny and Gordon had bickered about it a little. Sunny felt they should use two-by-fours, but Gordon, always the thrifty Scot, wanted to use some old scraps of the bigger timbers. She pushed the bag up behind the boards and tapped the wall back into place with an old shoe tree she found there.

Her task completed, she sat heavily on the double bed and looked around the room. The guesthouse was charming, but ever since the break-in three weeks ago it had seemed a little ominous to her. Thank God they'd only broken into the guesthouse.

Sunny would never have known about it if she hadn't been taking care of Marjorie's damn Peke. He was a nervous, yappy little dog, and he woke Sunny at five in the morning. Mr. Lee scrabbled at the window and so Sunny let him out. But she heard such a fierce yapping over by the guesthouse she was afraid the dog had got tangled up with a coyote. Most of the time dogs and coyotes managed to coexist without too much friction, but because Marjorie's dog was so unrealistically scrappy for his size, and because he was Marjorie's dog, the last thing Sunny wanted to do was present her best friend with a dead dog on her arrival home. So she switched on the light, rummaged for slippers, stopped to inspect small teeth marks all over one of them, and cursed the Pekinese once more. Then she slipped into a robe and went out into the dawn with a thick flashlight.

Instead of a coyote, Sunny discovered the guesthouse door yawning open. "Who's in there?" she demanded angrily, imagining that whoever had been there had left, because the door was open. They'd probably left when they'd heard Mr. Lee and seen the light switched on up at the house. Still, she didn't want to go inside.

She called her nearest neighbor, a retired military man, who appeared in robe and pajamas. Together they inspected the guesthouse. The bed appeared to have been slept on, not in. There was a definitely human indentation on the bedspread. Sunny and her neighbor examined the ground around the guesthouse. There were footprints in the sand, and some bent twigs.

Nothing was missing. Sunny didn't bother to call the police. She and her neighbor decided it might be some illegal alien holing up for the night or perhaps some amorous teenagers. Sunny rather liked this explanation, but her neighbor snorted. "Forget it. You're showing your age, my dear. Nowadays they do it in those vans with dark windows. Or in motels. Or in their parents' houses. It's not like it was when we were young.'' Colonel Lewis, with his eagle's beak and white wavy hair, looked nothing like the amorous teenager he might once have been.

Erik and Audrey had been terribly upset by the incident. ''Mother, it's dangerous living here alone. You should get a dog.''

Sunny, remembering the tiny teeth marks on her slippers, shuddered, but did allow Erik to arrange for a tamper-proof lock on the guesthouse. He also inundated her with pamphlets about burglar alarms, now stacked on her desk waiting to be read.

Could the break-in have had something to do with Billy and Alex? Sunny doubted it. She even doubted that her precautions with Harriet Grey's identity cards and cash were necessary, but no one would know the lengths to which she had gone. There was something comforting about living alone, she thought. No one knew when you were being foolish.

She looked down at her hands, dusty from her efforts inside the closet. Really, the guesthouse needed a good cleaning. Still, since the break-in she'd seen it as invaded space and had kept away. She'd need new guests to exorcise the place. But now that the children were gone she was more likely to keep guests up in one of their old rooms. She frowned again at her dusty hands and went into the bathroom.

She hadn't been here at all since the break-in. She had simply poked her head in the door to see if it was occupied. Colonel Lewis had inspected the shower. There was nothing in here but soap and towels. She found a cake of her favorite English soap, shaped and scented like a lemon, which she kept for guests. It seemed wasteful to use it now and ruin it. But after all, she told herself, I can afford any kind of soap I want. I'll use it now and take it up to my bathroom.

She lathered her hands and looked into the shaving mirror. She was startled and frightened all out of proportion to see that four letters had been scrawled in soap across the mirror. The four letters that floated across the image of her face were T, A, K, K. Could they be the intruder's initials? That left out the illegal aliens. There were no K's in Spanish.

"Takk," she said aloud to herself over the sound of water rushing from the tap. "Or Tock." That's how you said *takk* in Norwegian. And in Norwegian, *takk* means "thank you."

4

CHANDLER TRIED TO look alert, intelligent and not too curious. But of course he was curious. His own superior didn't know he was here.

As the old man busied himself with a manila file folder, Chandler noticed his hands. They were ancient hands, much older than the face, with brown spots on them and laced with gnarled blue veins.

"We've been wondering where this man is for quite a while," he said now in his cultivated voice. "At first we sought him actively. Then, it seemed less important. We'd ascertained he hadn't gone over to the other side or anything like that. Just seems to have disappeared. Now, however, something very important has come up. We must find him."

From the file folder he produced a glossy photograph. It looked as if it had been blown up from a smaller snapshot. The man was dark, with strong planes to his face, slanted cheekbones, and a straight nose. Chandler thought he looked like an ascetic type, except for the fullness in his lower lip.

"Alex Markoff. One of our agents," the old man continued. "Disappeared before your time. Heard of him?"

Of course Chandler had heard of him. Alex Markoff's disappearance was a source of a great deal of agency gossip. Chandler had heard various theories. He was indeed a suicide. He'd just arranged for his body not to be found as a final gesture of defiance, a last joke on the agency. He had escaped and now ruled a secret kingdom in the Himalayas. This last theory smacked of Rider Haggard, but there were some who believed it. At least there were some who said others believed it. Alex Markoff had become a Russian Orthodox monk. He'd had plastic surgery and now sold real estate in southern California. It was hard to sort out the jokes from the actual theories. But Chandler Smith knew that if a man tried to hide, and change identities, it was pretty easy to do. A bunch of sixties radicals had managed very nicely, despite the efforts of the FBI to find them, and none of them had the training an experienced agent like Alex Markoff had.

The old man leaned back in his chair. "We have an official investigation going on, and an official search for this man. But there is reason to believe another, more covert search is needed. You see, Markoff has some information of great value to the agency. Something which must not be compromised."

"Where should I start?" said Chandler.

"All the information everyone else has is there," said the old man. "Read it here in my office. Memorize it, if you can. Then, take what you think is the best tack. Remember, you'll be almost a free agent. I'll be your control myself. And we can meet only rarely."

"May I ask, sir, why I was chosen?" Chandler regretted the question instantly.

The old man didn't seem to mind. "Because I understand you have initiative. And common sense. That's all I've ever wanted in an agent. Some people don't like initiative, but when it's combined with common sense it's extremely valuable. And because you're nobody in this outfit, and nobody pays much attention to you.''

"I see." Chandler cleared his throat and caressed the file folder in front of him. "What if he really is dead?"

"Someone may want that very much," said the old man. "But I sure as hell don't."

Sunny's phone rang. Could it be Billy? She hoped so. She wanted to know why he'd broken the appointment and how to get his attaché case back to him.

"Sunny? Bob Dawson here." Why was Bob Dawson calling? For a second Sunny wondered if it wasn't another of those widow calls. Right after Gordon had died, she'd been amazed by the number of men they'd known socially who seemed to want to console her. Some of them were most unlikely—husbands of good friends. Sunny had heard about the phenomenon from other widows. Even more amazing than the clumsy attempts at seduction was the lack of embarrassment the men showed when she met them later in normal social life.

"Oh, yes." Sunny knew Bob's wife, Florence, and occasionally accepted invitations from them, and invited them over herself, for cocktails or dinner. She and Florence, a librarian who loved music, enjoyed each other's company.

"Florence and I are getting up a little golf foursome and hope you can come along. There's a nice young man we'd like you to meet." Bob's voice was always affable, but he sounded a little strained in his affability now. Usually Florence arranged invitations.

"That sounds nice," said Sunny vaguely, wondering if she really wanted to go along. She certainly wasn't interested in meeting any *young* men. Although Bob's idea of young might be sixtyish.

Then Sunny remembered some gossip she'd heard about Bob Dawson. He'd managed a small cargo airline out of

Tucson that was said to be a CIA front. Now, apparently because the airline's real ownership was common knowledge, the line had been phased out. Bob had taken a post in the business department at the University of Arizona. Was he still connected with the CIA? And did this call have anything to do with Billy? Or Alex? It all sounded silly, but Sunny thought the worst that could happen was a dull afternoon. She enjoyed golf anyway, so it couldn't be a total loss.

"I'd be delighted, Bob," she said. "When do you want to play?"

Florence and Bob's young friend turned out to be Richard Matthews. He was an unlikely acquaintance of the Dawsons, young and rather scholarly-looking. Perhaps he was a student of Bob's, but he looked less like a business major than a young poet. He and Sunny were partnered against the Dawsons.

"Damn this forehand," said Florence.

"Keep your wrist straight, dear," said Bob, chuckling. Sunny had once played bridge with the Dawsons. On that occasion, when Florence had overbid in clubs, Bob had been less charitable. Florence replaced a divot and pouted. "Why don't you two play on ahead."

Richard Matthews strode purposefully toward his ball, a good fifty paces down the fairway. He seemed to ignore Sunny. Perhaps it was because she was older. A young man like this probably found a middle-aged golf foursome tiresome.

Sunny tried to make pleasant conversation. "How do you know the Dawsons?"

"Dr. Bob was my professor," said Richard.

"Really? I can never imagine Bob Dawson as a professor; he always seems so . . ." What did she mean to say? Unprofessorial? Unintellectual?

"I was impressed, because he'd been active in the field

before taking an academic post," said Richard. "Oh, there it is."

He addressed the ball, seizing the club in his rather bony hands, squinting out over the green, and tossing a long lock of dark brown hair from his eyes. "Seems like most of my professors were kind of naive." He executed an erratic drive into some high brush. Sunny's ball was nearby.

"Well, I got into the same mess with one less stroke," she said, laughing. "But let's see who gets out first."

They strode over to the weeds and began thrashing at them with their irons. Richard sneezed.

"Bless you."

"Thanks. Hay fever. Never thought it'd act up in Arizona."

"It didn't used to," said Sunny. People used to move here because of asthma and hay fever. Then the same people planted Eastern-style gardens and now the air is full of pollen. She looked at him in a motherly way. He'd extracted a large white handkerchief from his pocket and sneezed into it.

"Here, let me find our balls. Stay back on the green, away from the weeds."

"No, never mind. Got to live with it." He smiled an engaging crooked smile. Sunny was charmed by his young face.

"Ah, here's one. Little green dot. That's mine I think." Sunny stirred up the weeds. "Better stand back. My nine iron sometimes acts like a weed eater."

"Weed eater?"

"Those automatic things you chop weeds with. I guess you're not a gardener with your hay fever."

He smiled ruefully. Sunny thought his eyes looked pink. "Nope." Then his pink eyes narrowed shrewdly. "But surely you don't need them here in the Southwest?"

"No, not really. My garden is strictly desert. Oh, I have a

few pots of geraniums in the shade. I read gardening magazines, though. Of course, they're never written for here, but it cheers me up to read about perennial borders even though I can't grow them.''

Sunny closed her eyes, said a quick prayer, and watched her ball sail back onto the green.

"You're from the Northwest originally, aren't you?'' said Richard now, still whirling his own club like a machete. Sunny, slightly miffed that he hadn't congratulated her on getting her ball out of the rough, said, ''That's right,'' and a second later she added, ''How did you know?''

"Mrs. Sinclair,'' he said, stooping over his own ball and growling at it, ''I've read your file.''

"What?''

"In Washington. You did something for your country once, didn't you?''

"Yes.''

"I'm asking if you'd like to do something for your country again.''

Funny. That was what Billy had said, thirty or more years ago in her mother's parlor. Billy was probably about this young man's age then, too. But Sunny was older now. She laughed.

Richard Matthews frowned. "I guess that sounds funny.''

"No, not at all.'' She resisted adding ''dear.'' He looked so young and vulnerable and rabbity. ''It's just that I'm much too old and set in my ways for that sort of thing.''

"I don't think so. You play an awfully good game of golf for an . . .''

"Old lady? Yes, I suppose I do. Nice game. All in the head I sometimes think. Maybe when you're my age, that slice of yours will have mellowed into something more useful.''

"Mrs. Sinclair, there's no need to be condescending.'' He smiled now, and she forgot his eyes were pink from hay fever. He really had a very nice boyish smile. "We need you. Again."

It was on the tip of her tongue to say, "To find Alex, I suppose," but she didn't.

"Whatever for?"

"To find someone. Someone you knew well. Alex Markoff."

"Alex Markoff! Haven't thought about him in years. Whatever do you want to find him for? And why do you think I would be able to do it?" Really, Sunny, she said to herself, you're overplaying the rich matron. You sound almost like Billie Burke. "Oh, let me guess. That file of yours."

"That's right. Your relationship was . . . close."

"And who exactly are you? You and Bob? The CIA?"

Richard bent down and flattened some weeds around his ball.

"What do you say, Mrs. Sinclair? Want some time to think it over?"

Sunny was annoyed at his confidence. He was sure she'd accept the challenge. Billy had been sure of the same thing, that's why he'd left the damn attaché case. What was it about her? Did she look like some Mata Hari, ready to plunge into idiotic men's games?

"Try relaxing the knees," she said sharply. "Think of them as a well-oiled hinge."

"Just be quiet a moment," he said politely, "and I think I can relax."

He swung, and weeds and a clod of earth arced into the sky. "Shit," he said. "I'll take an extra stroke." He pitched the ball back onto the green. "I'll be glad to give you some time to think about it. Maybe we should talk more, privately."

"The rough on the back nine is private enough," she said. "And, so far as accepting any assignment you might have for me, well, I think not." Now she sounded worse than Billie

Burke. I think not! Where did she get that? Next thing she knew she'd be tapping the young man with her fan.

Later, as the four of them had gin and tonics in the clubhouse, Sunny turned to Richard Matthews. Florence and Bob, acting like matchmaking double-daters, were feigning a great interest in some friends of theirs across the bar, waving and shouting. "But please bear in mind," she said solemnly, "that despite my refusal, I'll keep our conversation in strictest confidence."

Billy had said the CIA wanted to find Alex in order to kill him. This young man didn't look like a killer at all. Bob Dawson, a beefy man whose body seemed to hang from a thick pair of shoulders, shoved Richard Matthews and laughed. "Florence and I beat the hell out of you, Flo's hook and all." He chortled.

Sunny watched Bob, slitty blue eyes in a round red face. She wondered if he'd recruited Richard in some university office. She wondered what had attracted the younger man to the life of a spy. Patriotism? A love of secrets? The attention of an extroverted relaxed man like Bob Dawson when Richard himself was so tense and almost shy? She knew one thing. Richard Matthews had found the attempt to recruit her painful, embarrassing, almost uncouth. Bob, she knew, had no compunctions of that type. Probably he'd worked mostly on Saudi and Iranian nationals; there seemed to be hundreds of them at the University of Arizona. What had possessed him to recruit this pink-eyed poet? For an instant she hated Bob for it. Later, when she got home, she thought about what Billy had said, and she hated Bob again, for trying to get her to find Alex Markoff so that he could be killed.

It was then that she decided that perhaps she had better find Alex. Without telling Billy, without telling Richard Matthews, she'd find Alex, tell him Billy's story, and tell him that the CIA was looking for him, too, and let him decide for himself what to do. It occurred to her that Billy and Matthews were acting in concert. Billy to tell her about the CIA's wanting him; Richard to prove it. Then, she supposed they'd see which pitch she bought. And, if she bought neither, perhaps they'd follow her to see if she did exactly what she now planned to do. Find him on her own. Well, if she did find Alex on her own, she'd have to ditch every tail they had on her. She had to come up with a plausible way to disappear.

Of course, finding Alex when they had failed was probably impossible. But whether it was or not, her first task was to figure out how to disappear. She tried to recall Alex Markoff's face. Funny, his body was much easier to remember.

5

SUNNY WOULD NEVER have decided to do it if Billy hadn't vanished. The recruitment pitch on the golf course, the menacing episode at the mission, these had piqued her interest. But it was Billy's missing the rendezvous and failing to contact her again that finally pushed her over the edge.

She could think of three reasons Billy never showed up. The first, and most likely, was that he was off on a bender. The second was that he was in some kind of trouble. The third was that he thought Sunny would be more likely to look for Alex if she thought he was in trouble.

This last possibility had dissuaded her at first. Cheap theatrics from Billy, she thought. Then it occurred to her that if Billy was playing this kind of game with her then Billy must take the whole thing very seriously indeed.

She knew better than to look for Billy. She'd only draw attention to herself, and make it impossible for her to ever look for Alex. And, she knew if she were to look for Alex, she'd have to do it right. First, she had to disappear.

A few days later, Sunny had it figured out to the last detail. A healthy lunch of fruit, French bread, and yogurt, and then she and Marjorie changed into bathing suits and sat under the ramada, sipping iced tea. When the heat became intense, Sunny dived into the pool and swam a couple of laps. She had never become used to the heat, but with the perverse fascination of the Scandinavian for warm climates—after all, hadn't Ibsen died in Italy? hadn't Queen Christina died in Spain?—she felt luxuriant in it. And, with the Scandinavian passion for fresh air *("Frisk luft!"* Tante Ragnhild had shouted, opening windows with abandon), she felt it was a waste not to enjoy the outdoors.

Marjorie, sweet plump Marjorie, frowned as Sunny emerged from one of her quick dips, and surveyed her friend's lithe body in the black maillot. Marjorie rearranged herself uncomfortably in the wrought-iron chair, sucking in her stomach and stretching her plump legs out in front of her. She wore a tropical-print suit with legs cut like shorts.

"Goddamn it, Sunny," said Marjorie for the hundredth time since the two women had been friends, "you look terrific. It's obscene. No woman our age should have a body like that."

Sunny usually murmured something comforting, but today she stretched her arms above her head and threw back her head like a ballerina. "It's true," she said. "I am in great shape. I love being in shape. It feels so good."

"I'll take your word for it," muttered Marjorie in a good-natured way.

"You know, Marjorie," said Sunny, indulging in another stretch and casting her glance back at Marjorie to observe her friend's narrowed blue eyes, "you could look great, too. It's all a matter of exercise."

"Exercise." Marjorie shuddered.

"You and I should go to Rancho Salubre."

"Out of my league," said Marjorie, still sounding cheerful, but becoming, thought Sunny, a little annoyed. Sunny bent over from the waist and touched the hot concrete around the pool with her fingertips. Then, to drive the point home, she put her long elegant hands flat down in front of her, keeping her legs perfectly straight.

"Sunny!" said Marjorie sharply. "You're showing off. Forget exercise. I'm at the stage where I'll rely on expensive corseting to deal with my figure problems."

Sunny straightened up and came back to the ramada.

"Marjorie," she said firmly. "We're going to Rancho Salubre. You'll be my guest. Just for two weeks. You'll love it. Just two weeks can really do wonders—and get you started right."

"Sunny! That place costs a fortune. I can't let you! Besides," she said with a pout, "I'm not sure I want to be tortured into shape."

"Marjorie, you'll love it. You'll feel so good. Really."

"Well . . ." Marjorie looked thoughtful.

"Say you will."

Marjorie giggled, put a pink lacquered fingertip into her glass, and sucked it in a sensuous way. Sunny decided Marjorie had relied for years on childlike gestures when she felt defensive. They suited her well. She was round and soft and sweet-looking, with wavy blond hair, now frosted with gray, and guileless pale blue eyes.

"Come on," said Sunny.

"No," said Marjorie firmly, shaking her head hard enough to set her pale waves bouncing. "I couldn't."

Sunny leaned forward fiercely. "Marjorie," she said in a low voice. "Take a look at my thighs." She extended one of her legs and pinched the flesh on the inside of her thigh. "You can have thighs like this, too. It's just a matter of exercise."

"I'm almost convinced," said Marjorie. "But I don't know. A leotard is a cruel garment. Everyone else will have thighs like you." But she surveyed Sunny's thigh with admiration and envy.

Sunny put her leg back. "Remember Joan McDonald? *She's* been to Rancho Salubre."

"Joan McDonald? At the club?" said Marjorie incredulously. "My God, she must be a size twenty."

"If she can wear a leotard, so can you. And remember," added Sunny, "it's my treat."

"Hmmm." Marjorie leaned back in her chair. "At what they charge a day, how can I turn you down?"

A week later the two women sat in Sunny's air-conditioned white Mercedes, the desert flying by outside the firmly closed windows.

"I'm glad you talked me into this," said Marjorie, sucking noisily on a mint. "In a way, even though they'll probably work us like dogs, there's something terribly luxurious about devoting two weeks of my life to nobody but me."

She sighed happily. "I put two weeks' worth of dinners in the freezer for Ed. Oh, Sunny, you'll never guess what he wanted me to do!"

Sunny, in jeans, T-shirt, and sunglasses, turned to her. "What?"

"He told me to scout around for clients. He said *he'd* never get a chance like this to run into so many rich women in one place. He even gave me a handful of his cards!"

The two women laughed. Marjorie's husband, Ed, was a stockbroker, and a prosperous one. The idea of sleek Ed Devine hustling a group of flabby rich ladies was somehow terribly funny.

"Marjorie," said Sunny, figuring a moment of good humor was the best time to broach the unpleasant subject. "I've got a favor to ask you."

"What?" Marjorie's blue eyes grew rounder.

"I want us to register under each other's names," she said slowly.

"Why?" demanded Marjorie.

Sunny sighed. "I can't tell you."

"How can you ask me to do a thing like that?" wailed Marjorie. "And not tell me why?"

"Maybe because we're good friends. And I'd do the same for you."

Marjorie leaned back against the leather seat. Sunny watched her friend's face from behind the sides of her dark glasses. Would Marjorie remember? Would she remember how Sunny hadn't asked any questions fifteen years ago when Marjorie had come to her, grim, white-faced, asking if Sunny could help her find a discreet gynecologist, willing to perform a then-illegal operation? Sunny didn't want to remind her. But she was prepared to do it if she had to.

Marjorie seemed to remember. "That's fair," she said in a quiet voice. Suddenly Sunny felt a terrible stab of regret. How could she ask Marjorie to help? How could she rely on the tacit understanding between them that this might be repayment for an old favor? Maybe, thought Sunny to herself, waves of unpleasantness coursing through her, Marjorie saw this as some kind of blackmail.

"I . . . I'm sorry, Marjorie . . ." she began. The trace of vulnerability in her voice seemed to reach something in Marjorie, who put out one of her hands and touched Sunny's shoulder.

"If it's important, of course I'll do it," she said. "But it'll drive me nuts wondering why. Is there any more of this plot I need to know about?"

"Just this," said Sunny. "I may be leaving Rancho Salubre before the week is out. And I want you to stay. Under my name."

Marjorie looked angry. "Terrific," she snapped. "Really, I feel like I've been had. You should have asked me before we left."

"I know I should have," replied Sunny simply. "You probably would have said no."

"That's true," allowed Marjorie with a shrug, as if the fact made no ethical difference.

"I suppose while I'm dining on raw carrots and getting beaten up by sadistic masseuses, you'll be off having an illicit interlude with somebody else's husband."

"No. I won't. I'm not doing anything of the sort. Be

reasonable. If I were, why couldn't I tell people I was off to Rancho Salubre and then keep my rendezvous instead?''

''Private detectives?'' giggled Marjorie.

''You've been seeing too many movies. No, really, it's not sex. It's business, of a sort. And I can tell you later.''

''Sunny Sinclair.'' Marjorie rolled the name around in her mouth. ''It's a nice name. I'll take it. For two weeks.'' She held up an admonishing finger. ''If you *promise* you'll tell me about it when it's over.''

''I promise,'' vowed Sunny.

''And if you stop up at this place here on the right. I want to get some peanut brittle.''

''No! We're having a healthy two weeks. Or at least you are. And besides, we're not allowed to bring food. God knows what happens if they catch you!''

''I'll eat it in the car,'' said Marjorie. ''Now, don't nag me about this. Remember, I'm doing you one hell of a favor.''

Sunny switched on her turn signal and moved too quickly into the right-hand lane, nearly cutting off a blue Buick. She maneuvered out of its path and winced, waiting for the inevitable long honk from its horn. Instead, the car simply pulled adroitly around her. In the mirror she caught the glimpse of a young male driver, a smile of amusement playing on his features. ''Bastard,'' she muttered. ''Probably laughing at a woman driver.'' The Buick drove on.

She was rattled by the experience; normally she drove well. But Marjorie's last-minute threat had galvanized her into quick action. If Marjorie wanted peanut brittle, by God she could have it. The experience made her realize, however, how edgy she had become. Must stay relaxed, she thought to herself, if I'm going to get back in the field. And then, amused at herself for taking her spying so seriously, she smiled. After all, it was just a game, probably a silly game with only one player, herself.

''Sunny, are you okay?'' demanded Marjorie as the white

Mercedes nosed into a parking space. "First you nearly get us killed, then you smile."

"Sorry, Marjorie. Just nerves. Be glad you're getting your peanut brittle."

These establishments loomed out of the Arizona desert like strange neon oases. Sunny had never understood the phenomenon. Perhaps driving through the desert was so monotonous that a visit to a combination gas station-souvenir shop and peanut brittle stand made a welcome break for people. But why peanut brittle? Why not something healthy like Arizona grapefruit juice? Sunny decided to stay in the car and wait for Marjorie to get the sticky stuff.

By the time they'd reached the side road with its deceptively simple wooden sign pointing the way to Rancho Salubre, Marjorie, true to her word, had polished off a sack of peanut brittle. The whole car seemed to smell of the stuff, and Sunny was overcome with a desire to brush her teeth, though she'd politely refused to indulge herself. Peanut brittle was something other people ate.

"I'm getting nervous," said Marjorie. "You won't leave right away, will you? I mean, we'll have to sort this out. I'm not sure I'll be able to pull this off. If someone says 'Mrs. Sinclair,' will I turn around? And what if someone we know is there?"

"Simple," said Sunny. "Tell them you're using my reservation and they wouldn't let us transfer without me surrendering a deposit. Make it all very conspiratorial."

"That's believable." Marjorie shrugged. "Just the sort of thing the Rancho Salubre people would do, from everything I've ever heard. Stick you for a big deposit if you rabbit on them." After a moment she added, "How did you get so sneaky?"

Sunny laughed. "I don't know. Really, I think of myself as an honest person. But there's always been a part of me that could . . ."

"Lie?" finished Marjorie with a trace of malice.

Sunny smiled. She remembered, back in OSS training, what a good liar she'd been. They'd all had to come up with a fake life story. Instinctively, Sunny knew that including a good chunk of truth made a lie more convincing. She'd told them she was a Norwegian-American. But she'd transplanted herself to San Francisco, a city she'd visited with her mother several times. And she'd said her father was not a chandler but a steamship line owner. She said she'd been to a Galileo High School and then Stanford. And she'd given herself seven siblings, all with the most peculiar-sounding Norwegian names she could think of.

Telling it all to a circle of giggling post-debutantes who made up her class was curiously thrilling. "Oh, you're not from the West Coast," said one girl, the daughter of an ambassador. "And you certainly didn't go to public schools. And I doubt that you're of immigrant stock. Your cousins probably came over with mine on the *Mayflower*."

The parts that were real had been the parts no one believed. It was true, she was a bit of an anomaly in the OSS. The other girls were from upper-class Eastern families and, excepting a few bilinguals like Sunny, were singularly alike.

If any of them thought there was something a little different about Sunny, it was probably that her hair was dressed a little more glamorously than theirs, because she had learned to do it herself with a million pin curls every shampoo, and her uniform fit her expertly because she had the skill to alter it, which she did one night cross-legged in her slip with a spool of dark cotton thread and nail scissors. Of course, she didn't wear a uniform until after VE Day. That's when she got her gun, too, during the demobilization.

The car rattled on the asphalt road for a few more miles.

"My God," muttered Marjorie. "It's certainly secluded."

"That's the whole point," said Sunny. "It gives you a

marvelous feeling of being away from it all. Like Saint Somebody in the desert.''

"Sounds terrible," said Marjorie cheerfully. "But I do think I'm ready. And, you know, Sunny, it's almost wicked, but knowing I'm going to be impersonating you makes it all somehow exciting. Do you know what I mean?"

"Yes," said Sunny. "I know exactly."

Rancho Salubre was surrounded by thick white walls. At the gate a uniformed porter in sunglasses added a surrealistic touch to the proceedings. He bent over the driver's window, while Sunny searched in her purse for her registration papers.

"My God," complained Marjorie, "I feel like I'm visiting someone in jail or something."

"Security is tight," explained the guard. "We have famous people here, you know. Privacy is important to them."

As he spoke, Sunny saw her own reflection in his mirrored sunglasses, and behind it a rapid silvery movement. She turned to see a glimpse of blue traveling down the road. Could it have been the blue Buick?

"Wonder where he thinks he's going," said the guard, gazing over her shoulder. "There's nothing down the road. It dead-ends in about a hundred yards."

Sunny smiled sweetly. "Do you know," she said chattily, "I think there's something the matter with one of my tires. Will you look at it?"

The guard frowned. "Perhaps someone up at the main lodge can help you."

Sunny looked severe. "I see. Well, I didn't intend to be a nuisance, but I've just noticed this funny bumpy feeling. I'm afraid my husband would be very annoyed if something happened to the car."

The guard smiled. "Which tire, ma'am?"

"I don't know. I just felt they weren't balanced, you know, that lumpy feeling?"

She got out of the car. The man walked around it, scrutinizing the tires, nudging them with his toes. "None of them are flat," he announced. "Why don't you just get the pressure checked next chance you get?"

"Oh, all right," she fretted. Marjorie gave her a questioning glance and Sunny ignored it, following the guard around and looking questioningly at the tires.

Finally, a blue Buick sped back up the road in a dusty cloud. Sunny couldn't be sure that the car was the same car she'd cut off miles and miles ago on the main highway. But she was sure the driver was the same. He wore that same amused expression. She got just a quick glance at him, but she was sure it was the same man. And he was the young man with gray eyes who'd watched her at the restaurant that day. The day Billy had tried to recruit her.

Marjorie took a long swig of carrot juice. "Does this really purify the blood?" she asked Sunny. The two women sat in the dining room, a room full of white linen and crystal goblets, and the comforting sounds of female conversation. Across one wall was a huge window looking out into a grove of magnificent saguaro cacti. These must have been a century or two old. They were like great sculptures, and they were somehow at odds with the exceedingly civilized interior.

Sunny shrugged. "I suppose at these rates, we may as well believe it does." She smiled.

Marjorie swirled her carrot cocktail with a piece of celery, like someone stabbing ice cubes in a Scotch with a swizzle stick.

"Sunny, I'm going to go through with the switch," she said, her mouth set in a determined way Sunny had never seen before. "But I have to know a few more things."

"Like?" said Sunny, trying to sound as if impersonating one's friends were a normal occurrence.

"Like what if Ed calls. And you're gone."

"Thought of that," said Sunny. "I'll give instructions that any calls for me, Marjorie Devine, should be directed to you."

"How are you going to get out of here anyway?" said Marjorie. "I have a feeling you won't get far. Miss Fraser will probably send dogs after you."

"If I told you," said Sunny, "you might not act surprised. This way you won't have to act."

"You know why I'm doing this?"

"Because you're a good friend," said Sunny, placing a hand over Marjorie's. "And sometimes good friends don't ask questions."

"Well, that." Marjorie shrugged. "But I think partly because I've never done anything like it before. There's something almost seductive about becoming part of an intrigue, whatever the hell intrigue it is you're up to. And, because you *promised* to tell me later just what it is you're going to do."

"I will," said Sunny, hoping she could. Maybe there'd still be a need for secrecy. But, more likely, she was off on a fool's errand, and there wasn't any need for secrecy at all. Still, the man with the blue Buick and that supercilious expression, he must mean something. And then there had been that golf foursome. Gazing out over the sea of women in the room, Sunny suddenly felt very much at home. Women didn't get involved in silly spy games. They were much too sensible. Only men did that kind of thing. Was that why Sunny had liked the war so much? Because she'd been able to play with the boys? Was that what she was doing now? There was something there to analyze, but she didn't want to think about it now. Later. When it was all over, if there was ever any proper ending. Then would be the time to think about the nuances, the motivations. Now she had only to think about how. Like men did. They seemed to think about the how more than the why.

*   *   *

"Remember, girls," said Miss Fraser to the assembled women in leotards, "stretching is strengthening. And toning. Now, first I'm going to go over your warm-up. Watch me, and then we'll get to work."

The exercise room was a long oblong, with a polished wooden floor, broken at one end by a huge gray square of carpeting. Large mirrors lined one wall, and a ballet bar ran along the mirror. Sunny noticed several of the women observing themselves furtively in the mirror. They came in all shapes and sizes, but the weight in all of them seemed to have descended to the hips. Most of them were middle-aged, sporting tasteful silver coiffures. There was one younger woman with a good figure. She had a mane of tawny frosted hair, a wide scarlet mouth, and a perpetual frown. Unlike the other women, who mostly wore the classic black leotard, this woman wore a metallic pink, with green tights and black and white striped leg warmers from lean thigh to shapely calf. Marjorie seemed to be watching her in frank amazement.

Miss Fraser, a diminutive woman with the brittle look of an old ballerina, including an improbably dark chignon, demonstrated stretching maneuvers, lifting one long leg easily to the bar, bending over slowly, appearing to gaze at herself with rapture in the mirror as she did so. Sunny knew she was actually centering herself by looking at her eyes.

Miss Fraser moved to the side of the room, flicked on a tape, and filled the room with lush ballet music. The ladies all hoisted a leg up on the bar with effort, and some good-natured groans. They executed the stretches as Miss Fraser went the length of the room, pewter eyes framed by a becoming sooty makeup, taking in every muscle. When she came to the tawny-maned woman in exotic leg warmers, she gave an audible snort. *"You,"* she said accusingly, "are a jogger."

"That's right," said the woman. "I'm up to twelve miles a day."

"Your uterus will fall," snapped Miss Fraser, as if she

almost hoped it did. "And your breasts will bounce so much you'll get horrible stretch marks." Miss Fraser ran a scarlet-clawed hand over one of her own magnificent glands, which, despite its womanly roundness seemed to stand up all by itself and point smartly forward. Each nipple was centered exactly like a pair of headlights. "And," she continued, "you'll get all stringy, like a tough old chicken that's been walked to market."

The other ladies murmured sympathetically, but not without some satisfaction, Sunny felt. The woman whose uterus, breasts, and general tone had all been damned looked aghast.

Miss Fraser patted her on the shoulder. "But you're fairly young," she said kindly. "We can get you on a better program and we can undo some of the damage. Remember, beautiful bodies come from stretching."

Marjorie's leg, apparently exhausted, fell from its perch on the bar with a thump. She took it in both hands and replaced it, her knee trying to straighten with obvious quivers. "You mean I don't have to jog?" she said happily.

"Believe me," said Miss Fraser, "when I've given you a workout, you'll beg for a nice twelve-mile run."

The atmosphere became leaden. Miss Fraser tittered happily. "Oh, really, girls, it's not that bad. We'll build you up to it. Don't do anything that hurts too much. But remember, if it's not hurting, it's not toning, shaping, and"—she paused—"*stretching.*"

It was really too bad Sunny had to leave. She liked Miss Fraser's workouts. She liked the sharp burning that came when she'd reached the limits of each muscle. She liked the light feeling she had after executing good, strong maneuvers, straight extensions. She even liked Miss Fraser, who combined the patter of a master sergeant with nice little cooing noises when you did something right. She liked the lush violins on the tape and the pattery sound of Capezio shoes on the wooden floor.

But it was now or never. If the man in the blue Buick was out there, he'd have a hard time following her the way she planned to leave.

With a sigh, because she really felt a whole two weeks with Miss Fraser would do wonders for her, she placed her hand on the bar, bent her knees, lowered her straightened back down in a squat, and screamed. She held the position as long as she could, holding on to the bar with a white-knuckled hand and waving off offers of assistance from the other women and from Miss Fraser, who'd elbowed her way to Sunny's side.

"It's"—she inhaled deeply and held her breath, the way people in pain do, just when they should really be breathing —"my back."

Miss Fraser's eyes narrowed. "You didn't tell me you had a bad back. It wasn't on your card!" she shrieked.

With a little gasp, Sunny let loose her grip and collapsed onto the floor, her face tightened up the way she remembered it had when she'd been in labor.

Two burly men, who looked rather like lunatic asylum guards from the movies, carried her into Claire Carruthers's office, Miss Fraser pattering behind them, her Capezio slippers slapping the floor.

"Just put her down on the sofa," said a gin-and-gravel voice. Sunny resisted the temptation to turn.

"Back?" the voice said sharply.

"It isn't on her card," said Miss Fraser defensively.

"We'll have a doctor examine her," said Claire Carruthers. Sunny was now on the sofa, a pink silk Victorian arrangement, with a lot of buttons digging into her.

She'd seen Claire Carruthers on the brochure, of course. A platinum blonde with a porcelain face. In person Miss Carruthers looked a little more haggard.

Sunny looked around the office, a far cry from her own monastic room. There was a magnificent Oriental carpet on the floor and some pink silk chairs with gilt arms that seemed to match the loveseat or whatever it was. There was also a small French Provincial desk unadorned with papers. Sunny imagined Miss Carruthers handled one piece of paper at a time, which was then taken ceremoniously away to someone else's more cluttered desk.

"No," said Sunny. "No one touches my back but my own doctor."

"That's impossible," said La Carruthers. She wore a long white garment that could have been an evening gown or a bathrobe. She began to pace around the floor in a long, masculine stride that sent the garment rustling expensively.

"Look," said Sunny, "I'll sign a release. Anything. Just get me on a plane to Phoenix. You've got one, I saw it yesterday. The helicopter."

"You're being silly," said Miss Fraser. "We only use that for supplies. You want medical attention."

"Shut up," said Claire Carruthers. "The guests' wishes come first." She went to a desk, pushed a button, and in a moment an attractive, dark young man walked in. In spite of the fact they were in the middle of the desert, he wore a dark business suit.

"Raymond, get me one of our standard medical releases," she said. "Mrs. Devine here will sign it. Then get the chopper ready. She's going to Phoenix."

Raymond raised an eyebrow inquiringly, hesitated for an instant, and left.

Claire Carruthers came to Sunny's side. "Ice pack? Anything we can do for you?" she said softly.

"She was just doing the regular routine," said Miss Fraser, her hands clasped in front of her. "And all of a sudden . . ."

"That's fine, Myra," said Miss Carruthers. "Why don't you get back to your class? I'll see to this."

Relieved, Miss Fraser left.

"I should have told you about the back," said Sunny. "I

know there was a space for it. But I thought I was cured. Really I did.''

"Backs are tricky," said Miss Carruthers. "And while I think you should see our doctor, I'm acceding to your wishes. Of course, we must ask you to sign this standard form. After all . . .''

"Yes, yes," said Sunny. "I'll sign anything.''

"Well, don't ever do that.'' Miss Carruthers smiled. "This, however, is pretty innocuous. Just something our tiresome lawyers insist we keep on hand.''

6

THE FLIGHT TO San Francisco from Phoenix was uneventful, but Sunny felt an exuberance, almost giggling to herself, at the thought that no one in the world knew where she was and what she was doing. It was a heady, delicious feeling.

Yet, when she arrived at the airport, the feeling went away. Now she felt alert, energetic, and careful. She placed her passport and all of Billy's cash in a nondescript flightbag in an airport locker, and put the key to the locker in her compact, a loose-powder compact with a mesh circle that kept the powder in place, and now the locker key, too. Thank God they'd just X-rayed it, not opened it at the anti-hijack gate, not that it was illegal to travel with lots of cash.

She called Marina from the airport. Burlingame was only a minute or so away, she knew. She'd spent a lot of time in the Bay Area.

She hadn't rehearsed what to say to Marina. She just blurted out her name, Harriet Grey, and said she was an old friend of her father's.

Marina sounded surly, but surprised Sunny by asking her to come and talk about him if she wished, that afternoon. Marina had a low, monotonous voice, with little inflection and no social nicety. She sounded as if strangers were calling to ask about her father all the time, and it was part of her job to talk to them.

With a pang, a feeling of loss that surprised her, Sunny recognized Alex in his daughter's face even more keenly than in the photograph. There was the same Slavic tilt to the cheekbones, the broad intelligent forehead, the level dark eyes under strong brows that looked a little masculine on Marina.

"Mrs. Grey," said Marina, leaning on the doorjamb like someone exhausted or even a little drunk. The broad forehead pinched into a frown, the face took on a sullen cast. "You want to talk about Dad."

"Yes. May I come in?" Sunny didn't smile. It seemed pointless to try and charm this young woman. She looked too suspicious and too intelligent for that.

With a languid gesture, Marina ushered Sunny into a spacious suburban living room. It was a wide, light, tasteful room without much character.

"So," Marina said shortly when the two women were seated on beige chairs. "You're looking for Dad."

"That's right," said Sunny. Absurdly, she wished Marina would offer her coffee to add a feminine, cozy touch to their business. But Marina wasn't offering anything. Not even a social smile, or even eye contact.

"I guess a lot of people wonder where he is. Did you read about it in the papers?"

"No."

"It's all public domain." Marina rose and swayed toward a corner of the room. She rummaged in an obscure piece of furniture that could have housed a stereo system or linens, and returned with a bunch of faded clippings.

There was nothing new here. A straightforward account from the San Francisco *Chronicle,* a shorter account from the L.A. *Times.* Sunny noticed the source and dates were penciled neatly on each clipping in a schoolgirlish hand. Alex Markoff, retired executive, cast off for a solo sail from Tiburon, on the San Francisco Bay. His craft later washes ashore without him in Suisun Bay. There's a note, the contents of which aren't made public. Sunny was startled to see a small, smudgy, ten-year-old picture of Alex. It was the same face, but rougher, older, sadder. Still, there was a jauntiness to his expression. He seemed to be squinting into the sun, and he wore an open-necked shirt. There was a chain around his neck that disappeared underneath the shirt. When Sunny knew him, men didn't wear jewelry. Just dog tags. She couldn't imagine what he wore around his neck. Maybe just a chain. So many men did these days. More of them did ten years ago.

"What did he wear on that chain?" said Sunny. It was a ridiculous question, but for some reason she wanted to know.

Marina looked startled. "I don't know," she said. "No one's ever asked me that."

"I knew your father years ago," she said now, firmness creeping into her voice. "We were very close. Before he met your mother."

"Did you know Mother?" said Marina.

"No."

"She killed herself," said Marina, almost with satisfaction. "That's what his life is all about. That's all I ever need to know about him. He may as well have killed her himself."

"I'm sorry," said Sunny simply, years of experience having taught her there's nothing else to say.

Marina chewed on a fingernail. "You knew him in the war? Were you running around getting cheap thrills in the cloak and dagger business, too?"

"I was in the OSS," she replied, unaccountably dying for a cup of coffee. "A translator."

Marina seemed not to have heard. "Well," she said simply. "If I knew where he was, I wouldn't tell you."

Sunny sat quietly, counting on the fact that anyone, with

any socializing at all, no matter how strongly they feel about anything, will fill in a conversational gap out of habit.

"Why," said Marina, "do you want to find him? I suppose you're with the company still. They've been bugging me for years."

"At first they sent around nice young men who admitted they were with the CIA. Then they sent around a nice young man who didn't say. Unfortunately for them, I'm happily married. Since then I've received a variety of strange types. The last one was an elegant little man who drank too much. He wore a flower in his buttonhole and he had nice manners. He said he was with the CIA, but he wasn't really. Then there are the funny clicks and buzzes on the phone. And strange cars parked down the street. Kind of handy really. I have my own built-in security force."

Sunny was glad she'd called herself Harriet Grey. She smiled tentatively at Marina, but remained silent.

"Why do you want to find him?" repeated Marina.

"It's a personal matter," said Sunny.

"Yeah. Well, don't bother telling me then. I spent my whole childhood being told lies. Daddy was on a business trip. Daddy worked for the government. If the other kids ask you, tell them Daddy works for the government. It's the lies that killed Mother."

"And the grief, perhaps?"

"Mom took those pills before Dad sailed away into the sunset. Two years before."

"I meant, the grief of your brother."

"Who knows? She knew Ivan would never come back. She told me so. She turned to me and said, 'He's not like your father. He won't make it.' "

Marina turned to Sunny suddenly and scowled. "I don't know why you're here. But nobody who wants to find him is up to any good as far as I can tell. And how would I know if they were? In any case, maybe he is dead. He probably is. His bones are probably at the bottom of the bay. I hope they are."

"But your life will be hell until you know for sure, won't it?" said Sunny softly. From another room Sunny heard the quick, demanding cry of a hungry newborn. "A baby," she said softly, forgetting her errand entirely, smiling happily.

"Yes. Maybe you'd better go. I don't want you around my baby. Sounds crazy, maybe, but that's the way I feel. I don't want him to hear any lies."

She showed Sunny to the door. "If you find him," she said, a sort of smile twisting itself on her face, "let me know."

"How shall I find him?" said Sunny.

"I don't know. I've never tried. Go back into the past perhaps. Maybe you know him better than I do. You knew him at the beginning. Now, please leave. If you do find him, for God's sake don't talk on the phone. Call me, say you're Mrs. Grey from a realty, pick one out of the book, and say you want to sell our house. You know the type of call."

Sunny knew. She'd received dozens of calls from pushy realtors.

Marina shut the door. Through its thickness, Sunny heard her say, "Coming, darling" as the baby's cry grew more intense.

The airport motel where Sunny was staying was conveniently close to Marina's Peninsula address, and close to the airport of course. Sunny was at first sorry she hadn't stayed in the city, but after seeing Marina she had a sense that finding Alex was more than a lark. This was serious business, serious enough to have made Marina's life a living hell. She remembered the time in her own life when she had babies. As she looked back, it was one of the nicest times in her life. She became angry that Marina's time should have been ruined by Alex.

She surveyed the motel room gloomily. There were the usual pair of double beds. She'd never understood that. Did they expect four people to a room? These were covered with gaudy spreads. There were two massive lamps on the plastic wood bedsteads, but despite their size—they were orange ceramic globes with tall yellowish shades—they put out little light.

She collapsed on one of the beds and thought vaguely about dinner. She wasn't really hungry. What she wanted was a drink and some sandwiches. She didn't want to drink alone in the hotel bar, either. She'd call room service.

There was really nothing more to do. Marina had been Billy's only lead, and now she had learned Billy himself had tried and failed to contact Alex through his daughter. One thing seemed sure, however. Marina didn't believe her father was dead. She'd said "maybe." That was interesting, but where did it lead? The only other clue she had was Pamela. There'd been the photograph of Pamela. But judging from Pamela's clothes in the picture, it was at least twenty years old. What could Pamela tell her? Maybe what Alex was thinking twenty years ago. There might be a hint there of where he would hide. But all in all it seemed too tenuous.

She sighed, disappointed that her search had dead-ended so soon. Serves me right, she thought bitterly. Who do I think I am, anyway, tracking down old spies? She called room service and ordered a double Scotch and soda and roast beef sandwiches. She knew the sandwiches would come with pickles and rose radishes and little cellophane petticoats on the toothpick that held the rose radish to the sandwich. All she wanted was a plain old sandwich, but in places like this one paid for all sorts of vulgar frills.

She slipped out of her knit dress, planning to eat in her robe. Really, she thought cheerfully, I can make this a cozy evening if I have a nice stiff drink and some sandwiches in bed. In her slip she flipped through the *TV Guide*. If only there were a cozy old movie on television.

But then she decided not to give up. Marina had said "go

back into the past.'' Maybe that's what she would do. She certainly had enough money. She'd fly to London, see Pamela. Pamela had known him later, in the fifties. She couldn't tell much from the old nightclub photo, but it was clear they were all relaxed and enjoying themselves. She'd see what Pamela knew about Alex Markoff then, after the war, after he'd married Gloria.

She asked the desk to connect her with Pan Am and was pleased to be able to book a night flight to London. Perhaps it was crazy, but why shouldn't she try one more approach?

There was a knock at the door. Room service was certainly efficient, even if the atmosphere was depressingly cheesy here. ''Just a minute,'' she said, rummaging through her suitcase for her robe.

The door burst open, and for a moment she was simply annoyed to be caught by the room service man in her slip. The next moment she knew room service might take another half hour.

A short man in a dark suit closed the door quickly behind him. She wondered how he got in. She knew she had locked the door.

''What do you want?'' she said severely, surprised at the calm in her own voice.

''Put on some clothes,'' said the man. ''Then come with me.''

''I'll put on some clothes,'' she said. ''But you'll have to leave.''

''We have a mutual friend,'' said the man. ''Marina Markoff. That was her maiden name, anyway,'' he added precisely.

''I can't talk to you now,'' she said, awkwardly getting into her robe. ''Perhaps we can meet in the coffee shop.''

The man looked at her thoughtfully and shook his head. ''Sorry. Won't do.'' He opened the door and another man came in. This man was much larger, though his face was round and bland, with a bulbous tip to the nose. His eyes were the blank eyes of a dullard. But they searched the room quickly and methodically as if placing all the doors and windows.

The short man was now sorting through her suitcases, and the task of putting together a female outfit seemed to frustrate him. Finally the larger man grabbed her knit dress from the dresser chair and threw it to her.

She threw the dress back in his face and dived across one of the beds for the phone.

The man with the bland face wheeled and pawed the phone out of her hand like a bear. It landed with a crash and a short jingle.

"Room service is on its way," she said.

The bland man spoke for the first time. "Then we'd better hurry." He tore off her robe and handed her the dress. She hated the moment when she pulled it over her head, because she couldn't see the two men for an instant and it made her feel even more vulnerable. She hesitated. Should she stall? She was too frightened to stall. She was afraid they'd help her dress, and the thought repulsed her. Besides, her chances were better in the lobby or the hall than alone with these men here.

She struggled with the dress for a moment, then pushed her head through the V-neck opening, struggling for breath. The first man handed her a pair of black calf shoes with straps and her purse. The large bland man threw her raincoat over her shoulders. The short man made an impatient little noise, like a husband all dressed and ready to go whose wife is taking too long. She was bending over the shoes now, trying to buckle them. Impatiently he pulled the first one off and handed her instead a pair of canvas espadrilles. They were navy, and she couldn't help but realize they were ridiculous with the rather formal salmon-colored knit dress.

"No, the heels are better," said his companion.

"We're going out into the lobby and into a waiting taxi," said the first man now. "Naturally you're distraught, Mrs.

Grey. Your husband and your physician have had a great deal of trouble finding you, but you've been known to wander off before. Sometimes you forget to take your medication. The desk clerk was terribly sympathetic. Mr. Grey here"—he jerked a thumb toward the bland man who was now taking a moment to smooth out the bedspread and replace the bedside phone—"is a patient, loving husband. He's so sorry for any inconvenience to the hotel."

"I'm old enough to be Mr. Grey's mother," said Sunny. The bland man was probably in his early thirties, but remarkably self-possessed in a way younger people didn't seem to be these days. Perhaps he was some kind of throwback.

The thin man shrugged. "The desk clerk is about eighteen. Everybody over twenty-one looks old to him. Besides, Mr. Grey was too upset to do much more than mope while I explained. No one paid much attention to him."

"What if I scream bloody murder on my way out?"

"You'll just confirm what I've told them. Paranoid schizophrenic. Assaultive." He opened his bag. "If you do get hysterical, Mrs. Grey, I'll have to give you an injection. To calm you."

"But really, it's not necessary. I'm sure you're as eager to talk about Marina's missing father as we are. It's just that it isn't safe to chat about such things in the coffee shop. Really, I'm used to these things. I'm sure you'll agree my arrangements are very sound."

Sunny didn't want an injection. "I guess I have very little choice," she said simply. Why hadn't she known she'd been followed to Marina's? Or had they heard her conversation with Marina on the phone? That would explain how they knew her name was Harriet Grey . . . unless the desk clerk gave it to them.

The doctor nodded to Mr. Grey and the three of them went out into the dimly lit hall. There was thick carpeting in bright orange and wall sconces that gave out a sickly orange light in garish patterns. The hall was deserted. As they got into the elevator and the doors glided closed, she heard the chime of another elevator and the cheerful rattle of the room service cart. There was her Scotch and soda, probably, and the roast beef sandwiches.

In the lobby Mr. Grey put a protective arm around her shoulder and murmured to her in a proprietary fashion. "The doctor has taken care of the bill, dear, and we'll have the bags sent on." Sunny went rigid and pale. His grip was fierce, and she felt the muscles in his arms and hands squeezing her tightly.

The doctor set his bag prominently on the counter. A little theatrical, that touch, she thought. Behind the counter the desk clerk, a young man with short oily hair and a downy mustache, nodded respectfully and gave her a furtive glance. A few bills changed hands. Sunny's eyes met the clerk's, and she glared at him. He averted his gaze, blushed, and pretended to be interested in a box of file cards.

She started to say something. She wanted to let him have a look at her again so he could be able to identify her again, and to attract the attention of the other people in the lobby, but Mr. Grey's hands dug hard into her shoulders and a second later she was being spun around with one man at each side of her. She could tell by the way they guided her they had done this sort of thing before. Their elbows prodded her along, and her feet practically left the ground. She knew, though, that to anyone who cared to notice, she'd look like a distraught woman fortunate to have the protection of two calm men.

The taxi, an old Yellow Cab, stood at the curb with its heavy door yawning open. She was pushed into it, landing on a hard green plastic seat. This certainly looked like a real cab, right down to its cracked vinyl, mended with electrician's tape, and the smell of stale cigarettes.

They left the curb as soon as the door touched close. Mr. Grey still had his arm around her, and the doctor sat in front with the driver. He turned to look into the back seat, but said nothing. If she spoke, if she said something, surely the driver would pick up that there was something odd about the arrangement. But the fact that although he'd pushed the flag on his meter down, he'd left without being given an address must mean that this wasn't a real cab. There was something else missing. She wasn't sure what. Oh, yes. The radio wasn't crackling as in a real cab.

She tried to extricate herself from the grip of Mr. Grey. She wriggled a little and he released her, then he pushed her to the floor.

She tried to bob up again and he put his foot on the small of her back. He brought it down heavily. She thought for a moment of Rancho Salubre. What an idiot she was, faking a back injury so she could go out and get this oaf's foot cracking her spine anyway. There was some kind of justice there. Lies often come true.

She tried to turn, to look up, but he maneuvered her back in place with his foot. She was furious that he only seemed to need one foot for this operation.

"Better check her bag," said the driver. He had a slight accent. Sunny wished she knew what his face looked like.

She heard the click of the clasp of her purse, and from underneath Mr. Grey's large foot she tried to adjust her eyes to the dark. All she could see was a cigarette butt, which loomed very large from her vantage point, more mended vinyl, and the corner of a dusty rubber floor mat. She thought of the compact. It occurred to her he wouldn't search that. Very few women nowadays used loose powder. The only reason she did was because the compact had been a gift from Gordon. He began flinging objects from her purse onto the floor. She saw a handkerchief on the floor mat beside her now, and her wallet, and her credit card folder. Then the compact. She was right, he hadn't expected it to be loose powder. It flew all over her and all over the floor.

"You idiot," snapped the driver. "What are you doing?"

"Looking for a weapon."

"No, you're not. You're looking for anything. Like an address book. Passport. Anything."

The man shoved her over with his foot and bent to collect the assemblage. While she was free for an instant she got her hands on the compact. She could feel the locker key in the powder. It was still there, wedged behind the clasp that held the gauze filter in place. She palmed it and said, "You idiot! There's powder all over me. What the hell are you doing?"

He brushed off some of the powder from his trousers, and Sunny actually enjoyed the comforting smell of her Charles of the Ritz powder. It was familiar and pleasant.

"Shut up," he said, sounding embarrassed. Sunny wriggled around some more so that her hand, the one with the key in it, was pushed up against the front of the seat. She peeled back a little of the tape that mended one of the cracks and pushed the key in as far as she could, into what felt like stuffing. She was kicked back away from it an instant later, but she rolled over the spot with her back, hoping the tape would stick again. It was the best she could do.

That done, she took a deep breath and screamed as loud as she could. They wanted her to be scared. She'd given them what they wanted. Besides, it made her feel better. And also, it probably annoyed them. She was amazed at the sound of the scream. It was truly frightening.

Gary Wayne Liddel sat at the wheel of his mother's Pontiac. The car was still now. In the dark he could barely make out the profile of his cousin David. David was scared, he could tell that. But David did whatever Gary told him. And besides, David's dad was a cop. If anything happened, they'd probably stay out of trouble. They could be released into David's dad's custody. Gary thought this was shrewd on his part, to have foreseen the possible consequences. A lot of guys were too stupid to figure out something like that.

Not that anything would happen. Gary knew how to

dismantle the part of the alarm system by the last loading dock. The warehouse manager was a slob of a guy, and stupid too. He'd rigged up that little part of the system so he could get in and out to help himself to a few things now and then. Gary had thought of telling them that the day he got fired. But then he had the brilliant idea of not telling. It was better that way. That way the warehouse manager would get blamed maybe. Or he could get fired when they discovered the missing stuff. Not that they ever seemed to care. It seemed like everyone helped himself to a few things now and then. Gary hadn't taken a thing. Not one little thing. And they canned him anyway. He should have taken what he could. Instead he'd tried not to screw up. And look where it got him. Well, he'd get what he had coming now.

It wasn't just the stuff. Gary looked forward to exploring the warehouse in the dark, all by himself, without anyone hassling him. Of course, David would be there, too, but that was okay. He even thought of going into the office, maybe trashing the place. That'd scare the old bitch of a secretary when she came in the morning, to find all the little plants kicked around, and Mr. Karcek could see the pictures of his kids all torn up in little bits.

"Ready, Dave?"

Dave grinned a sickly grin. The boys got out of the car, closing the doors quietly, and walked around the dumpster to Loading Dock G. Gary took the screwdriver out of his pocket and smiled. This would be fun. It'd get all that frustration off his chest. He knew he'd feel better, and wasn't that the most important thing? It wasn't good to walk around all frustrated.

Having the gags taken out was worse than she'd imagined. She began to retch, and she hated the man who'd said he was a doctor, sitting across from her, his knees touching hers, looking at her with false concern. The handkerchiefs themselves made two hideous sodden lumps. He laid them out on the desk beside her and examined them, like a doctor examining some hideous things he'd removed in an operation.

Her throat ached, and she put a hand to it gingerly. She had closed her eyes throughout the removal of the gags, much as she did at the dentist's office. She opened them now and looked around her.

She was sitting in a bleak office, a glassed-in cubicle of an office in what seemed to be a warehouse. They'd gone past rows of boxes marked "Fragile."

It was an old-fashioned-looking office, with an oak desk and chair in an orange stain. Sunny sat in a straight-backed chair of the same oak. There was a carpet on the floor, an electric blue and olive green shag square, unraveling at the edges. It must have been a remnant. In a glass case stood some examples of cut-glass crystal: a sherry decanter and glasses, a gaudily ornate champagne tulip, and some tumblers. There was a typing table with a row of plants behind it. They were succulents, like the plants that grew in Arizona. That was probably all that grew under the dim fluorescent lights. The lights crackled a little, and cast unpleasant green shadows. On the desk there were pictures of gap-toothed blond children in cheap gilt frames.

Around her stood the three men: the man she thought of as the doctor, Mr. Grey, and the cab driver. His cab driver ensemble looked overdone—a central casting cabbie circa 1940, with a proletarian-looking cap, a leather aviator jacket, and baggy tweed trousers. For the first time she could see the face of the cab driver. It was round and blond, not unlike the gap-toothed children's portraits on the windowsill, with metal-rimmed glasses that made a pair of pale blue eyes look grotesquely large. The cab driver looked concerned. Perhaps he hadn't known how rough the evening would be. But she was still convinced he wasn't an ordinary cab driver.

The doctor leaned toward her. "We're so sorry for the discomfort we've caused. Are you more comfortable now?"

She was delighted at the opportunity to speak. "Comfortable? I'm terrified. Who the hell do you think you are?" Her voice came out a frightening rasp. The gag had done more damage than she thought.

"I'm so sorry." He sat gingerly on the desk, moving aside an old-fashioned green blotter and a dangerous-looking memo spike to make room. "I imagine you aren't used to this sort of thing. Perhaps it's because you're involved in something a little over your head."

"Apparently," she said.

"Why were you talking to Marina?"

"Do all her visitors get run through your mill?"

He smiled, revealing gold dental work. It gave him a foreign appearance.

"Now, Mrs. Grey, don't be sarcastic. Our business should take very little time. We're on your side. That is, if you're on Alex Markoff's side, we're on your side. We need to find him, too."

"Why?"

"We're asking the questions here. Why were you looking for Alex?"

"Sentimental reasons," she said. "I had no idea . . . What's going on anyway?"

"Sentimental reasons?" echoed the doctor.

Sunny guessed this man was about the age of her son, Erik.

"You wouldn't understand," she said simply.

"Ah, Mrs. Sinclair, of course we understand. You were lovers. And now you're wondering whatever happened to him. When one grows older one wants to find out about the past. Unfinished business, they call it in therapeutic circles."

What a fool this young man was. He knew nothing about what happened when one grew older. There wasn't any urge to settle unfinished business. There was a whole brand new life that was much more vivid than the past. My God, people moved from their ancestral homes to trailer parks in Florida.

The past was often of less interest to the old than to the young. But in his ignorance he'd given Sunny a way out.

"That's true," she said softly, still appalled at the gravel in her voice. She sounded like a gin-soaked lady.

"So you wondered what became of your old lover?"

"I suppose so."

He stood erect, and Sunny noticed how short he was. "Wrong. You *do* know what happened to him."

"I do?" She was genuinely surprised.

"Alex Markoff was in Tucson two months ago."

"He was?"

"That's right. Perhaps driven by the same impulse as you are. To reestablish the past?"

"I never saw him."

"No?" He nodded to Mr. Grey, who approached Sunny. She noticed with some satisfaction that Charles of the Ritz powder clung in patches to his dark suit. He struck her hard across the face, palms open, with the back of his hand. She felt the knuckles against her cheek, and a sharper pain, too. When she caught her breath and looked incredulously at his hand she saw a heavy ring there. It was a large opal.

"Don't you know opals are unlucky?" she said inanely. She felt blood trickling down her cheek from the wound.

Mr. Grey looked nervously at his ring.

"Mrs. Sinclair, please don't prolong this," said the doctor now, seating himself cozily back on the desk.

"Could I have some water," she croaked.

The taxi driver, looking genuinely appalled at the turn of events, made as if to leave the office in search of water.

"There's some booze in the left-hand bottom drawer," said Mr. Grey.

"Even better," she said.

She bided her time as the taxi driver produced a bottle of some yellowish liquid. The doctor nodded toward the display of cut-glass crystal, and the taxi driver, after a moment's pause, very correctly chose a tumbler. He poured it out for her and handed it to her, sympathy radiating from behind his scholarly Coke-bottle lenses.

"Slivovitz," he murmured.

She took it, smiled a Scarlett O'Hara smile at him, and took a deep sip. If anyone was a potential ally here, it was this man. She surveyed his body. It was squat and powerful-looking. But against Mr. Grey? There was probably nothing he could do. Still, she clung to the sympathy in his eyes. As she sipped, she thought. Her best tack, she decided, was to act helpless. A sappy menopausal lady, who'd wandered into something by surprise in a sentimental quest for an old lover. It was a ridiculous story, of course, but so was the truth.

The doctor sighed.

Sunny remembered a party in London during the war with some Yugoslavs, and she remembered slivovitz. It was powerful, as strong as Scandinavian aquavit. Right now, that was just fine.

The doctor fiddled with his lapels. He wore a gray suit, much too old for him. "Mrs. Sinclair," he said, sighing heavily. "Please tell us what you know about Alex Markoff. We are determined to find him. For his own good. We know he was in Tucson."

Sunny thought of the mirror with "Takk" written across it in soap. It couldn't be. He couldn't have been so close and then disappeared. Absolutely too corny.

"There's nothing to tell," she said, trying to inject her voice with pathos. "I wish I had seen him."

"Very touching," said the doctor. He nodded to Mr. Grey again, who came forward dutifully, like a child in school called upon to recite.

"Stop!" said the taxi driver. The two other men stepped back. The taxi driver moved forward slowly, pulling another oak chair toward Sunny. The doctor and Mr. Grey stood against the sides of the room, hands folded in front of them. "Get me a glass," he said. Sunny was somehow comforted by his accent. He sounded cultivated, well educated. But what kind of accent was it? German? Slavic? He sat, and without looking, accepted a glass of slivovitz from Mr. Grey, who poured out like a well-trained waiter.

"I detest this sort of thing," he said apologetically. "I'm sorry my colleagues are so crude."

So this was their game. Mr. Grey and the doctor played cold. Then, when Sunny detested them both, the taxi driver came forward and played hot. It was an ancient interrogation technique.

For her sake she'd appear to buy into it completely. She sagged in her chair, looked at the taxi driver with cow's eyes, and allowed tears—tears of rage, but she wouldn't let them know that—to well up in her eyes.

"I don't understand . . ." she began, and trembled. This was involuntary, but that was fine, too. It suited her purpose.

"I'm sorry, Mrs. Sinclair, but we must know where Alex is. We don't want to harm him. You must understand, you have stumbled into something very important. For his sake, and yours, too, you must tell us what you know."

She closed her eyes and took another sip of slivovitz. "I wish I knew more."

He put his hand on hers. To her amazement she found comfort in its warmth. Their eyes met. As if he sensed the intimacy of the moment, he removed his glasses, almost unwrapping them from his face. He looked rather sweet without them, blinking for a moment to make the adjustment.

"He must be warned, Mrs. Sinclair. You can't do it. It's too dangerous."

She jerked herself back to reality. There was no one better to warn Alex than she. She was a totally disinterested party. She kept her hand under his, however. "If I knew, I'd tell you," she said.

He stood up suddenly. "But you do know."

"No," she said, sighing. "I don't."

"If you knew, would you tell me?" He looked over his shoulder at Mr. Grey.

"Yes," she lied. "I would."

"I don't want you to be hurt."

"I suppose I remind you of your mother," she said angrily.

He laughed. She liked his laugh. "No, my mother is not so chic as you, and she is more easily frightened." He raised a palm upward in a gesture that was anything but Germanic. He wasn't a German. Or even an Austrian. Sunny had made a hobby of guessing nationalities during the war in London. He was too blond to be a Frenchman. Whoever he was, whatever he was, his accent was the accent of a well-educated European. It was English-English with a low buzz to the "th" sounds.

"Does your mother know what you've become?" she said sadly.

He turned his back on her. "Don't be so clever," he said. "You're in no position."

From outside the office they heard a strange keening sound, followed by smashing crystal. After a second Sunny recognized the first sound as an adolescent whoop.

"What the hell?" said the doctor. Sunny was delighted to see genuine fear cross his weasly features.

The foreign man put down his glass. "Stay here," he said to Mr. Grey. He beckoned the doctor and the two of them left the office together. As they crept out the glass door she heard a long laugh from deep in the warehouse. It was definitely the laugh of someone very young.

Gary Wayne Liddel took another cardboard box full of white wine glasses and expertly removed the cardboard cross-hatch. Then he upended the box, and was rewarded with a satisfying crash of glass on the floor.

David looked nervous, but Gary nudged him, then stomped on the shards with his boots. David giggled and followed suit. There was only a second of the really exciting stuff in each box. Most of the glass broke on contact with the cement floor.

Gary moved on to another box. He felt so good. All his anger was getting out. That was what his therapist said was a good thing. Not that his therapist would hear about this. He was interested to see that most of the glasses broke off right at the stem. His foot had to shatter the cylindrical part. He figured he and David could tear up quite a few thousand dollars' worth in about twenty minutes. They would be too tired to do the whole warehouse. And maybe they should save a few boxes to sell. After all, that was what they were really here for.

Sherry decanters maybe. They were the most expensive item. He was disgusted with Mr. Karcek. Gary knew what the sherry decanters cost him. And he marked them up a hundred percent. "Keystone plus," Karcek had said to someone one day, fondling one of the things. There were two kinds. Square ones and round ones. Keystone meant a hundred percent. And plus. Karcek was a creep, making so much money on this stuff.

He took out his Swiss Army knife and started on the filament tape on another box. Then David came and grabbed his arm. He pushed David off, but David said, "I hear someone."

Gary stopped for a moment, his thin arm poised over the box.

David was right. Gary heard pounding feet coming toward him. He repositioned the Swiss Army knife in his hand. If he had to cut someone, he had to cut someone.

The footsteps came closer, and Gary dropped the box, grabbed David, and ran toward the office. Maybe they could barricade themselves in there and call David's dad.

Sunny sat in her chair, watching Mr. Grey. He looked annoyed, perhaps because he hadn't been invited to go out and see what was happening. They'd heard another cascade of crystal.

"You have powder all over you," she said to him.

He looked at her vaguely.

"Why don't you have a drink, too?"

"Shut up," he said with finality.

He came toward her and raised a hand to her. She turned her head to fend off the blow, but before she did she saw two pale faces in the doorway. She let out a semi-stifled scream.

He turned toward the direction of her gaze. Mr. Grey wheeled toward two young men. One was dark and thin, with a few spots of acne on his face. The other was shorter, with a full, wet mouth and light brown hair. As Mr. Grey turned, Sunny leapt up and turned the typewriter over on his foot. She was delighted to see the spasm of pain cross his face. She grabbed the memo spike.

"Shit," said one of the young men at the door.

Mr. Grey's face looked livid with anger. He braced himself on the desk and prepared to leap toward Sunny. She gazed down for a second at his hand, a second that seemed like forever, and looked at the bone structure. The bones that led toward the fingers were raised in tension. She brought the memo spike down between them, hard, pinning his hand to the desk. A pool of blood began to form around the spike. The metal base of the memo spike had little felt ovals on it, so it wouldn't mar a desktop. It quivered a little after she had plunged it down, and she marveled at her own strength. She brushed past him.

The two young men stared at her. She looked at their faces. The hint of a sneer began to come to the dark-haired one. The fair one looked toward his companion for a clue as to what to do next. Sunny knew immediately that they operated as one, with the taller, darker young man as the motivating force. She slapped that one hard across the face. The shorter fairer one began to weep. She pushed them both aside and went out into the warehouse.

It was dark in the outer warehouse. She knew she was making noise, as her heels clattered along the concrete, but she didn't care. She heard low voices, very far away, perhaps behind rows and rows of the cardboard boxes that surrounded her. If she could only remember how they'd come into the building, she could leave, perhaps in the taxi.

She found the door through which she'd been dragged. It was a fire door, heavy metal with a thick-looking lock on it. She twisted the catch, but it was clear she couldn't get out without a key. She closed her eyes for a moment and thought. Where would another door be in a warehouse? This one led to the offices. The others might be along loading docks, along the other side of the building.

7

THERE WERE TWO phones on the bedside stand. One of them emitted a low purr. The old man woke instantly. His wife, Lois, shifted comfortably under the blanket and turned over. The old man swung his pajamaed legs over the edge of the bed and took the call.

"Jackson here. Sorry to disturb you, but my orders are to call you on anything about the Marina Markoff survey," said a voice.

"That's right."

"Let me patch you through to our guy in San Francisco."

A new voice came on after some static. "Our routine surveillance of the daughter's phone picked up a Harriet Grey. Harriet went to see her. Seeing as she wasn't on any of our lists, we followed her. She's checked into a hotel near the San Francisco airport."

The old man sounded testy. "And?"

"She's been abducted."

"What?"

"We've traced her to a warehouse on the Peninsula not far from the airport. The warehouse belongs to a Karl Karcek. Crystal and cut-glass importer. Czech, left in 'sixty-eight. Still has relatives there. We've known about him for some time. He's in touch with the Czech consulate and we haven't been able to ascertain whether or not he's being coerced or whether he's a plant.''

"Never mind all that now," he said testily, searching for his glasses. "Who's Harriet Grey?"

"Want us to check with the FBI here?"

"Forget it, keep them out of it." If ever there was a national security case, this was it. Besides, he was close enough to retirement to forget about any jurisdictional niceties.

"Can you go into the warehouse and get her out?"

"I suppose so."

"Without anyone knowing who she is? Without her knowing you got her out?"

"Yes, sir," said a nervous voice.

"What's this Grey woman look like?"

"An older woman," the young man began, then after an embarrassed pause where he'd obviously remembered to whom he was talking, he added, "that is . . . older than Marina Markoff."

"Has she got good legs?" said the chief.

There was a puzzled silence. Did this young idiot think he was going off the deep end?

"As a matter of fact, I noticed them on the videotape as she came out of Marina's house. They were nice legs."

Women changed over the years, but their legs remained the same. Maybe it was Sunny Sinclair. The old man remembered Sunny from the war. He remembered her legs, too. He had read the report of her attempted recruitment by that boy. And of course they'd tried to recruit her because Markoff, or someone looking like him, had been spotted in Tucson. Maybe she was taking on the case as a wild card, an agent without a control. Or maybe someone else was controlling her.

"I want that tape transmitted to Langley. And I want her out. Then I want her followed. Get someone from there to start. And I want them to keep in touch."

When he'd hung up, he bent over his wife and kissed her,

and went to the kitchen for a glass of milk. From the kitchen he called to have a car sent around to take him to the office.

She decided to start checking for other doors as far away from the office as possible. She didn't know what the frightened-looking boys would do; it was clear they were just delinquent kids who'd broken into the warehouse and stumbled into the scene, but she didn't imagine Mr. Grey would stay pinned to the desk for long, and she didn't want to meet him again.

To her left was a long thin passage lined with boxes. She ran down the length of it trying to minimize the clatter of her heels. She clutched her raincoat and her purse, although she'd be prepared to let them go if she had to. All she really had to get was the locker key, wedged into the upholstery of the taxi. And then she had to take off.

She stopped to catch her breath at the end of the passage she'd just come down. Now she was in total darkness. She was sorry she had her light raincoat over her arm. It would make her easy to spot. Her hand touched a handle, like a bicycle handle, and as her eyes adjusted she realized it was a hand truck, for carrying stacks of boxes.

Suddenly she heard feet coming her way. Ahead of her she saw the two figures of her interrogators, the doctor and the cab driver. They were running now, and she heard the crunch of glass under their feet. Quickly she pushed the handtruck toward them. It collided with the cab driver, who fell into the broken glass. Sunny heard him scream and saw the figure of the doctor bending over him. The cab driver looked up at her. Blood was streaming down his face, and he held his palms up incredulously, examining the stigmata there. In the dim light, a shard of light glistened from his cheek.

"Get her," he said to his companion, his voice losing control. The doctor was caught up in his role; he took an extra second to bend over the injured man. He took another to clamber over him and the hand truck. Sunny took off down another dark box-lined passage. "Get her," she heard again.

She heard his feet pounding behind her, she even heard his breath. He wasn't used to running. Damn these heels, she thought.

She saw a square of light ahead of her, on the left, and another a little farther away, on the right. She thought the first one might lead back to the office, so she turned quickly down the second. Once she was around the corner, she stopped and listened for footsteps, examining in the short time she had, the arrangement of boxes around her.

He was close now, very close, and he turned down the first passage. Sunny pulled hard at two boxes near the bottom of the stack next to her. In what seemed like an agonizingly slow time, the boxes acted like a pyramid of oranges at the grocery store and collapsed in a jumble, sealing off the passageway. She began to run again, and heard the doctor scrabbling at the boxes and breathing hard.

Should she stop and pull over more of the boxes? No. It would take time, and she could seal herself in as well as seal them out.

If only she knew in what direction she was going. She wanted to stay away from the office, away from Mr. Grey and the boys, although they must have taken off, too.

She ran until she came up against another concrete building wall, lined with a workbench. The bench was covered with excelsior and rows of long-stemmed glasses. At the end of it was a large metal door with a large "A" painted on it. It looked like a garage door, and Sunny fiddled with the handle, but it wouldn't budge.

If there was a door marked "A," there had to be at least a door marked "B" somewhere. And the boys had come in somehow. She felt her way past more workbenches and came to the second door. She brushed a glass with her raincoat as she hurried toward the door, but caught it with her hand just before it hit the concrete. She sat for a moment on the cold concrete floor and exhaled with relief.

A moment later she was glad she was sitting, because she saw the huddled figures of the two boys, silhouetted against the end of the row of boxes, and she was sure they couldn't see her. They might know where she could get out of the building. She kept down and crept toward them, the glass still in her hand, her purse and raincoat over her other arm.

They were walking alongside the boxes, half in shadow, the smaller figure leaning against the larger. They made slow progress, past doors marked "C" and "D." There was one more door to go. That must be the way out. Sunny was thrilled to see a small sliver of light underneath it. It was open. Should she wait for them to go out?

Before they reached the door, a huge hulk of a figure leapt out at them from behind more boxes. "I've got them," came the voice of Mr. Grey.

"Where are you?" called out the doctor from far away.

The slightly accented voice of the third man yelled, "Forget them, get the woman!"

From what she could see, Mr. Grey wasn't following orders; he was grappling with the two boys. The crack of light under Door E gleamed tantalizingly at their feet. She heard grunts of exertion from the trio and huddled under the workbench as far as she could. There was a second shelf sharing the space with her and it was a tight fit.

From elsewhere in the warehouse two sets of feet could be heard. One fast, the other slower. She imagined that the shards of glass in his face and palms, maybe even in his chest, were slowing down the cabbie. The two boys were like limp puppets hanging on Mr. Grey. The taller one seemed to be pounding on his face while the other was crouched lower. She peered into the darkness. The smaller boy was biting Mr. Grey's leg. He batted back, but the boy stayed clamped onto his calf. Mr. Grey lost his footing and fell backward.

A second later the three of them cascaded into more boxes. There was the sound of glass breaking. She decided to move now—rushing toward Door E and discovering that it slid easily open. She opened it just about two feet and prepared to slide underneath. She dropped the glass. The sound of its breaking couldn't be heard above the scuffle still coming from the fallen boxes. She gathered her raincoat and purse around her and slid underneath. She was almost under when she felt a hand on her ankle. She was being dragged back under the door. The doctor was squatting next to her, a look of triumph on his face. She grabbed the broken glass beside her by its stem and raked the broken edge across his face. She saw a line of blood form wetly across his face, from his forehead, across one eye and down his cheek to his mouth. He released her and she rolled under the door.

She heard him thud heavily on the floor. Perhaps he'd fainted. She scrabbled across the ledge of the loading dock and jumped from it—a distance of about three feet—to an asphalt surface below. She was in a vacant parking lot of old asphalt. Weeds and California poppies had pushed through the cracks.

The ledge from which she had jumped ran the length of the buildings—from Gate E where she was to Gate A. There was a space underneath the ledge, a narrow space, between the building and the heavy timbers that held up the ledge. She squeezed between a couple of the timbers and crouched in the dark. Above her she heard the voices and the door opening. She made her way with difficulty through the narrow space, catching a glimpse through the timbers of the area. Across the parking lot was a sagging, rusting cyclone fence. In the adjacent parking lot she saw the shapes of German shepherds. They began an angry, hungry medley of barks.

Their noise covered the sound she made as she half walked, half crawled. She wasn't sure where she was going;

she just wanted to get as far away as possible. She heard voices above her, and footsteps, but couldn't detect any pattern in them. It sounded as if chaos reigned. Beneath her was hard dirt with broken glass here and there and plenty of cigarette butts.

When she came to the end of the tunnel-like passage, she crouched and looked out. Her face hurt, where she'd been struck. She explored the gash with her fingers. The bleeding had stopped, but it was quite a deep scratch. Her hands themselves were filthy, and one of her fingernails was broken off. Her purse was still strapped to her, and now she tied the raincoat to it by the sash. She wasn't going to give up her Burberry without a fight.

There was another two or three feet of building beyond the end of the loading dock where Sunny hid. She crawled out gingerly now, on her hands and knees, the way they'd taught her years ago in training, pulling herself along by her elbows.

The activity on the loading dock seemed to have stopped. She heard the cabbie cry out, "One of you lock those kids in the office. Knock them out first. And pull the phones. I'll cover the back here, and the other one checks out the front and seals off the entrance."

The dogs were still yelping and there was more walking overhead. At the corner of the building, crouching in a bunch of dandelions covered with dust, she was able to see a car, parked near a large blue dumpster. The parking lights were on. It must be the boys' car. Maybe they'd left the keys in. If they were smart they had, to ensure a quick getaway. But why had they parked it so far away from where they had presumably entered? Maybe so they could walk around the building on their way in and not disturb the dogs.

She took a deep breath and ran for the car. She got in easily and smiled to see the keys in the ignition. She turned the key and tried to pull the door in simultaneously.

''Wait a minute,'' said a voice at her elbow. She screamed. Mr. Grey stood there, his hand on the door. She slammed the door closed on his hand, watched the metal squeeze the fat fingers, glanced in horror again at the opal ring. Good. It was the same hand.

She threw the car into reverse and pulled away. The weight of his body pulled his hand out. Then she opened the door and slammed it shut more securely.

The yelping of dogs and the rotting cyclone fence gave her an idea. Making a great arc in the parking lot, she rammed the car toward the dogs, toward a corner of the lot where the fence seemed to be coming loose. She reversed and went out and saw that she had made a triangular shape in the fence where the rusty fencing curled away from the posts. She watched with satisfaction from her rearview mirror as the two rangy animals pushed their way through.

She doubted whether the doctor had had time to secure the boys in the office and get to the front of the building. The cabbie had said he'd take the rear. And from the screams and frenzied yapping of the dogs she decided Mr. Grey was out of action. She decided to go after the key. She wheeled the car around the building, passing precipitously over a couple of speed bumps.

She had a brief moment of panic when she pulled the car toward the front of the building and found herself headed up against another cyclone fence. This one looked impenetrable. After all, this car seemed to be a Pontiac, not a tank.

She reversed, made a Y-shaped patch of rubber, and set out to go the way she'd come.

The dogs had Mr. Grey down now. Unlike the police dogs she'd seen in films, they weren't simply standing guard over him. One was worrying at his throat, the other dancing barking circles around him.

The cab driver stood paralyzed on the loading dock, watching the grim scene. If he had any brains at all, he'd get out of there; the other dog would be up on the dock in a few seconds when he'd lost interest in watching his friend work over Mr. Grey.

The cab driver ran down the loading dock as she flew by, and jumped off. She guided the car toward him and came very close, hearing a chunk of wood splinter against her car as she took the corner.

She still thought she had time. He was in bad shape. She'd seen his frightened face as she'd swerved toward him. It was bleeding from the broken glass, and his pale blue eyes without their spectacles looked terrified. The fact that he was without his glasses might give her an advantage, too.

This time her way was clear. She whipped around the building and pulled up alongside the cab. It sat there very sedately, next to some Roman brick planters with a few sickly marigolds in them, as if it were waiting for a fare.

The key was where she had left it, tucked inside the vinyl crack, inside the stuffing. The whole back seat was covered with Charles of the Ritz face powder. She checked the cab. There were keys in it, too.

Something told her that the cab would be more convenient. She wanted to make her way to the airport, and she could leave it there in the cab stand. She slid into the driver's seat. It was too far from the pedals, but she slumped down and was able to reach them. Just as she was about to take off, she remembered the keys in the Pontiac. She went back and yanked them from the ignition. In the back seat she noticed a set of golf clubs. This must be the boys' parents' car.

Through two sets of windows she saw the front door open. The doctor stood there, looking confused. She pulled a club from the back and threw it at him. He ducked and she rushed to the cab. While she coaxed the car to life, the club sailed through the plate-glass window by the entrance to the office. An alarm sounded, louder than anything she could ever remember hearing.

She took off as the startled doctor lost his balance and fell back into the broken window.

* * *

Chandler Smith came into the old man's office. He'd wondered if he should shave. And now, as he saw how impatient the old man looked, he was glad he hadn't.

"So, they found you at last."

"Yes, sir."

"In the future, while you're working on a special assignment from me, sleep at home." He looked fiercely at Chandler Smith. "And alone, if possible.

"The Markoff thing heated up," he growled. "You know we've kept an eye on the daughter all these years."

Chandler nodded. Since he'd received the special assignment he'd read everything in the old man's private files.

"Nothing for years. But lately she'd been receiving visitors. The latest one is the Sinclair woman. At least, I think it is. A couple of Czechs picked her up tonight. Took her to an abandoned warehouse. I want her released and then I want her followed. If those guys are interested, we should be, too. Maybe she can lead us to him. You read about the Sinclair woman in the stuff I gave you?"

"Of course." Chandler had been intrigued by Alex's old lover. Her wartime photograph showed her to be a real beauty. He'd rather enjoyed imagining old Markoff and this smoky blonde screwing madly while the blitz raged on outside their window. The whole Markoff file was fascinating stuff, and over the past few days he'd become more and more intrigued with his mysterious quarry.

"Well, since the alleged Tucson sighting, we've kept her in mind. You know one of the guys on the regular investigation talked to her. He got nowhere. But now she's in the case. I think she is anyway. Could be someone else.

"I thought a connection between Alex and Mrs. Sinclair, as Sonia Magdalena Isdahl is now known, farfetched at the time we heard about it. But it was the only thing that connected Alex Markoff with Tucson. Besides of course the fact that Tucson is a border crossing—to Mexico and points south.

"Whoever this woman is, Harriet Grey or Sunny Isdahl,

she's the only one who's been able to get some sparks going from a branch office of the KGB.''

The old man broke off and answered a ringing phone. "You've got San Francisco? Good." He switched a button on the phone so Chandler Smith could hear both sides of the conversation. "These are the guys on the ground," he explained. "They should be flushing her out now. They should have done it twenty minutes ago."

"We're at the building," said a nervous voice. Chandler could imagine how a CIA stringer in San Francisco felt. He probably knew his career might be over soon if he didn't handle the situation so the woman got out and the police and the FBI and the press didn't hear about the incident.

"Is she in there?"

"I don't know, sir. The situation is pretty chaotic."

"What the hell does that mean?"

"We've got an alarm going off, and I hear police sirens. I've got a man down at the back of the building, with a communicator, but all I can hear from it is barking dogs."

"Hang around till the cops show," said the old man. "Tell them you're FBI; I don't care what you tell them. Just make sure the woman gets out and on her way. Then follow her." He paused, still holding the phone.

"I quit smoking last week," said the old man to Chandler. "But I sure feel like one now."

Chandler felt in his pocket and came up with a crumpled pack of low-tar cigarettes. The old man tore off the filter and accepted a light from Smith while they listened to crackling noises from the speaker.

"What's going on now?" bellowed the old man.

"Nothing. The cops just pulled up," said San Francisco.

"Well, go and introduce yourself."

"Right."

"Tell him you're linked up to Washington. Say it's the FBI."

A half hour later the old man had smoked all of Chandler's cigarettes. The latest they heard, before the man in San Francisco closed off, was that the police had rounded up two scared kids, two badly lacerated men, one a Czech consular official, and a local thug the police knew and called "The Arm" badly mauled by dogs, with a hand that had been punctured and crushed.

"Any sign of a woman at all?"

"There was a lot of face powder on the guy the dog got," was the reply. "It appears the kids are part of a separate incident. The car's here. But no sign of any vehicle the Czech was driving."

"Are you going to be able to keep this quiet?"

"I think so, sir. The kids are related to one of the cops—not one of the officers here, sir, but a member of the force . . ."

"Okay, okay. Who's got the Czechs?"

"The cops are turning them over to the FBI."

"Great! Who's going to help put together a story for the FBI? Got any ideas?"

"I'll try and get the local police to keep them in a cell till tomorrow, sir. That'll give us some time."

The old man slammed the phone down.

"Fly out to San Francisco," he said. "Check the hotel. I'm putting a passport check out on Harriet Grey. And we'll get someone in Tucson to see what happened to Sunny Sinclair. Could be this woman calling herself Harriet Grey's someone else altogether. Whoever she is, she sure can dish it out.

"Call me from the airport, Smith. I may have some new details."

Sunny peeled out of the parking lot in the cab. It reminded her of her father's old Chrysler, high off the ground with a deep gurgle of an engine. She imagined it was roadworthy, but she wished it weren't so conspicuous. On the dashboard sat a Yellow Cab hat, with checkers around the brim. Perhaps it belonged to whoever really drove the cab.

She put it on and couldn't resist a look in the mirror. She adjusted the cap at a more rakish angle. She couldn't help but laugh. She looked ridiculous, but from the road she'd look less peculiar.

From farther away she heard sirens. The police must be responding to the alarm. She didn't want to meet them coming out of an industrial park. She turned off a side road that ran alongside the freeway. She was in a strange area of warehouses and low office buildings, mixed with scrap yards. The roads here were a strange, convoluted mixture of private roads and public streets. She pulled in between two huge trucks in front of a concrete bunker of a building and killed her lights. The sirens went past her and she nosed the cab back out onto the road that ran along the freeway and headed toward what looked like an on-ramp, although it was hard to tell without her lights. Maybe she'd have to cross the freeway somehow to get back on the southbound lanes to the airport.

She'd have to turn her lights on when she rejoined the freeway. She flicked them on now and was shocked to see another police car looming toward her around a corner. She swerved and he went on his way, but the encounter scared her. If the police discovered a bunch of wild dogs, wounded men, not to mention all that broken glass, they might wonder who she was.

She better get on that freeway fast. She pulled quickly into what looked like an on-ramp, only to come up short at a red sign that said "Do Not Enter." She slammed the car into reverse—there was an awkward shift knob on the column and she ground the gears and winced before she got into reverse—and planted her foot firmly down on the pedal to get out.

She whipped back onto the road that hugged the freeway. Sooner or later it had to get her onto Interstate 5.

It took Sunny almost forty-five minutes to make the airport, cruising slowly through a jumble of industrial buildings, running up against dead-end streets. A couple of times she cranked down the window to listen to the comforting whoosh of the freeway so she could place it. Once she found herself overlooking an inky San Francisco Bay.

When she did make it she was pretty sure she wasn't being followed. She almost would have preferred a high-speed chase. The frustration of patrolling the darkened, confusing maze between the freeway and San Francisco Bay had been enormously frustrating. A few times she'd spotted blinking red lights from control towers, so she knew she was close.

When she did arrive she pulled into the taxicab stand, threw her cap on the dash and practically staggered to the first ladies' room she could find. She was a mess. Her scratch looked nasty, and a purple bruise spread over her face. She was covered with dirt and she had holes in both knees of her stockings. She rinsed off her face and ran a comb through her hair. Her nails were dirty and broken and she washed her hands perfunctorily, then put on a little lipstick and put a quarter in a machine that dispensed a blast of cheap cologne. She removed her stockings and threw them away. Thank God she had a tan.

Her shoes were impossible, one heel was almost off, so in a fit she tore off both heels. She was now wearing a rather peculiar pair of flats.

Her rumpled filthy raincoat she put on over everything and buttoned it to the collar. Then she set out for her locker. The flight bag was there. She patted it proprietarily. It was her only escape route, her only means of continuing the search.

The Pan Am ticket agent, a young black man with velvety brown eyes like pansies, said, "What happened to you, ma'am?"

"I was mugged in my hotel room," she said. "And I've lost my ticket, my credit cards, everything. I missed my flight and I have to get to London. Tonight."

The clerk wanted to credit her lost ticket against a new one, but Sunny stopped him. "Please. I'll have my travel agent take care of all that. Fortunately I can pay for a new ticket in cash."

"But it's very simple. It's all in the computer."

Sunny burst into genuine tears. "Just let me buy a ticket. I've had a horrible experience. They took my luggage—everything."

"But the police . . ."

"I just want to make a flight to London," she said between tears.

He handed her a large handkerchief. This one was a crisp linen square, much nicer than the hideous thing she'd had smashed down her throat. She took it gratefully.

"Okay, okay. But you have to have a passport."

"I do. I have my passport. It was in the hotel safe." She fished in the cheap plastic flight bag and came up with Harriet Grey's passport.

"The next flight is in three hours," he said. "Don't you want to talk to the police or anything?"

"I talked to the hotel people. I have to make a flight soon. My daughter's getting married. They told me not to leave, said I had to stick around and make a report. I wouldn't be surprised if the police sent detectives here after me."

The clerk looked dubiously at her now.

"I know it sounds crazy," she said. "But if I can just get to my daughter's wedding I know the unpleasantness of it all will go away. I just want to get on that plane and be left alone."

"Don't worry," he said. "They never care enough about muggings and stuff to send anyone to the airport after a witness."

He looked over his shoulder. Sunny followed the direction of his gaze and saw two men scanning the crowd. There was a long line at most of the gates.

"I'll tell you what, ma'am, I'll write up your ticket now and we'll put you in the Clipper Club."

Sunny knew about the lounge the airlines reserved for their best customers. She was sure she'd feel safe there.

"Oh, thank you," she said, patting the man's hand. He looked a little concerned, perhaps that he was letting a disheveled lunatic into the Clipper Club, so she added, "My late husband traveled a lot, and we always had that little secret code punched onto our tickets."

He smiled now, sure he'd done the right thing. He tapped into a machine and produced a folder. "Smoking or Non?"

"Oh, smoking I guess. What the hell?"

"And I do have to look at your passport." Sunny handed it to him.

"Thank you, Mrs. Grey."

"You've been so kind," she said. "I'm writing down your name so I can tell the airlines how helpful you've been."

She didn't dare look behind her, but Clarence Wilmot, the clerk whose name she was copying from his nameplate, seemed to be looking over her shoulder with apprehension. He had been ever since she'd sputtered on about detectives following her to the airport. He accepted her handful of hundred-dollar bills.

"Have a nice flight," he said automatically, beckoning to a porter to take her to the airline's private lounge.

She turned and noticed the two men. Whoever they were, it was clear they were looking for someone. So far, all they'd seen of her was the back of her head. She sidled away, maneuvering herself between the porter and the men. One of them, she could see from the corner of her eye, seemed to be moving toward her.

A young girl with a glazed expression came up toward Sunny and pressed a leaflet in her hand. "Are you happy?" she said.

The porter brushed her away. "Damn nuisances," he

mumbled. "Hare Krishnas. You used to be able to spot them in their orange sheet things, but now they wear civvies.

"Excuse me a moment, ma'am, I've got to pick up a bag for someone else in the Clipper Club. Man left his briefcase in the restaurant. I'll be back in a sec."

He darted into a restaurant and Sunny felt suddenly alone and vulnerable. She turned to survey the crowded lobby and saw one of the men who'd obviously been searching the lobby come toward her purposefully.

She flashed him a radiant smile and handed him the leaflet. "Are you happy?" she murmured. He threw the leaflet down and marched on.

Chandler Smith kept a flight bag with a toothbrush and a change of clothes in it at his office. It was a convenience mostly for his erratic private life, but it came in handy now. He proceeded directly to the airport, and within the hour he was waiting there. He called the old man.

"A few new facts, Smith. The San Mateo County Police say they almost collided with a Yellow Cab leaving the area of the warehouse when they answered the alarm. Our little lady could be in it. No sign of it since. But the hotel confirms she made an outside call from her room earlier this evening to Pan Am. I've sent a couple of men to the airport. The hotel's right near there.

"When you get there, call me again. This is strictly between you and me. No one knows I'm sending you out. As a matter of fact, no one knows you're involved in this operation at all. We've talked about this; I won't repeat it on this phone.

"Listen, Smith, those bums on the ground in San Francisco aren't worth shit. All I can say is, you better be.

"Nothing from Tucson yet. Our man there knows her socially. Says he saw her a few days ago. His wife says she's at one of those fat farms. Though from the video they've sent back here, I can't see why. Anyway, we're working on that angle, but apparently the fat farm has better security than a few government agencies I could mention, so nothing yet.''

The porter knocked on a door that to the casual passerby looked like a janitor's closet. ''Tell 'em Joe sent you,'' he said with a chuckle. Sunny inwardly blessed the man for pretending not to notice she'd been beaten up lately and that she was dirty. She gave him five dollars.

Behind the plain door was an elegantly appointed room with framed prints of old sailing ships, a collection of fake antique furniture and an Oriental rug. Free booze was standard in these places, and Sunny wasted no time ordering Scotch and soda from a polite Chinese attendant. Either he was unflappable or the ticket agent had called to say a recent crime victim was on her way. She thought of explaining, but was too weary. The collection of dark-suited businessmen glanced at her and went back to their *Wall Street Journal*s. She might have been in a men's club.

Sunny hadn't eaten, and she took a handful of salted nuts. They tasted divine. The attendant asked her to sign the guestbook. She signed Harriet Grey in the handwriting she'd practiced and ordered another drink. It went straight to her head. She leaned into the deep cushions of the sofa and relaxed. She really ought to sort out what she'd learned so far, but a polar-route flight would give her time for that.

She wondered idly how Marjorie was doing, posing as Sunny Sinclair. She couldn't believe she'd faked her back injury that very morning. It seemed like part of another life. She gazed thoughtfully at her drink. Perhaps it was a cousin of the Scotch and soda she'd heard tinkling merrily on the room service cart as the elevator doors closed on her. That seemed part of another life, too.

She thought of the broken crystal goblet, of the jagged line of blood running vertically down the doctor's face. She took a quick sip. Maybe that's why she'd felt it was another life. Since then, she'd been initiated in blood, like little English children who have the blood of the fox smeared on their foreheads at their first hunt.

Hours later the attendant pushed at her gently. "Mrs. Grey," he said. "Your flight."

She thanked him, tipped him lavishly, too, and made her way to the gate. Those few hours of sleep had really helped. She felt fresh enough to notice with sympathy a young good-looking man, obviously red-eyed and in need of a shave. Chandler Smith hurried past her to a bank of phones and called in.

"Nothing new here," growled the old man. "Those idiots didn't find her."

"She's been here all right," said Chandler, triumph in his voice.

"Yeah? How do you know?"

"Just a hunch. Before I called you I went out to the cab stand in front of Pan Am. There's an old Yellow Cab there. Full of face powder. Smells like expensive face powder. She must be an old-fashioned lady."

"What?"

"Loose powder. Only my mother uses that."

"She's young enough to take three pros and a couple of delinquent kids. And get out of the country without us knowing about it. Maybe what we need around here is a few old gals like that," he growled. "See if you can track her down. If the trail's cold, get on a plane and pursue the Central American angle. We think that's where Markoff's keeping his money. You'll be briefed at the embassy."

8

SUNNY SIGNED THE register H. M. Grey in a firm hand. She was exhausted from the transcontinental flight. Even in a wide-bodied plane, the flight was grueling. She wanted nothing more than to check into a quiet hotel room, put the Do Not Disturb sign on the doorknob, and relax. She'd better relax before she called Pamela. It would seem odd enough, her arriving unannounced.

The bellman looked slightly askance at her small amount of luggage. She'd managed to cover the bruise with makeup from a flight attendant. She didn't care. She tipped him with an American dollar bill, apologized, wondering vaguely what the exchange rate was these days, and closed the door on him. The dim hotel room looked terribly inviting. She stripped off all her clothes and walked into the bathroom. Damn. She should have chosen the Hilton. This very British hotel, one she remembered from the war, didn't have a shower. Just one of those deep tubs with a shower gadget that looked like a telephone receiver hanging from a graceful chrome hook. Tubs like this were marvelous when you wanted a deep soak. What she wanted now was a brisk shower. She drew a tepid bath and turned on the television. A lady in tweeds was instructing dog owners in their proper handling. Ah, she thought, there'll always be an England. There was something peculiarly soothing about the lady's drill sergeant voice.

She stepped into the tub and nestled in up to her neck. Her ankles were puffy from the flight. She rotated them and luxuriated in the feeling she was doing something for her body.

Even in her short trip from the airport she'd discovered that London had changed radically from the war. She and Gordon had been there in the early sixties. All she remembered of that trip was an enchanting hat she'd bought—turquoise flowers bristling with stamens. Could it be she'd worn such an anachronistic hat just twenty-odd years ago?

But during the war things had been different. She had thought it was a cosmopolitan city then, bristling with people from all over the world. But actually they hadn't been from all over the world. Most of them were white. Now the city was truly cosmopolitan, with streets full of Pakistanis and Chinese and West Indians and Africans. The Old Empire had come home to roost.

She wondered if she could find the old flat, where she and Alex had met. It was in Chelsea. Rather arty but very respectable. She closed her eyes and thought of the last time she'd seen Alex Markoff.

"I can't help it," she said. "I want to see." She stood at the huge window and reached up to open the blackout curtains just an inch.

"Come away from the window," he said.

"It's all right. The light's out in here."

Sirens keened. The wounded London skyline was black against the eerie red glow of the sky. In the street below Sunny heard cockney voices and the sound of rubble settling. Beneath the window she could barely make out two mushroom-cap helmets and the crouching figures with shovels, illuminated by the erratic hooded flashlight one of them held.

"There must have been a hit on this street earlier."

"Don't be silly. All the windows would have been shattered if it had been anywhere close. Is anything on fire?"

"Not that I can see. The fire brigade isn't out there."

She heard the sound of his shoes falling to the floor. "Come here," he said softly in the dark. She pulled the blackout curtains together and turned, barely able to make out his figure. He was pulling off his tie and opening the buttons of his shirt. "I've made you a drink." He turned on the lamp on the nightstand.

Sunny wore a peach-colored silk slip, real prewar silk cut on the bias, with thin straps over her white shoulders. She stood against the curtain for a moment, like an actress.

He smiled at her, his wide Slavic face with its slanted cheekbones and dark arched brows strangely at odds with his open American smile. He'd made them two Scotches with a splash of soda—there was a magnificent silver soda siphon in the flat, engraved with a crest—two generous drinks in heavy crystal tumblers. "No ice, I'm afraid," he said. "Do you mind?"

"No. I'm becoming very continental. Besides, there's a war on, you know." She sat next to him on the bed and accepted her drink. He put his hand on her thigh under her slip where the top of her stocking met bare skin. Outside an eerie buzzing sound was followed by a great crunching explosion. The windows rattled. She started, but the pressure of his hand on her thigh didn't change.

"God, it's right in this street," she said. "If they find our bodies wrapped in these monogrammed sheets under the rubble, everyone will know," she added flippantly. It seemed important not to let him know how frightened she was. If he were ever afraid, it wasn't here in London. It was wherever he went when he left London, places Sunny couldn't ask about, somewhere over the choppy gray sea.

"I'll have to speak to Billy about the ice," he said easily, pushing her abundant, fine blond hair away from her broad forehead.

"Don't talk. Just kiss me," she said.

He took the glass from her hand, set it on the nightstand, and kissed her. She felt the warmth of his hands through the peach silk as he pulled her to him, and she was suddenly trembling.

"Is that me, or the goddamn blitz that's making you do that?" he whispered, teasing her ear with his breath.

"Both, I think," she said truthfully, but where fear and desire overlapped she wasn't quite sure. Fear heightened desire. And of course, there was something terribly exciting about making love in such sumptuous surroundings. The flat reportedly belonged to some very rich people who were waiting out the war with South African relatives. How Billy St. Clair came to have charge of it, and how he managed to keep the linen sheets ironed, the bar stocked, and the brass basket by the fireplace stocked with dry wood, no one knew. One thing Billy hadn't arranged, besides the ice, was the heat. There wasn't any. Even by British standards, the place was cold.

Sunny and Alex spent most of their time there in bed. Once they had a breakfast in the flat, in front of the bedroom fireplace. They ate one precious fried egg each, a gift from Billy, Alex said, with slices of bread on paper-thin china plates with a Jacobean pattern, using heavy silver monogrammed forks. Everything in the flat was monogrammed or crested or both, and they joked about it. But it was silly to eat there when restaurant meals didn't require ration coupons, and besides, there was so little time for anything besides lovemaking.

In the morning Alex would slip out from underneath the crisp sheets when he thought Sunny was still sleeping and make a fire.

She would lie on her side, her head turned to watch him move about the room, enjoying pretending to sleep. Men, she felt, could walk around naked so much more naturally than women. She watched all the muscles in his long swimmer's body work together.

The very last morning they were together she'd watched him like that. Once he had started the fire, he walked back to the bed, stood over her for a minute, and then pulled back the satin-covered eiderdown. She felt a blast of cold, and she felt vulnerable, yet excited by his bold assessment of her. He put one hand on her shoulder and turned her over on her back, her long hair spilling over her face in a red-gold cascade. Still feigning sleep, she murmured, then opened her eyes and brushed the hair from her face.

There was an emotion in his face she'd never seen before. Its strangeness, its intensity, frightened her. She reached for him, grasping his hands. He shook her loose.

"I just want to look at you," he said. "I hardly ever look at you, just look at you, without touching you. I'm hardly ever more than a foot away from you. I want to look at you and never forget Sonia Magdalena Isdahl at twenty-two."

Sunny had never seen Alex Markoff again.

Dear Madge. Billy gazed fondly on Madge's rigid back as she sat at her typewriter. Secretaries turned over quickly at the CIA. But Madge had been here, if Billy remembered her file correctly, since 1959. Like most of the girls, she'd been recruited right out of high school from a small town in Virginia. Once, over a third drink, years ago, Madge had told Billy how thrilled she'd been when her high school typing teacher told her she could have a government job. "I thought it was because I was the fastest typist at John

Marshall High,'' said Madge, her soft Virginia accent coming out more strongly after the third drink. "Later I found out the company gets all its clericals from small towns around here because it's easier to run background checks on hicks who've never left little two-cornflake towns like mine.''

Now he put an arm around her and felt her flinch a little at his touch. She stopped typing. No matter. "How's my dear old Madge?'' he whispered. "I had another one of those wild dreams about you, so I thought I'd drop by and see you in the flesh.'' A prerogative of age. Men his age were supposed to be dirty old men. And harmless, too.

Madge smiled nervously. She liked Billy St. Clair. She really did. He'd always paid attention to her, remembered her name. They'd had a couple of drinks together a few times. She didn't remember if he was married then or not, but it didn't really matter. They'd just had drinks. Madge liked Billy because he seemed to remember, the way the others did less and less, that she was a woman. And that was comforting, even from an old fool like Billy St. Clair.

"How about making a little addition to the passport flagging list?'' he said. "Oh, what a good shade of green for you.''

"Well, you know, redheads should always wear green,'' she said. She watched him examine her hair and she wondered if the shade she was using was too vivid. A couple of days ago she'd seen an old photograph of herself, taken when her hair really was red, not streaked with gray, and she'd been shocked to see how much paler it was compared to the rinse she used now. And come to think of it, the roots didn't quite match anymore. She'd have to soften it.

Billy really was very nice, but of course it was completely unauthorized for him to be asking her this. Somehow, though, Billy was such a fixture around the place, it was easy to bend the rules just a little. And then, of course, there was the other thing.

"Oh, Billy, you really shouldn't," she said, smiling.

"It's a matter of the heart," he said dramatically. "I've been playing around with this woman for years, and I think she has a pair of my cufflinks. Terribly compromising. I've got to know where she is."

Madge giggled. "This is the first time you've asked me to put a woman's name on the list. Who is she?"

Billy wrote quickly a name and number. "Harriet Grey. Why, Billy, she's already on the list."

Billy raised his eyebrows. "Oh, really? Who else has that slut been playing around with?"

Madge didn't want to tell him how Harriet Grey made the list. But she did.

As he ambled back through the maze of corridors, Billy thought hard. So the old man had a handle on Sunny now, too. Well, maybe that was okay. Thank God for Madge. And thank God for that Russian embassy chauffeur a few years ago. Poor Madge. When Billy confronted her with him, ever so delicately, she swore up and down he'd told her he was a West German. It didn't matter. And when he showed her the photograph, taken surreptitiously at a Washington singles bar catering to those who'd been around once or were beginning to fear they never would, her face, surprisingly young and radiant, turned up to the chauffeur's, he knew he had her for life. Madge didn't want to go back to that two-cornflake town.

Still, Madge was a good sort. Billy always tempered his requests with a little friendly flirtatiousness, a kind word here and there. There was no point stripping the poor woman of whatever dignity she had left. She was much more helpful this way.

"Don't worry, Madge. I've suppressed this," he'd said calmly when he showed her the photograph. "Because you're a nice girl.'' Madge, bless her heart, had taken the more pleasant option and their relationship was carried on under the pretext that the incident was dead and buried. Of course, they both knew it wasn't—it was always there, ready for Billy to spring whenever he had to. But Madge was a well-brought-up Virginia girl. She didn't like unpleasantness any more than Billy did.

Sunny spent most of the next day asleep. When she woke, the light from the window seemed to indicate that it was afternoon. She examined her face in the mirror. The bruise didn't look much better. She'd give herself another day to heal before she contacted Pamela. She had to buy some clothes and respectable luggage anyway.

In the street outside her hotel she saw that there was a light drizzle. Good thing she had her Burberry. She bought a newspaper at a stand and went into a depressing-looking sandwich shop to get a bite to eat. Wedging herself by the wall against her precious flight bag, she opened the paper. The first thing she saw was the date. ''Oh, my God,'' she said.

The old man hung up the phone. His face was grim, but there was a glimmer of resolute satisfaction in it. Gone, completely gone. His people were trying to track down her airline ticket, but the airlines weren't cooperative, and thousands of people flew through there every day. Well, it had to be on a computer somewhere. If she was flying under the name Grey. But by the time they got the information, she could have gone on somewhere else. He took out his copy of Sunny's file one more time. It was there in brief detail, what she'd been up to since the war, which on the surface didn't look like much. A husband. Two kids. His eyes flicked over the data again. Then a date leaped out at him. Today's date. She had a daughter, Audrey. And today was her birthday. He'd get a tap on the daughter's phone by any means, fair or foul. It had probably better be foul. There was just a chance . . .

Sunny chewed her sandwich slowly and thought it all over carefully. If she didn't call Audrey, Audrey would worry. It all came from this ridiculous Norwegian preoccupation with birthdays. Birthdays were so sacred in Norway that important ones were put in the newspaper—when you turned sixty or seventy. And *everyone* got congratulated on your birthday—your mother, your brother. *Gratuleren med dagen.* Congratulations with the day.

Audrey wouldn't believe her mother could forget her birthday. Sunny felt a horrible pang of guilt that she had, but then she reminded herself that things were not at all normal in her life right now. If she had a phone credit card—but it could be traced of course. Everything could be. Would there be a tap on Audrey's phone? It seemed unlikely. If the CIA was looking for anyone, it was looking for Harriet Grey. Still, she didn't like it.

She steadied herself and thought some more. If Sunny didn't call, would Audrey call Rancho Salubre? Make a fuss? They'd give her Marjorie. Marjorie wouldn't be able to handle that. Her whole careful cover would be blown.

She had to call Audrey. She'd call her from the hotel. Pay for the call in cash. And check out. She'd have to speed things up. Get to see Pamela sooner, bruise or no bruise. England was a big place. Once she'd left her hotel, how could they find her?

And what would she say to Audrey? She hated to lie to her own daughter. She counted on her fingers, figuring the time difference. If Audrey was at work and had that damn machine on . . .

Back in her hotel room she made the call. Audrey's voice on the machine filled her unaccountably with tears. She choked them back, made her voice as normal as possible and said, loudly, in case the transatlantic connection was a poor one, "Happy Birthday, darling. I'm sorry I missed the day itself, but as soon as I get back we'll have a special lunch and I'll give you your present. *Gratuleren med dagen*. Marjorie and I are getting in terrific shape. Wait till you hear about my workouts. Bye." She hung up and thought fleetingly of the moment in the hospital, this day some twenty-eight years ago, when they'd handed her that tiny bundle. She pushed the thought out of her mind. Mothers, she decided, couldn't be good spies. She gathered up her things and prepared to check out.

"London," murmured the Old Man. "England. She's in England. Now, what the hell is she doing there?" He picked up the phone and, after some trouble, got through to Chandler Smith in San Francisco.

"We found Harriet," he said simply. "And she's Sunny Isdahl. She called her daughter's answering machine. From a hotel in London. She's already checked out. Better get over there. I'll put a man on it until you arrive. Yes, I know London's a big place. All we can hope for is to keep tabs on her known associates. Actually, there's only one. Her old roommate. Pamela. I remember her from the war. I'm getting on it right away. I'll be in touch."

Pamela looked lovely. Sunny was always startled to see old acquaintances. But Pamela looked like nothing but a softer version of her youthful self. Funny, she thought, because she herself had grown tauter, more sinewy, while Pamela had blossomed into a dewy-looking English rose. Eyes like periwinkles and cheeks like roses.

Pamela wore stout tweeds, like the dog lady on the BBC. Sunny suddenly felt terribly citified in a too-tight lavender cashmere sweater from Marks & Spencer. She'd thought she looked country English, but she looked raucously American.

Pamela grabbed her bag in a red-knuckled hand.

"You look maddeningly slim," she said. Why at our age must we always comment on one's preservative powers? thought Sunny ruefully. "Lars will be absolutely captivated. Tell me, what you are doing in England? Just traveling on your own?"

For a second Sunny felt like saying she was embarked on a walking tour. She had read about walking tours somewhere, maybe in Agatha Christie or Dorothy Sayers.

Pamela lived in what she called a cottage, but what in America would have been called a Tudor mansion. It was a rambling half-timbered structure, with blowsy roses climbing over the gate and leaded-glass windows.

They walked up the path to the yapping of dogs, and Sunny admired a perennial border full of delphiniums and hollyhocks, columbine, lupines, and stock.

Lars, whom Sunny remembered in uniform, now looked casual in a nubby hand-knit sweater and twill trousers. He greeted them with a trowel in one hand and a clay pot of some hopeless looking vegetation in the other. "Working on the herb garden," he muttered, in a voice more English than Scandinavian.

"Lars has great ambitions for the herb garden," drawled Pamela. "He's found some old tract by a medieval monk and he's trying to train them all into a knot." Pamela pronounced Lars in an unabashedly English fashion, making the *s* into a *z*.

Soon they were all sitting in a sitting room out of a Noel Coward comedy. There were baggy chintz slipcovers on the wing chairs, a clashing chintz print on the sofa, a forest of small mahogany tables including a sofa table bristling with silver knicknacks, and a tray with a silver tea service—Earl Grey tea in one teapot, hot water in another, a plate of sliced lemon, sugar lumps, and cream in silver containers, and a plate of sandwiches spread with what Sunny remembered as

potted meat and also sandwiches of cucumber and watercress. There was also a yellow cake swirled with jam.

Sunny helped herself to everything and wondered how
England's upper-class could ever sustain life between a
kippery breakfast, a boiled lunch and dinner, with such fare.
Wasn't it in the *Importance of Being Earnest* that everyone
had lived on cucumber sandwiches? Watercress sandwiches
had even less substance.

Pamela and Lars talked about the garden, the children, the
cottage, and Lars's business. He was an executive in the
English branch of Volvo.

"Do you remember Alex Markoff?"

"I certainly do. Your old flame." Pamela looked arch.
"We were all terribly impressed. He was tall, dark, and
handsome."

"I wonder what ever became of him."

"We saw him. After the war. Years ago." Lars poured out
brandy in small glasses.

"His wife," said Pamela, raising her expressive brows,
"looked exactly like you."

"Really, darling," said her husband. "She wasn't nearly
as attractive as Sunny."

Pamela ignored him. "Slim and blond, with waves around
her face. Smooth brow."

Sunny slipped off her shoes and curled her feet cozily
underneath her in the deep sofa. A large orange cat bounced
up next to her and made itself into a puffy ball.

"If you don't like cats, kick him off," said Pamela.

Sunny shook her head and stroked its fur.

"She seemed, as I recall," said Lars, "rather unhappy. A
brittle sort of woman."

"Rather too refined, if you know what I mean," said
Pamela. "There's such a thin line between refinement and
vulgarity, isn't there?

"They had a couple of children. A girl and a boy. With
Russian names. Rather fanciful names, I thought. I can't

remember them now. Ivan or Boris or something. And Alexandra or Natalya. I can't remember. Strange for a Cold Warrior.''

"When was all this?'' said Sunny.

"Let's see, it must have been in the early sixties. He was stationed here, at your embassy. Very vague about his job. Lars and I just assumed he was, you know, at the same old stand.

"We saw a bit of them. She gave little dinner parties. They had a magnificent flat. And wonderful help. Honest to God British servants.'' Pamela paused and looked thoughtful. "As to what he was like, how he had changed since we first knew him—well, he was older, of course. Less intense. Quite an affable man, a polished host. Although that may have been part of his job. There were always quite a few quietly influential people at his parties. I always imagined we were there as part of his cover. To make it seem as if he were what he was supposed to be, a commercial attaché, while he was picking up the odd bit of political information.

"I can only think of one time when the facade, if it was a facade, slipped. I asked him if I could see the children. They were sleeping. He beamed, he positively beamed, and I remember thinking how touching. You know, our son is a wonderful father, and our son-in-law, too. Changing nappies, kissing the children. Not like in our day.''

"I beg your pardon,'' said Lars huffily.

She waved a hand in the air. "Oh, you know what I mean. Anyway, he took me by the hand and led me up to their rooms. The girl was in a cot—what you call a crib. Very pretty little child, but with a serious little face, like her father's face. The boy was in another room. Alex bent over the child and kissed him, and he told me, 'Pamela, nothing makes me happier than these children.' He looked down at the boy—of course, they always break your heart when they're asleep, they look all dewy and innocent, don't they?—and he said, 'I'd give my life for this little boy if I had to.'

"I was rather embarrassed by the intensity of it all, but moved, too."

Of course Pamela would have been embarrassed, Sunny thought. English people wouldn't say a thing like that. But what Pamela didn't know, and what Sunny did know from reading the dossier Billy had shown her, was that Alex knew what it was to risk one's life. And that boy had died before Alex. The story was the closest she'd come to learning about Alex. And somewhere, from that new knowledge, had to be the germ of a plan.

The plan came to her later as she lay between wakefulness and sleep in one of the narrow guest room beds in Pamela's house. If Alex could be reached, if he was still alive, if Marina could communicate with him. It was a slim thread, but it was her only chance. She had to get back to Marina as soon as she could. If she failed, she'd go back to Tucson and hope that Harriet Grey would die a quick and painless death.

But that alternative seemed very grim to her. Why? Was she frightened after her abduction? Did she think she'd be safer if she found Alex? She pushed all these questions from her mind and fell asleep, still thinking fitfully of the plan.

Sunny had decided she had to get back to Marina without alerting anyone—neither Billy, nor the CIA, nor the men who'd taken her from her motel in San Francisco. She needed a new passport. At first she thought of going to the embassy as Sonia Sinclair and claiming hers was lost. But if anyone was keeping track of her movements—and Billy had given her the strong impression that the CIA would do anything to get to Alex and kill him—she really needed another passport. Harriet Grey was compromised, too.

"If only I had a double," she said vaguely. Then she remembered that of course she did. Her second-cousin Ingrid. The resemblance had been striking when they were teenagers. Ingrid's own grandfather had mistaken Sunny for

Ingrid on the street in that little fishing village during the war. She had to get to Ingrid, hope Ingrid had a passport—all in all she thought it likely; most Europeans did—and take it. It was all incredibly easy. She'd go to Norway without a passport, the way she'd gone before. During the war. With Alex.

9

SUNNY FIRST MET Alex Markoff in a drafty Scottish castle. She'd been called to Scotland, she assumed, for routine translating duties. She was never told, and of course one couldn't ask. She'd only been told to bring warm clothes, and it was good advice. She could see her breath in the air of the cavernous main hall where she stood with her small suitcase.

A moment later she was installed in a grim bedroom, an old servant's room under some eaves, with a bird's-eye view of the unkempt grounds and of craggy mountains in the distance. Then she was taken down one flight to what had apparently been a much grander bedroom, with Victorian wallpaper and a brass fireplace. Now, however, it was fitted out like an office, with gray filing cabinets and serviceable desks and chairs. A thin, balding man with steel-rimmed glasses sat behind the desk, and lounging by the fireplace, wearing a dark sweater and gray flannels, was Alex. She recognized him at once as someone very handsome, very serious, and very young.

"Sit down, Miss Isdahl," said steel spectacles. He had been introduced as Colonel Huntington. He had a file in front of him, and he seemed to be consulting as he spoke. "You're of Norwegian background?"

"Yes."

"And do you know a Hjalmar Halvorsen?"

"There are lots of Halvorsens in Norway. But I have a relative named Hjalmar Halvorsen. He's my mother's uncle. My great-uncle."

"What do you know about his politics?"

"Nothing much. I met him before the war. Just briefly."

"Miss Isdahl, your great-uncle is a pretty important man right now."

"Uncle Hjalmar? Impossible."

"Impossible?"

Was she being told Uncle Hjalmar was a collaborator? Would they send her home as a security risk?

"He's a very simple man. Very kind, very simple, but never important. He's an enigma even to the family."

"Kind of a loner, you'd say?"

"No question about that." She smiled. "He's a lighthouse keeper. Or he was."

"He still is. That's why he's so important. As you are no doubt aware, the Germans have taken over the Norwegian lighthouse system. They've kept a lot of the same people. And they've kept the lighthouses dark except when they need them, and then they send out a special order."

"If he's still on the payroll, it doesn't mean he likes the Germans," she said heatedly. She glanced nervously at Markoff, by the fireplace. He was smiling at her, amused no doubt at her family loyalty. It must seem a little naive. She gave him a stern look.

"Not at all, not at all," said the colonel soothingly. "Let me tell you our problem. We need a light on at a specific time for a specific reason. Your uncle's light. We need his cooperation for just one night, then we're prepared to get him to Sweden. He won't talk to anyone. The reports"— the colonel looked embarrassed—"indicate he may not be quite right . . . that is, the strain . . ."

"Uncle Hjalmar was always eccentric. I don't think he's nuts," said Sunny. "He's a painfully shy man."

"Would you say you got along well with him?"

"It's hard to tell. He does have family feelings. And I look like his granddaughter—my second cousin. He liked that."

"We've gotten nowhere with him. We can't even get anyone near him. We were wondering if you could talk to him."

"Go into Norway?" Sunny's eyes glistened. "But you never send women in."

"It's a special case. And of course, you're free to turn this down. The Americans have said we can borrow you."

"I'll go. I'll talk to him. But I don't have the training to get behind the lines. I haven't been to jump school."

"Don't worry about that. We have a guide for you. The Americans wouldn't let you help unless they sent along an American guide." The officer seemed annoyed that the loan of Sunny was conditional. "Alex over here. He's been in and out a dozen times. And you're not jumping in. We're sending you on the Shetland Express."

Sunny looked hard at Alex. "How's your Norwegian?" she asked him.

He answered in Norwegian. "You can do the talking. I'll do everything else." It was passable Norwegian and she was surprised. He was too dark to be a Norwegian.

"You're dark for a Norwegian," she said. "Don't you stick out there?"

"You'll be safer with me than I'll be with you," he said.

Sunny was trained and retrained. She'd memorized the message to Uncle Hjalmar, the important date, the contacts he'd make for the escape to Sweden, the appeal to patriotism. She'd memorized the route, and she'd been assigned a bundle of worn-looking clothing with Norwegian labels. Skiers' clothing, with a hand-knit sweater. She'd been given a small capsule containing cyanide.

She crossed the sea on a beat-up fishing boat manned by fishermen from the Shetland Islands, and she felt a great spasm of fear when she set foot on Norwegian soil, but she was sure Alex Markoff didn't know how frightened she was.

By the time Uncle Hjalmar came into the little coastal town for supplies, they'd waited two days at the farmhouse of a Norwegian resistance member. Alex and Sunny spent long hours together waiting for word. They spoke very little, Sunny out of fear that her fright might become evident, and because Alex Markoff didn't seem to want to talk. There was a military aspect to the whole thing. She'd always thought that there'd be a playful element to under-cover work. She knew now it was really a cold feeling in her stomach. And the dark man with her was of absolutely no comfort.

She stopped Uncle Hjalmar on the street. For a second he thought she was her cousin Ingrid. He looked terrified when he realized who she was. But when she did manage to talk to him with Alex, who said nothing, at the farmhouse, he embraced her and wept. He listened carefully to her appeal, sucking noisily on a pipe, running gnarled hands through his wavy silver hair.

"There'll have to be a change in the escape plans," he said finally.

"What do you mean?"

"I've got a couple of people with me at the lighthouse. The widow of an old school friend and her child. They're Jews."

"No wonder you've kept people away," said Sunny in awe.

"I've been terrified. I've managed to move them around and keep them out of sight whenever the Nazis come in and tell me how to run my lighthouse. But I don't think I can keep it up."

Sunny didn't know if she had the authority to okay a change in the plan, but Alex nodded when she looked at him questioningly. She said that the widow and child would be taken to Sweden, too. She gave him the Norwegian contact who'd make the final arrangements. When he'd left she said to Alex: "Now I hope to God nothing gets all loused up."

"It's not your problem anymore," he said. "And if you

make it your problem, you won't be any damn good anymore yourself.''

''Thanks for your sympathy,'' she said wearily. ''I've just got a sweet old man, my mother's uncle, in pretty deep. And I feel lousy about it.''

He took her by the shoulders. ''He was already in. If the Gestapo found out about the Jews he's hiding, he'd be imprisoned or killed. You may have saved his life. And theirs.''

She relaxed a little, and smiled.

He had let his hands drop to his sides. ''But I'm only telling you that because you're an amateur. My first advice is best. You did what you were told. Now your responsibility is to get the hell back to London and in one piece. We're only halfway through, you know. And now's the time to be extra vigilant. You found him; you talked. You made the deal. Don't give him another thought and don't relax. There's a lot of miles ahead.''

''When are we getting out of here?''

''Tonight. We're spending the evening in a barn on the hill about a mile from here. We're going back the way we came, and we set out at dark.''

They shared the barn with a couple of fragrant cows. Alex threw his knapsack into a hayloft and stretched out in the spiky yellow hay. ''Try and sleep a few hours,'' he said. ''It'll do us good.''

She was too nervous to sleep. She sat on the floor, watching the cows chewing their cud and rolling their brown eyes at her in curiosity.

Alex Markoff's breathing became regular. She watched his sleeping profile. He looked very gentle now, his lashes resting on his cheek. She smiled at him. Who was he, anyway? How did a young college kid, or whatever he really was, get so hard so fast?

She crept on her hands and knees closer to where he slept. Maybe some of his calm would rub off on her. Her stomach had been full of butterflies for days. But, she had to admit, there'd been moments when she'd felt marvelous. When she knew that Uncle Hjalmar would help, when she knew she'd come in and done the job.

Suddenly, from outside the barn, she heard dogs barking. A second later she heard voices. "I tell you there's no one in there, and if there is I'd like to know about it."

"We'll find out soon enough," said another.

She found herself clinging to Alex. His eyes were wide open but he hadn't moved. They heard a rattling noise at the barn door, where a wooden board fit into brackets. The cows shifted nervously.

She felt him wrap his arms around her. "There's one damn good way out of this," he whispered into her hair. "Act indignant, you've had a roll in the hay rudely interrupted."

A second later he'd ripped off her thick cardigan and wrenched open her shirt beneath it.

"Open the door please, now," came from outside the door.

"Just a second, just a second. Now don't go stomping around in there putting the cows off their milk" was the reply. Sunny admired the man's coolness as she herself pulled off her shoes. Alex was peeling off his shirt, and he'd started at the belt on her ski pants, when the door swung open. He pulled her to him, she felt his chest against her naked breasts and his mouth on hers, his hands twisted up in her fine, red-gold hair.

A second later he pulled away from her, and they turned to see three men by the light of kerosene lanterns. Sunny screamed and clutched his shirt to her chest. Alex let out a frustrated sigh and fell back into the hay. *"Svarte helvete,"* he said, a curse, in perfect accent.

Sunny turned modestly away, but through her hair she saw the men. Two men were civilians, the third wore a German uniform.

Sunny began to cry. She sniffled loudly.

The German eyed her lasciviously, a foolish grin on his face. The smaller of the two civilians said testily: "Our reports were correct. Your barn is occupied."

"We must ask them for their papers."

Sunny and Alex had papers, but she was terrified to think about an interrogation. Her cyanide capsule, in a compartment in the hell of her boot, was meant for just such a contingency. She knew Alex's Norwegian wasn't good enough. And she knew whatever happened she'd never take the cyanide capsule.

The farmer laughed. "You can't be serious. It's clear what these young people are about. Weren't you young once, too?"

"They could be dangerous."

"Look at that lovely pink glow on the girl. She's only interested in one thing."

The German asked for a translation of this last, and the small man gave it to him. He laughed appreciatively and slapped the farmer on the back. *"Ja, ja. Sehr schön,"* he said. The little man frowned and began to remonstrate in German. The officer just waved at him and he fell silent. Then the German clicked his heels together and bowed to Alex and Sunny.

"I don't know who you are," said the farmer now. "But I want you out of my barn by dawn. Sooner if possible. My cows have had enough excitement for one night."

They left, shadows from the swinging kerosene lamps ricocheting over the old walls. "Want a little drink, gentlemen?" said the farmer amiably. "I've got some old aquavit back at the house."

Sunny collapsed, sobbing tears of relief edged with the hysteria of fear. He put an arm around her neck and pulled her to him. They lay together, locked in a desperate embrace, while he pushed her hair from her brow and said softly, "It's okay. You're all right now. You're safe."

She clung to him, trying to control her sobs, her face buried in the hair of his chest. After a second her sobs were interrupted by laughter, no less hysterical, but more exhilarating than terrifying. He began to laugh, too. They looked at each other, gave each other a hug of triumph, and laughed again. He kissed her exuberantly on the mouth. She began to pull wisps of hay from his hair and kissed him back. Suddenly she remembered her naked breasts. She pulled away and her blue-gray eyes became large and solemn.

His face became grave, too, and then he smiled very slightly, a sideways smile that didn't include his eyes. He reached out and traced the curve of her breast with his fingertips, lingering for a second on the pale pink nipple. He took her slowly, silently in his arms and they kissed—a leisurely, long kiss—as if they had all the time in the world.

Ever since that time, her first time, Sunny had felt a little leap of excitement at the smell of fresh hay.

She was sure Pamela and Lars had been bemused by her visit. She hadn't written them that she was coming, she must have seemed edgy during her stay. And there was the bruise, covered more or less successfully with orange makeup, but still visible and now turning a sickly green, that they'd been too polite to mention and that Sunny had been too weary to explain with some phony story.

It occurred to her that they felt sorry for her, alone and widowed. On the railway platform, waiting for the train back to London, Pamela had taken her arm and whispered into her ear: "Look, there's a distinguished-looking man about our age. Maybe you'll have a nice chat with him on the train."

Sunny looked rather nervously in his direction. He seemed engrossed in the *Times*. She was jumpy, she knew. She wished she hadn't called Audrey. Still, it was absurd to suppose that someone would be watching her on the platform of this poky little railway station.

"You're sure you'll be all right?" said Lars, with a frown.

Sunny had told them she was going up to Scotland to look up some of Gordon's relatives. She didn't know a thing about Gordon's Scottish relatives, and neither had Gordon, but it seemed plausible.

"Oh," Pamela had said. "Sinclair. Yes. I believe there are Sinclairs in Aberdeenshire and in Northern Scotland as well. Which lot were your husband's family?"

"The Aberdeenshire Sinclairs," Sunny had replied. Actually she was going north to Lerwick, and when questioned it seemed wisest to lie as much as possible. It was amazing how easy it became. They had provided her with a railway guide and she'd planned her itinerary.

"Of course I'll be all right," said Sunny now. "This train will take me to Euston Station, then I'll go over to King's Cross and take my train to Scotland."

"You're very brave to travel alone," said Pamela.

"I suppose I am," said Sunny with a smile.

She was relieved when her train arrived and took her away from Lars and Pamela and their quiet life. She had felt so false staying with them. Had her life with Gordon seemed as tranquil? She supposed it had.

Euston Station was modern and vaguely depressing. British railway stations, Sunny felt, should be monuments to Victorian grandeur and optimism.

She consulted her pocket map of London. It was a short walk over to King's Cross. She decided to go by Phoenix Road. She was sorry she hadn't had more time in London. Her short walk between stations wasn't taking her through anything very scenic, either. There seemed to be a lot of urban renewal going on in the area her map told her was Somerstown and which she certainly didn't remember from the war. The noisy construction, the mess of excavating and building, reminded her a little of the blitz. At Pancras Road she turned right, and then beheld another station—not King's Cross, but St. Pancras Station. There was certainly no dearth of train stations in London.

She stopped a moment to admire it, looking up and smiling. St. Pancras looked exactly like a British railway station should look. A huge Victorian Gothic monstrosity. There had never been and never would be anything like it in Tucson. She looked back down for a moment. She had the uncanny and uncomfortable feeling she was being watched.

Two thuggy-looking young men were watching her as they lounged against the front of a West Indian restaurant, reggae music blasting from inside. They were an unprepossessing duo. One was tall and thin, with a cheap plastic-looking jacket, tight jeans, and orange hair in tufts springing from a lean, pale face. The other was squat and florid, wearing a shabby black overcoat and sturdy boots.

She thought fleetingly of the two teenagers in the crystal warehouse. These two looked older, meaner, and more desperate. She must have looked odd to them, too, obviously a tourist, her head craned upward to see the railway station that to them must appear simply as old and dingy, her Pan Am flight bag conspicuously on her shoulder. In her other hand she carried the small suitcase she'd bought to hold her new things, but it was the flight bag, with the cash, that she felt most possessive about, and she hitched it up on her shoulder nervously in a protective gesture.

They followed the gesture with their flat, cold eyes, and she knew that she'd let on there was something valuable within. She set off purposely away from them, down a small lane to get closer to King's Cross.

A minute later she was sorry she hadn't taken Euston Road, the main street, because they were following her. She was more annoyed than frightened. But she kept up a good, businesslike pace and she didn't look back. She doubted they'd try anything. After all, this was England.

When they swooped down on her, it was without warning. Only later did she remember the sound of heavy boots running toward her for just a second. Then she felt hands on her shoulder and felt their hot breath on her neck. They'd managed to push her into a little cul-de-sac. She had no idea where she was, and was dimly aware of brick wall on all sides.

The tall one was twisting at the strap of the flight bag. She held on to it like death and managed to swing around. It was tough at close quarters, but she managed to kick him right underneath his knee, pushing up with as much force as she could muster, a maneuver, she knew, which could dislocate a kneecap.

Whatever she'd done to him, it was plain that it hurt. "Ow," he said, indignantly, the first word she'd heard from either of them. He hopped on his other foot for a minute and looked at his companion. She knew she should take this moment to try and break free, but the short square one stepped in front of her, blocking her path. A second later—she never saw him actually pull it out—she saw a long shiny knife, held underhand, gleaming against the background of his dark coat. He smiled, his face widening even more. She stepped back, and the knife made an arc. It was clear she wasn't the target. He was trying to slash the strap on her flightbag.

She decided she'd have to scream. She couldn't afford to give up that cash. But what if there were an investigation? She'd have to show the police her false passport, explain what she was doing wandering around London with a flight bag full of dollars and the few pounds she'd exchanged.

She stepped back another pace. She couldn't keep this up indefinitely. She was just getting herself in a worse position. The boy with the knife took another step forward and beckoned with his hand, indicating she should hand over the flight bag.

Behind him she saw a man in a khaki-colored raincoat. She tried not to look at him. The young men in front of him weren't aware he was there, and she wasn't about to tip them off. Instead, she bought a little more time and stepped back one more pace.

The man in the raincoat acted swiftly. He slammed the tall skinny one against a wall, then twisted the knife out of the fat one's hand with an expert flip. Sunny didn't stand there while he took on both of them. She went over to the skinny boy and gave his kneecap the coup de grace. Now he actually screamed and slid to the ground, sprawled against the damp paving stones. She looked over at her rescuer, who was holding the point of the knife against the thick neck of the other one.

"Right," he said to Sunny. "Get out of here. Now."

Sunny was about to thank him. She looked at his face. With a swift intake of breath she recognized him. He was the man on the railway platform back in Lars and Pamela's little village.

She decided to do as he asked, gathered up her things, and ran out into the lane.

She didn't stop running until she reached King's Cross. There she bought two railway tickets. One would get her north to Scotland. The other was for the boat train to Paris.

Whoever that man had been, he didn't seem to want her harmed. Although, she imagined, he was still following her. She got into the train to Paris without looking around to see if she was observed. She stood conspicuously at the window of her compartment, leaning out and looking over the platform. After a while, she checked her watch, counting on the fact that British trains ran on time, and, leaving it to the last minute, drew the shade, gathered up her luggage, and went down the corridor. At the very end of the train, she slipped out onto the platform and made her way in a hurry to the train bound for Scotland. It was a long trek, through milling travelers, but she didn't see the distinguished-looking man anywhere—not until she was settled in the compartment of the train to Scotland. She peeked out behind the shade for just an instant. And then she smiled. He was in a telephone box, speaking hurriedly and looking over at the boat train. She hoped that he was telling someone else to arrange to have that train met by another operative. When her own train pulled out of the station, he was still on the phone.

After that it was easy. She took her train north, then a boat, and eventually ended up on a dock lined with fishing craft in Lerwick.

She shifted her flight bag from one shoulder to the other and smiled shyly down at a nice old weather-beaten fisherman. She could tell from his craft that he was Norwegian. The smack looked uncannily like the one on which she and Alex had been smuggled into Norway. Except the barrels on board undoubtedly contained fish, or would soon, instead of Colt machine guns.

She said hello in Norwegian. *"Goddag."*

"Want to sign up and go fishing?" joked the man. "Real pleasure cruise."

"I've been out in these waters before. Three days to Norway. It was a rough crossing."

He looked curious.

"In the war," she explained.

"Ah. The Shetland Express. I sailed with old Shetlands Larsen then myself. Of course, I was in the Royal Norwegian Navy then. Now I do the same thing for myself. And just after fish these days."

"The smack I was on looked just like this," said Sunny.

"Could be the same one," said the man, fiddling now with a pipe. "Want to come aboard and look her over?"

"Sure." Sunny clambered aboard and the captain showed her around. There were some young, blond hands aboard who looked at her curiously, wondering no doubt if this lady in advanced middle-age was the captain's girl in this port, she thought to herself.

"Food's better now," he said. "We had regular military rations, remember?" He looked at her sharply. "You look Norwegian, but you don't," he said finally.

"I'm American. An American tourist. And what I'd like

right now is to go out on one of these again. Can I buy a passage?''

He looked thoughtful for a minute. ''Hell, I'll take you over. You want to go to Norway?''

''Sure.''

''And don't mention a passage. We were old comrades in arms, remember? We've got another woman on board. The cook. Actually she's my niece, likes to come over with me and do a little shopping in England once in a while. You can bunk with her. Got a passport?''

''It's back in London. In the hotel safe.''

''No problem. No one cares about those things anymore. Besides, you didn't have one last time, did you?'' He laughed. ''Got any luggage?''

She patted the flight bag that now carried everything. Money, passport, and the few articles of clothing she'd bought in London.

''I'll show you where to stow your things.''

Gerhard Mannheim was fifty-nine years old. Fifty-nine seemed much younger than sixty. He turned away from the long-legged black woman who slept at his side. The sheets were twisted around them. He pulled them straight with a little frown and tucked them around his companion, glancing for a moment at her coral-painted lips, full and soft. He'd seen lips like that, smiling out at him from a hundred revolutionary posters. Was this a revolutionary act, sleeping with a woman who in the posters would have a fist raised against the capitalist imperialist oppressor? He sighed. No. He had simply wanted a novelty. And this girl had been a sweet girl. Her bottom had stuck out like an athletic boy's, and he'd caressed it, and her full, pointed breasts, but only out of boredom. She was different, but not that different, from the German peasant girls who during the war would have done the same for a pair of nylon stockings. Cherie, her name was. And, no doubt, she'd been fully vetted by the

CIA. He'd never paid for sex in his life. And he told himself he wasn't paying for it now. The CIA was. Something to keep him occupied. Like the color TV and the fully stocked bar. They'd even found his favorite Scotch, and the refrigerator was full of dark Heineken.

If only it would end. The sooner the better. He should have defected to the English. The Americans weren't safe. But then, that's what he had to offer them, the knowledge that they had a traitor in their midst.

The sooner they found the man he'd almost seen in that cabin in Norway so many years ago the better. Then he'd be able to lead a normal life.

Cherie murmured in her sleep. He worried about her. She'd shown him pictures of her children, two little boys with wide gap-toothed smiles, who spent this time with their grandmother, he knew. Did the grandmother know what Cherie did to provide them with the things they needed? He hoped not.

She was a product of the West. It was evil, the West. He'd learned that from the television. He'd seen the daytime game shows, playing on an obscene greed. This country would swamp him with the fat of the West, like wallowing in a vat of curdled cream. But, for all its evils, it was better than the East, better than the terror, the knock on the door, like the knock he'd feared so much as a youth. Gerhard Mannheim remembered no time when he'd been free. First there'd been the Saxon kings, then the Kaiser, then the Führer, then those who acted in the name of the People.

"But Sonia, you should have told us." Ingrid ran her hand through her short-cropped silver hair.

"I didn't really expect to come to Norway. I was in England, and I made a short hop over."

Ingrid looked surprised. "Well, you're here now. I'm so glad. Come in, come in. Will you stay with us?"

"No, no. I have to catch a plane tomorrow."

"Stay with us, Sonia. You must."

Perhaps she should. It might take a while to find the passport. Ingrid looked different.

It wasn't just the hair. Perhaps they were at the age where one's life and soul showed in one's face. Ingrid looked squarer, somehow. There were a few more lines in her face, more strong angles, and she was generally more robust-looking. Healthier, more strapping, with a fine, high color to her cheeks and eyes that looked clear and guileless, without the trace of smoke to mar the blue. Still the two women looked very alike.

Ingrid laughed, a full, hearty laugh. "I can see what you're thinking, Sonia. Do we still look alike? I think so. But you look more elegant. And so brown. Why, we've just come back from Spain and I thought I looked like a Spaniard after lying on the beach. But I look like a cod next to you!"

Good, Ingrid probably had a current passport.

The evening passed heavily. Ingrid's husband, Sven Carlsen, an engineering professor, was a silent man, rolling interminable cigarettes and saying little. When he talked it was to complain about the cost of living in Norway, how taxes had killed the middle class, how expensive everything was. "The oil, what good is that to us?" he said. "Everything still costs a fortune, and our coast will be ruined for nothing. All kinds of foreigners here now." He shook his head.

Ingrid hauled out the family album. "And here's Uncle Hjalmar. With that Jewish lady he married after the war. Tante Rosa. Remember?" They sipped liqueurs in a room full of spare, teak furniture with rough, modern weavings on the wall. Ingrid's husband seemed to eye the liqueur decanters—creme de menthe, brandy, Cointreau—nervously, probably thinking of the prices.

Later Sunny was put to bed in what appeared to be a study with a fold-out sofa. In her nightgown she tiptoed to the desk and slid the drawer out. It was a meticulously kept desk, with piles of receipts paper-clipped together. Sunny remembered laughing when her father had told her, in all seriousness, that a Norwegian had invented the paper clip. "Such a simple thing, but really brilliant," he'd said seriously. What a funny country.

Thank goodness the teak desk was beautifully made. The drawers worked silently. She couldn't believe her luck when she discovered two passports, in an envelope full of Spanish pesetas. For all Ingrid's husband's complaining, they lived well, it seemed. Expensive furniture. A nice flat in a nice part of Oslo. Spanish vacations.

She opened the first passport. A sour-looking Sven. The other had a rather pretty picture of Ingrid, smiling shyly. Her teeth weren't showing, thank goodness. Ingrid had a lot of gold dental work in one of the incisors. Sunny had noticed that at dinner.

She took the passport to the mirror and compared herself. She had to cut her hair. She looked too glamorous the way she was. It wasn't that the faces weren't the same, it was the style. Funny, even in a passport picture, you could sense something about a person.

There was a small knock at the door. Sunny leapt into bed, pulling the feather comforter around her neck. She still held the passport.

"*Ja?* Come in."

Ingrid's voice asked her if she wanted anything. "And what time shall we wake you?" She came into the room.

"Whenever you wake up," said Sunny.

Ingrid frowned at the desk and shut one of the drawers.

"We have a careless maid," she said. "A Turkish woman. Very sinister. I hope she hasn't been going through our things."

"Lot of foreigners these days, I guess," said Sunny.

"And Arabs, too. Something to do with the oil. It has changed so much. Of course, you wouldn't know about that."

"In Arizona," said Sunny, "we are the foreigners. And the Mexicans are our maids. Very funny how history works."

"One must be philosophical, I suppose," said Ingrid vaguely. "One egg or two tomorrow?"

"One," said Sunny, thinking that Sven would prefer an economy, and knowing that by answering now she might be saving Ingrid a sleepless night planning tomorrow's breakfast. Food and money—*mat og penger*—she remembered now, had been the chief topics of conversation in cousin Ingrid's family when they had been girls, and apparently nothing had changed, offshore oil and Spanish vacations and Turkish maids notwithstanding.

The next morning, in the ladies' room at the Oslo airport, Sunny cut her hair short with a pair of nail scissors. At first she was appalled. She looked out from under the cap of silvery hair like a frightened French collaborator in wartime newsreels. But perhaps it looked rather striking. She swept up the locks from the sink and put them in the trash. She gave the attendant, an amazed Turkish-looking woman, a crown and went to board her San Francisco-bound plane.

10

SHE REMEMBERED MARINA'S code. She called from a public phone in Burlingame, on El Camino Real.

"Hello, Mrs. Cooper. This is Harriet from Coast Realty. We were wondering if you'd be interested in one of our free market evaluations."

"I don't think so."

"Well, can I leave you my number in case you change your mind? Perhaps you want to discuss this with Mr. Cooper."

"Sure."

Sunny couldn't tell from Marina's tone whether she knew to whom she was speaking. Did she use the same code for everyone? Marina simply sounded like a bored housewife in a nice suburb, tired of the incessant real estate pitches.

Sunny gave her the number of the booth. How long would she have to wait? She kept her hand on the receiver, and with the other pushed the hook down so the phone could still ring and so to the casual observer it would look as if she were still on the phone. Tired after the flight from Oslo, she leaned her forehead against the smudgy, cool glass. Outside there were rows of old eucalyptus trees, their strips of orange bark and button-shaped seeds strewn about the gutters and sidewalks. A group of teenage girls walked by, wearing shorts and bare midriff tops. They were laughing, she could see, but she couldn't hear them through the glass. She could only see their faces crinkle up, and their mouths agape. They whispered to each other and laughed again.

She felt a strange sense of dissociation. What was she doing, mumbling codes into a phone booth, anyway? Outside, life went on and her own intrigue seemed trivial all of a sudden, and foolish. There was nothing keeping her. She could walk away any time. If Marina called back, she didn't have to answer. She didn't have to tell the horrible lie she'd prepared.

The phone rang. She smiled and picked it up.

"Hi. You came back." It was Marina.

"That's right."

"Did you find what you were looking for?" There was sarcasm in Marina's voice.

"No. But I want to very badly. I didn't tell you why before. Will you let me now?"

"Maybe." Again the coldness.

"Not on the phone."

"No. Of course not."

Sunny arranged a meeting in the ladies' lounge of the St. Francis Hotel. If either of them were being followed, a meeting place that automatically excluded men gave them a better chance.

Marina agreed to the meeting. "I can't help you," she said. "But I don't mind knowing why you want to find him."

Sunny hung up. She wasn't sure why she'd chosen the St. Francis. Now she had to get back into the city to make the meeting. But maybe that was all right. If she was being followed, she had more opportunity to lose her tail that way.

She walked back down Burlingame Avenue, past elegant little shops, parked Mercedeses and BMWs, and tanned suburbanites. She felt at home here.

The train station, an elegant relic from the twenties, was

at the end of Burlingame Avenue. She bought a return ticket although she had no use for the return portion, but she thought it made her less conspicuous.

Looking out the train window at the sprawl of the peninsula, she could see beneath the layers of development to a time when there was simply a row of small, quiet towns leading up to the city. It had all changed so much since she'd first known the area.

The ladies' lounge in the lobby of the St. Francis was at the end of a short corridor lined with pay telephones, behind the famous old grandfather clock that had remained a permanent fixture of the hotel for years. Sunny remembered it well. She and Gordon had always stayed at the St. Francis. San Francisco had been one of their favorite cities.

The clock told her she was right on time. Marina sat inside, at a long dressing table in the marble-lined outer area. She wore jeans and a sweater, and strapped to her chest in a corduroy carrying bag was the round form of a baby, its fuzzy head barely showing over the top.

Sunny sat next to her and began combing her hair. She looked at Marina in the mirror.

"What I'm about to say isn't easy," she began.

Marina surveyed her warily in the mirror. Sunny's eyes could take in the whole room behind them—the row of marble booths with gilt handles, a knot of older ladies at mirrors farther down, a slim black woman in a maid's uniform, with white apron and cap.

"Frankly, I'm curious," said Marina. "No one has ever wanted to find my father for personal reasons. It was a long time ago. I can't imagine what keeps you interested after all these years. He never made any real friends that I knew of. Even his family."

Sunny slipped her comb back into her purse. "Your father and I were together many years ago, it's true. Something has happened recently which makes it all different."

"They must be desperate, to have looked for you and sent you after him."

"By 'they' I guess you mean his old employers."

"Them. And others, too."

"Someone else sent me." She turned now and faced Marina in person. Marina seemed to start, as if it were easier to talk into a mirror face than a real one. "Your brother sent me."

"My brother is dead," said Marina. "I identified the body. What there was of it. So don't tell me he crawled out of the jungle. That story's been tried. A very convincing woman from the POW-MIA families' group talked to me several years ago. But it won't work. It was," she added with dignity, "a very cruel way to try and flush my father out."

"I'm talking about another brother," said Sunny slowly. "A half-brother you didn't know you had."

"What?"

"I never said good-bye to your father," began Sunny. That part was certainly true, so it was best to linger there for just a second. "We were together one night, like many other times, and then he left. I never saw him again. I never had the chance to tell him about the baby I was expecting." Her eyes glistened a little, at the thought of this imaginary betrayal, only a little greater than the actual betrayal.

"Why? After all these years . . ." began Marina.

"The child was adopted." Sunny sighed and fished in her purse for a lipstick. Something about grooming oneself was very comforting when one was either lying or revealing an awful truth. "Recent court decisions have made it possible for adopted children to find their birth parents. The young man came to me. I promised him I would try and find his father."

Marina stroked the sleeping child. "Why isn't he talking to me himself?"

Sunny sighed. "I don't want him to be hurt any more

than he has. If his father is alive and doesn't want to see him, I'll be glad to tell him his father is dead. But, more, I want a chance to talk to Alex myself. To convince him to see the boy. Well, he's a man actually.'' She turned boldly to Marina. ''He looks like you.''

Marina looked startled. ''It's impossible,'' she said. ''My father's dead.''

''I don't believe that,'' said Sunny. ''I'm not sure why. I think it's you. Something about you tells me he isn't dead.'' And something Billy had said, too.

''You see,'' said Sunny, glancing at the sleeping child, ''I don't think I did the right thing when I gave the child up. I think I have to do the best I can to make up for what I did. And that includes doing everything I can to make sure the boy meets his father. I'm sure you'd do the same for your son. I'm only happy that I have the financial means and the nerve to search for him. Can you help me?''

''I want to meet him first,'' said Marina.

Sunny hadn't counted on this. But one word of Marina's had answered her question once and for all. First. I want to meet him first. Alex was alive.

''No, I couldn't do that,'' said Sunny.

''He's my baby's uncle,'' said Marina. ''My baby has no relatives anymore. I want to meet him first.''

''If I allow that,'' said Sunny, ''you might not let me find your father. And it's so important that he find him. His life,'' she said, applying lipstick to her upper lip in two careful points, ''hasn't been happy. I don't think he's capable of happiness until he finds out about his parents. Both of them. Then you can meet.''

''I have to think,'' said Marina. ''I'm so surprised. A brand-new person, a person I've never heard about. A son for my father.''

''Do you think he'll want to see the boy?''

''A son,'' said Marina bitterly. ''You know, Dad was never the same after my brother died. I often felt that if I'd died, things would have turned out differently. He might not have changed so drastically. Might not have . . . turned against everything he'd ever done. And because of the pain of losing his son, he willingly gave up his daughter.''

"Not entirely," said Sunny, searching Marina's face. "There's a way to get to him, isn't there? You're in some form of communication. How you've managed . . . it must have been difficult.''

"How would you know?"

"Because I've been looking for your father, and I've learned I'm not the only one. Why haven't they broken you down?"

Marina smiled ironically. "I was trained by one of the best. My father. But we can't communicate. It's only one-way. I can get a message to him. Whether he's alive to get it, whether he'll respond, I don't know. I tell him when people are looking for him; we have a code. I have a code to tell him if I'm in any danger because of him. I haven't had to use it yet. And I have a way to tell him other things, too. I told him about his grandson here. But if he got that message, he didn't respond.''

"Will you tell me the code?"

"Of course not."

"Will you send him the message?"

"I might. I have to think. Are you being followed?"

"I was. I don't think I am now."

"Well, I am. We can never meet again. You may have picked up a tail if we've been seen together.''

"I did last time we talked. But I've lost it."

Marina nodded. "That's the way I like it. It's a little screening device. The CIA keeps track of my visitors. Gives me a margin of safety. Since the baby I'm even more concerned about safety. I beg you, if I help you, don't compromise my safety. Or my child's.''

"I understand."

"Where are you staying?"

"Nowhere."

"Good. Don't. Get on a train. Not a plane; that'll take

you back down the peninsula and you might be spotted. Take a cab to the train station—not the SP, but the Amtrak station. There's a cab in front of the hotel. Maybe you better take two cabs. Get on the first train there is, in any direction. Later, transfer and get yourself going north. Do you know the Northwest?''

Sunny grinned. ''I'm from Seattle originally.''

''Perfect. One week from today go to the main branch of the public library. There is a main branch, isn't there?''

''There was. I'm sure there still is.''

''Be there at two P.M. exactly. In the history department. No, that's probably a busier department. How about art? The art department. I'll call you there. With further instructions if there are any.''

''Is there a back-up plan?''

''No,'' said Marina. ''You have one chance. What name are you using? Your own?''

''No. Ingrid Carlsen.''

Marina raised her eyebrows. ''For a retired spy, you've got yourself in pretty deep. Do you have papers in that name?''

Sunny nodded. Was Marina suspicious now?

''How can I trust you?'' she said.

''I can tell you the date the child, your brother, was conceived. Your father can check it against his memory. It was in August of 1945. August fifteenth. The last time we met. He had to leave the next day. For years.''

''Okay. But can I tell him anything else, anything to prove you're who you say you are?''

''You've seen my old photo.''

''It's a pretty old photo,'' said Marina. ''And I can't necessarily convince him.''

''We were together on a mission during the war,'' said Sunny. ''The name of the mission was Sporløs.'' She spelled it. ''With one of those slashes across the final o.''

''What does that mean?'' said Marina.

"It's Norwegian. It means 'vanished without leaving a trace.'"

The scholarly-looking young man in seersucker, the man Sunny had met as Richard Matthews on the golf course in Tucson, sat outside the ladies' lounge in the St. Francis Hotel lobby. Marina Cooper was his only tangible lead. Everything else had petered out—the Sinclair woman, if that's who she was, had vanished into the health ranch. Then she'd resurfaced, according to the old man, as Harriet Grey. The man in seersucker wasn't sure. The videotape they'd taken outside Marina's house wasn't that clear, and the health farm people were adamant that she was with them. Their attorney wouldn't let him near the place. If the jerk beside him now, the San Francisco operative, hadn't botched it that night at the warehouse, they'd know who she was. But the fact that the woman had met with Marina Cooper, and then left behind some wounded men after a nighttime abduction, made Marina Cooper hot again. So here he sat, on a round red plush banquette, reading the San Francisco *Chronicle*.

"Hasn't she been in there a long time?" he said to his companion.

"I told you, she ducks into ladies' rooms all the time. Nice ones, like they probably have here, so she can nurse the baby. It took me a while to figure it out."

The man in seersucker made a mental note to suggest to the old man that they have a woman tail Marina Cooper. This was ridiculous, a powerful agency of the U.S. government, blocked at the ladies' room door. Rest rooms were horrible for electronic surveillance, too. Lots of cold, bouncy surfaces and running water. And besides, the best electronic gear in the world wasn't as effective as a tenacious, warm body in pursuit.

He could try and recruit some passing female to tell him what was going on in there. She'd probably report him to the house detective. Besides, his last recruitment attempt—the attempt to recruit Sunny Sinclair on the golf course in Tucson, hadn't been a mad success.

"Shit, I can't stand it," he said now. "Flash a maid or someone your FBI badge and get the attendant to come out."

"I can't use that unless things get really tight," said his companion. "The repercussions. Jesus. One thing I've learned," he added philosophically, "is that women spend a lot of time in the can. Women spend even more time in there when they're on their own than when they're out on a date or something."

Seersucker Suit sighed. This man was a jerk. "So what's the total now? She's been in there a good twenty minutes."

"Everyone who's followed her in has been accounted for. Except an older lady."

"Christ. Like the Sinclair woman?"

"I don't know, I just saw her from the back." The man looked nervous. "Her hair has been changed," he added slowly.

"If Marina comes out first, you follow her. I'm taking the old lady. Does she have nice legs?"

Obviously uncomfortable, the agent nodded.

"She knows me," said Seersucker through his teeth, his rage barely suppressed. "But I'm taking her anyway, if it's her."

"Okay. Okay."

Sunny booked her ticket all the way through to Vancouver. That was the last point on the Coast Starlight, and if anyone was paying attention to her, they'd have a lot of points between San Francisco and Seattle to cover. Besides, if Seattle turned out to be as dicey as San Francisco had the first time, when she'd ended up in the warehouse, it might be nice to have a ticket out of town ready for a hurried exit.

She collapsed into her sleeping car berth. She wasn't coming out, not for anything. She'd instructed the porter in her Norwegian accent that she was not to be disturbed, that she'd ring for anything if she needed it. Then she tipped him twenty-five dollars and slept. Her last thought before she fell asleep was that her hair was dirty; she thought about washing it in the basin in her room. If she was going to keep up this grueling pace, it probably made sense to have short hair like this.

Her first thought when she awoke was that it was dark outside the windows. Why was she awake? She'd heard a scream, that's why. Without thinking, she ran to the door. There were people outside, their voices raised. She heard someone call for a doctor.

It would seem unnatural not to open the door. She did and saw a cluster of bathrobed travelers and white-jacketed porters clustered around the door to the next compartment.

Inside lay a man, a large patch of blood staining the front of his shirt and his seersucker jacket. He lay half propped up against the sofa—it hadn't been folded down into a bed. The young man's face was contorted with pain, but he seemed to summon the last of his strength. From beneath a shock of fine hair, blue eyes looked at Sunny beneath heavy lids. His eyes were strangely alert. He said one word. "Sinclair." It was barely a whisper, and then a cascade of blood came from his mouth and dribbled down his chin. His eyes glazed over. It was Richard Matthews, the young man with hay fever. Bob Dawson's friend.

A blast of cold air engulfed the small group outside the compartment. The window was open. Smeared along it was a trail of brownish-looking blood. She could hardly believe that he'd pulled himself back through the window, but it looked like that's what he had done.

Next to her, the porter's hand reached for the emergency cord.

"No," she said. "The sooner we get to the next town the sooner he can get help."

"He's dead, ma'am," said the porter. "I've been a soldier."

A moment later Sunny was retching in the basin in her compartment. She cleaned out her mouth and spat. How would Bob Dawson back in Tucson feel about his young recruit now? Was anything worth cold-blooded killing? But then, who knew what the young man was? Maybe he'd been sent to kill Alex.

She sat on the bed and thought hard. The authorities would be talking to her soon. What was she going to tell them? Well, the truth, obviously. The current truth. She was Ingrid Carlsen. She didn't hear a shot. She heard a scream. The porter's scream, she had since learned. She wondered about two things. First, was the killer on the train? He had to be unless he'd jumped off. She knew that could be done. But she knew it hadn't been done. Because the killer was probably as interested in her as he was in the young man. But maybe not. How could she know anything?

The second possibility was that she would be implicated. He'd said her name. But maybe only she had heard that. She decided to say she wasn't sure what the dying man had said. After all, she was a foreigner. She may as well play that up to the hilt. She could make her Norwegian accent as heavy or as light as she wanted, and she was glad now she'd used it with the porter. It proved again that a false identity should be assumed completely. And, she decided, she'd get off the train as soon as she could. She didn't think she could crawl back into the train if she'd been shot and thrown out a window.

But first, before any investigation, she'd demand a Scotch and soda from the porter. He managed to deliver it to her, despite the commotion.

"Get another one for yourself," she said huskily.

"Right."

They sat gloomily together in her compartment and drank. Something about having seen the body together gave them a bond. He was a middle-aged black man with gray hair.

"He rang," the man said. "And when I came, I found him like that. God, I feel awful. I could have come faster. Maybe if I had, he'd be alive."

"Not a chance," said Sunny. "I've seen things like this. In the war, you know. In Norway. The man was dead."

"Did you hear what he said?" said the porter. "Think that was the name of the guy who did it?"

"He muttered something," said Sunny. "But I couldn't hear."

"It was a name," said the porter. "Sinclair. I heard it. Boy, lady"—he shook his head—"you wanted yourself a rest. You picked the worst stateroom in the train." He took a sip. "Or I guess I should say the second worst. Your neighbor there got himself the worst place for a calm trip."

The interrogation was much better than she'd imagined. She started off on the right foot with a nervous-looking young deputy from a small Oregon town by loudly bemoaning the fact of violence in America. "How can you people live this way?" she demanded in an accent like Ingrid Bergman's. "People shot and hurt. My children told me to be careful here. You are crazy people. I want to go home. I must go back home." She switched to Norwegian next. The sheriff looked at her passport, noted the number and name. He replaced his Western-style hat, a felt Stetson with a sheriff's badge in the center, and hitched up the belt that held a holster with a long black Colt in it. "I'm sorry, ma'am. I know how disturbed you must feel. I'm sorry you had to be involved in a homicide on your vacation." He handed back the passport. The young man looked so sincere Sunny burst into laughter, semi-hysterical laughter. "You people are all crazy," she said.

"I need to know where you can be reached, ma'am."

"My address is on the passport. Believe me, I'm going right home. You can reach me there."

He laboriously copied down the foreign address and left.

Sunny collapsed back onto the pillows. She'd been probably the first and last Norwegian that man would ever meet who acted like an Italian under stress.

Right before she slept for the second time, she changed her mind. She'd get off in Seattle as planned. The train was underway now, with the sheriff's deputies aboard. The porter had told her other deputies would be boarding the train at each county line. Leaving the train early might look suspicious. Besides, the train had been delayed for hours now. And Marina had been very specific. She had only one chance to reach Alex. There was no back-up plan.

Chandler Smith lay naked on the small cot in his hotel room. Goddamn humidity. He hated Central America. Everything smelled like rotten fruit. And the whole place was about to blow. He'd known that for years, but now he was here he could feel it in every pore, a cloying muggy kind of precursor to blood in the streets. The embassy people were practically in a state of siege, and even with the old man behind him they were hard-pressed to help him track down the bank account Alex Markoff was rumored to have here, when the guerrillas were in the mountains, in the city, and probably on the embassy payroll. The air conditioner wheezed and sputtered. The juicy little pops that came from the machinery were, he knew from previous visits, nothing to do with the general rundown shape of the equipment, but the sound of bugs being sliced up by the blades.

The telephone at the side of his bed rang. The desk had an urgent message for him. "Slide it under the door," he said. He wasn't opening any doors in the middle of the night for anyone. Not here. He crept to the door and stood beside it, his gun in his hand. When the piece of paper came, and the footsteps had gone away, he read it. It was written in block capitals, all run together as if it had been dictated letter by letter to someone who spoke no English: COMETOTHEEM-BASSY.

Dammit, he'd lost too many suitcases in his career, and this time he wasn't going to repeat the experience. After a message like that he wasn't coming back to this hotel. He packed everything, scrambled into a pair of jeans and a shirt, and got together enough cash to check out.

As he stepped into the street, he heard gunfire from a few streets away. He wasn't stepping into any cabs tonight, either. He made his way on foot, clinging to the sides of buildings, the walls nicked with bullet holes from previous revolutions and slogans emblazoned from the one that seemed to be underway now.

This better be important, he thought to himself. If it isn't, it's my resignation. If I live to resign.

"Have you got Chandler Smith yet?" snapped the old man, on the line from Washington.

"He's coming now. He just made the compound." A pause.

"This better be good, damn good." Chandler was obviously furious. And the decoding clerk in charge of the special line obviously hadn't told Chandler that the call was from the highest level.

"I'll ignore that. Listen hard. That son of a bitch in San Francisco stumbled back onto the Sinclair woman. Or Harriet Grey. Whoever she is. Thank God another agent was with him, or he would have let her go again, no doubt. If he isn't working for the KGB, we should arrange it. Our regular man on the case was there. Your less covert colleague, Richard Matthews. He followed her. Our man in San Francisco didn't know where. But unfortunately we do."

"Unfortunately?"

"He was killed tonight. On a train. The Coast Starlight. Near Bend, Oregon. That's B-E-N-D. The information we have is scanty, but we do know there's a Norwegian national on that train. Stuck out, because of the Sinclair woman's background. We cross-checked the name with her file. Ingrid Carlsen. Sunny Isdahl has a cousin named Ingrid Carlsen.''

''Killed Matthews?''

''That's right. I told you this was pretty important stuff. That woman has to be the key to it. I want you to fly to the West Coast. You won't be able to intercept the train, but get yourself to Portland or Seattle, whichever is faster. We'll try to keep an eye on her. But now that we've lost one agent, you're it, the whole goddamn thing. Don't mess up. And I expect to hear from you as soon as you touch down. Get a military flight the hell out of where you are now.''

The old man put down the phone. Chandler Smith was his last hope now. And he had to keep the trail hot for him. Even if it meant bringing in another agency. He didn't like that at all. They were such clods, they'd probably pick her up, scare her off. He'd have to make his request low-key. She was going to find him, and so was Smith—if he could find her and hang on hard. Someone else was already close to her. Close enough to kill.

11

SUNNY WAS SURPRISED to see how the area around the railroad station in Seattle had changed. When she'd been there last it was practically an abandoned area of old brick buildings, full of broken glass and drunks with nests of shopping bags in their hands and layers of old coats on their bodies against the Seattle rain. Now it was apparently becoming chic again. She'd heard about the renovation of the area. The brick buildings had been cleaned, spindly maples had been planted along the sidewalks, and there were shops and restaurants. There were still a few bums, but they seemed to coexist with the professional-looking crowd drinking white wine and eating late-afternoon snacks at sidewalk cafés.

She went into a coffee shop, something less aggressively chic than most of the restaurants in the area. This looked like an old diner that had withstood the area's decay and subsequent renewal without change. The waitresses were motherly-looking older ladies in starched uniforms. She sat at the counter, near a pay phone, and ordered a cup of coffee.

No one seemed to be following her now, but that didn't mean anything. She'd proved a dismal failure as an agent. She'd managed to hide her tracks by checking into Rancho Salubre and then made herself conspicuous by visiting

Marina. She'd escaped surveillance again, she thought, in Europe, but must have picked up the boy in seersucker, Richard Matthews, through Marina. Or maybe Marina was having her followed. For all she knew, Marina, who seemed to resent her father, could be working with the CIA. And if Billy was right, the CIA wanted Alex very badly. That someone involved was willing to kill was clear now. And that was, no doubt, someone other than the CIA. Someone who was following her and wanted the CIA not to follow her.

It was absolutely impossible, she decided, to ascertain what was going on. She knew only that Billy, who hadn't kept his meeting with her, was concerned for Alex, and that Billy was right—Alex's whereabouts were important to at least two groups of people. She had decided at the beginning that whatever trouble Alex was in was not for her to discover. She wanted only to warn him. To tell him everything that had happened to her on her search, and let him decide what to do. Then her job was over.

She couldn't stay in a hotel. Whoever had killed Matthews was probably in Seattle, following her. She had one advantage. Seattle was her home and she knew the area and had family there. She'd call her brother, Magnus, and ask him to help her. He was an engineer at Boeing, a logical man, a chess player. He would be able to help her plan. But she couldn't call him at home. He wasn't home now anyway, and who knows, the CIA or anyone else who knew she was Sunny Sinclair could tap his phone. The work phone though, that would be more difficult. After all, Magnus worked in a sensitive area, on a new missile system.

She asked the waitress for more coffee and change. There was a long list of numbers for the Boeing Company, and she knew that finding an individual employee was a little like finding someone in a small city. Boeing had thousands of engineers. There was a general information number, though, and fortunately she remembered the name of the missile system on which her brother was working. She remembered because Magnus had joked about it when they'd last talked. "They love those mythological names," he said. "You know, Poseidon, Trident, that sort of thing. But some congresswoman on the Defense Appropriations subcommittee wanted a woman's name. So it's Athena. Goddess of defensive warfare, among other things."

"Rather pretty," said Sunny. "The gray-eyed goddess Athena. Gunmetal-gray eyes this time."

Sunny told the general information operator the name of the project and spelled out Magnus Isdahl.

"Well, I'll see if I can find his extension," the woman said dubiously. "You don't know which plant, or whether he's at Kent, Tukwila, Everett, or where?"

"He's working on Athena."

"How do you spell that?" Sunny tried not to let irritation creep into her own voice. Finally she was put on hold. She sipped coffee and looked around the café. Nobody seemed to be watching her. There were only a few people at the counter, and from the way the waitress joked with them, they all seemed like regulars. It was that kind of place.

On the counter was a copy of the Seattle *Times,* and Sunny glanced at it while she listened to the vague buzz of electronic sounds as she held the earpiece.

The headline was about a new Boeing contract. She remembered that new orders or cutbacks were always big news. Seattle depended highly on Boeing for economic strength. A smaller article talked about a Central American revolution that seemed about to happen.

The operator came on the line again. "I'm transferring you," she said. Sunny wanted to ask where, in case she was cut off. But she wasn't cut off. Another phone was ringing now.

She flipped over the paper. And saw a small story that caught her eye immediately. "Amtrak passenger slain," datelined Bend, Oregon. She was surprised to see something so soon, but then she remembered she'd spent another twenty-four hours, practically, on the train since the murder.

"Authorities have no leads in the case," the article said, "and the county sheriff's office has requested help from the FBI, as the crime occurred on an interstate train. The victim, tentatively identified as Donald Sawyer, a salesman for an electronics manufacturer, was shot at close range with a small caliber weapon. Speculation that the shooting was drug-related has received neither confirmation nor denial from investigating officers."

A voice came on the line. Sunny tore her eyes away from the article and asked for Magnus. "May I say who's calling?" The tone was suspicious. "His sister," said Sunny. Magnus was so respectable she didn't want to have the secretary wondering what mystery woman was calling him at work. "Mrs. Sinclair," she added, after the woman said suspiciously, "His sister?" She regretted it immediately.

"One moment." She was back on hold again, and she turned back to the article.

"Authorities refused to comment on the statement of a porter, Mr. Aaron Cummings, that the man uttered a name, 'Sinclair,' before he died, leading to speculation he may have named his killer."

"Hello," Magnus's familiar voice came on the line.

She said nothing, frozen by the newspaper story. She couldn't ask Magnus to help now, not without a lot of explaining. If he read the story, and wondered why she'd arrived unannounced, he might suspect.

"Sunny? Are you there?"

She hung up the phone.

Kikuko frowned at her husband. "The pool filter is broken again," she said.

"Why is it always my fault when things break?" Billy demanded.

They were in the spacious living room in a Virginia suburb. Kikuko was stretched out on a long sofa, propped up at one end by pillows. She was beautiful, even when she was glaring at her husband, with a beautiful smooth round face, set off by hair in a style that few Asian women over twelve wore, a neat, short bob with bangs, like a doll's. The effect of the childlike hairdo with the dramatic makeup, wings of taupe and gray eyeshadow and vivid orange-red lips, was striking.

Billy stood at the bar and watched her in the mirror as he mixed them both drinks.

"Well, what are you going to do about it?" she demanded.

"For Christ's sake, call the pool people," he said.

"Why pay someone when it's probably just some leaves or something?"

"Well, get the leaves out yourself. But then, of course, you'd have to pay for a new manicure."

She surveyed her long red nails, curving over at the tip, and smiled. Billy knew she liked to think people thought of her as "Dragon Lady," and her fingernails were straight out of *Terry and the Pirates*.

"Well, figure it out yourself," he said, handing her a drink in a wet glass. He noted with satisfaction that a few drops fell on her turquoise silk blouse. "I have to go into the office. Something's come up."

Billy never called it his den. That sounded too middle class. But it was hardly an office; he didn't work there much. Mostly it was a way to get away all by himself and think. It was a small, square room far away from the rest of the house, paneled in warm oak, with shelves of books, mostly about espionage, and a small fireplace with a clutter of knickknacks on the mantel. There were some rather bawdy old eighteenth-century prints, and a kidney-shaped desk.

He sat at the desk and took his first sip of Scotch, the best sip of the glass. Damn. Things were happening much faster than he'd assumed. Thank God his contacts within the agency still came through for him.

The young CIA agent in charge of finding Alex Markoff was dead. But Billy had never believed the old man would have entrusted something so important to him. There had to be another more covert search.

He had to find Sunny. He had to tell her the old man wanted to kill Alex, and that it was very likely he had a more covert operation in place.

But Sunny had disappeared. She'd disappeared in London. Harriet Grey had disappeared, too. Her passport wasn't used, her credit cards weren't used. And there was no activity on Sunny Sinclair's own passport.

Dammit, why had she lost his man in London? Didn't she want protection? It was clear she didn't know how dangerous it all was. It was very possible she would have to die, along with Alex.

He had to find out what the old man knew. He had to find Sunny. And especially, he had to find Alex Markoff. He sighed and looked thoughtfully at his half-empty glass. Maybe he would have to get back into the field himself, after all these years.

Sunny paid for her coffee and left the café. As she left, a man in a navy blue windbreaker and tan slacks watched her leave. He was leaning against the jukebox, seemingly reading the selections, but he watched her in the ornate mirror. He'd seen her last at the mission San Xavier. He'd been wearing a khaki suit then.

She imagined she was still followed. Hadn't the murderer been following Richard Matthews, who'd been following her? It seemed the most logical explanation. She had to get away for a moment and think. Seattle seemed strange to her now. The people on the street looked so much more sophisticated than she'd remembered, and they all looked younger, too. There was a more festive air about the place. Even the stately Smith Tower, once the tallest building in town, a white, pointed thing that looked out over the Pioneer

Square area where the train had delivered her, now sported a canvas Japanese-looking fish flying from its rooftop.

She went downtown, walking the ten blocks or so, to the one landmark that never really changed. Frederick and Nelson's was an old-fashioned department store. Old Seattleites felt a great loyalty to the place; Sunny herself still maintained an account there, and sometimes had the specialty of the candy department sent to friends at Christmas. Frederick's was the kind of place where liveried doormen helped old ladies into cabs. When she was a little girl, she'd always been rewarded with a lunch in the tearoom for good behavior on a shopping trip. Mama always had an old-fashioned before lunch, and sometimes there was a fashion show with an elegant young man playing dreamily on the piano.

"I'd rather pay just a little more at Frederick's than go somewhere else and have them treat you like you just got off the boat," Sunny's father would say fondly. It was rumored that certain light-fingered ladies from better families were followed discreetly by floorwalkers, who noted their thefts and had them put on the monthly bills.

Sunny had always been amused by the ladies' lounge. This cavernous room, sprinkled with banquettes and little chairs and tables, was a sort of club for genteel old ladies. They whispered to each other, and sat at the desks, and took care of their correspondence on the Frederick's stationery that was provided.

Now that she was older, she thought with a smile, she'd fit right in. Except the ladies always wore little white cotton gloves. She'd sit there for a while and regroup. She couldn't imagine a safer haven than the ladies' lounge at Frederick and Nelson's.

The old white marble structure was a comforting sight, rather like seeing an old aunt. There were signs that a lot of slick young marketing types were doing their best to bring Frederick's into the last half of the twentieth century, but the old atmosphere prevailed. The elevator girls were gone. They had all been diminutive brunettes who pointed at arriving elevators. The bronze plaque, however, with the solemn list of Frederick's employees who had given their lives in World War II, was still there in front of the elevators.

Sunny made no moves to indicate she suspected that someone was following her. She tried to look around, but saw nobody who seemed to be trailing her. He'd have more trouble in Frederick's. The place was crawling with women in tan raincoats and silver hair.

The ladies' lounge hadn't stood the test of time. There were a few old dears around, and the writing desk, but the place had lost its genteel atmosphere. It no longer smelled of lavender water, but of cigarettes, and instead of old ladies whispering, there seemed to be a collection of young women in jeans trying to shepherd broods of children into the bathrooms that opened off the main lounge. Still, Sunny felt safe here. She collapsed into a low chair and thought.

She really couldn't bring Magnus into this. She'd have to tell him everything, he'd insist on it, and he'd tell her she was crazy, pick up the phone, and call the police or the FBI. His wife would become hysterical. And if she lied? She'd never been able to lie convincingly to Magnus. She squirmed at the thought. Most lies appeal to some emotional need of the target. Magnus had no pressure spots that Sunny had ever discovered. And, if he heard that a someone named Sinclair could be connected with a murder on a train coming into Seattle, and connected it with Sunny's unannounced arrival and desperate desire to lay low . . . well, it was hopeless.

Who else did she know? She closed her eyes, reflecting on the serenity she felt here, knowing she was surrounded by women. She'd felt that way at Rancho Salubre, and later, with Marina in the ladies' room at the St. Francis. Women's enclaves. After all, it was men who raced around, played spy, and shot each other. If she had been a man, would she have ended up like Alex, hiding in fear? Or like Billy? Bitter and alcoholic? If they'd had women's enclaves to run away to now and then . . .

Her eyes shot open. Cousin Margaret! Cousin Margaret was Tante Ragnhild's daughter, born late in life. They had played together as children. Both little girls were physically active and loved climbing trees together and swimming in Lake Washington. But when they were adolescents, they parted ways. Sunny became a beautiful young woman, athletic and lean, and had lots of boyfriends and nice clothes. Margaret became very tall, muscle-bound, and surly. No one knew why she was so unhappy, given to bursts of tears. She didn't want to socialize with anyone anymore, and everyone assumed her unfortunate looks had something to do with it.

When the war came, and Sunny joined the OSS, Cousin Margaret surprised the family by joining the WACs. She looked quite handsome in her uniform. A military carriage and diet turned her rather square body into something Junoesque. She seemed very happy, and although women in uniform always had a bad reputation, no one could mistake Margaret for a camp-follower. The family was relieved that Margaret seemed to have found herself, until she and another girl were dishonorably discharged under circumstances that made it clear to everyone that cousin Margaret and the woman were lovers.

Sunny's father declared he didn't want her in the house. Sunny hated him for it. She remembered how unhappy Margaret had been, and now she understood why. She felt that the family had somehow betrayed Margaret, and she'd kept in touch with her through the years. She lived now on a small farm on an island in Puget Sound with her lover of many years, not her fellow WAC but a fluffy lady who worked as a secretary. Sunny had met her once or twice.

While she couldn't find a lie to tell Magnus, she had a perfectly good one for Margaret. She remembered how, on a visit to Seattle, Margaret had been eager to see Sunny, but

tried to maneuver Gordon and Erik out of the invitation.
Over Gordon's protests, Sunny and Audrey had gone to visit
the two women. The farm had an unworldly air about it.
Margaret had managed to make herself a little enclave, an
enclave for women only.

She telephoned Margaret from the pay phone in the ladies'
lounge. Sounding slightly hysterical, she burst out with a
story about a man, a man who was following her and
persecuting her. A love affair gone wrong. Sunny had to get
away from him. He was pathologically possessive. Could she
stay with Margaret for a few days?

"Of course, of course," said Margaret. Her voice was low
and calm.

"But it's very important he doesn't know where I am,"
said Sunny. "He's crazy. Oh, I don't want to put you in any
danger."

"Don't worry," said Margaret with grim satisfaction.
"You'll be safe here. The mailman doesn't even make it onto
our land. I'll come into town and get you. Where are you?"

"I'm at Frederick's."

"It'll take an hour or so. Want a bite or something before I
come? I'll meet you . . ."

"At the side by the doorman," said Sunny, checking her
watch. "At exactly one hour from now."

"Make it an hour and a half. The ferry can sometimes be
late. I'll come and get you, and Mildred will get a room
ready for you here."

There had to be a way out of here that would throw off
anyone following her. She remembered a time when she'd
fallen at Frederick's when she was a little girl. They'd taken
her to a nurse. Did they still have one? She'd find out.

A white uniformed attendant was emptying ashtrays and
polishing mirrors. "Excuse me," said Sunny. "I feel as if I
might faint."

Sunny slumped back in her chair. A few moments later a
cheerful middle-aged nurse with brass curls was pushing her

in a wheelchair through the crystal department. Sunny didn't know if she imagined it or not, but a man in tan slacks and a windbreaker seemed to look at her with more than curiosity. He seemed perplexed. The nurse took her to a room with narrow white cots and curtains between them. "Slip off your shoes, honey, and lie down. You ever faint before?"

"No, that is, a few times. I guess I shouldn't have skipped lunch."

"Well, you just lie down until you feel better."

"I feel so ridiculous," murmured Sunny. She imagined everyone said that when they arrived here. The nurse wore an old-fashioned crisp uniform and a nurse's cap. So much nicer than these modern nurse getups. Frederick's still managed to maintain some of the old standards. Sunny closed her eyes. Really, she did feel like a little nap. The sheets were so cool.

The old man wore evening clothes. They were in rather shocking contrast to his rugged face, but he wore them with the same ease he wore his usual battered tweeds. He rose from the bridge table, patted his wife's hand, and excused himself. He'd let her have the bid, even though he suspected she'd never make it in no-trump, because he wanted a moment to telephone.

In the bedroom he adjusted the black tie and went to the red telephone. "Patch me through to Smith in Seattle."

"Good, you made it," he said when he heard Smith's voice. "Listen, I'm glad you're there, because she is, too. Unless it's a plant. Listen to this. Her brother works in a sensitive area at Boeing. There've been some leaks and there's routine surveillance on the lines in and out of Athena. We think we picked her up, calling him. It was just dumb luck because we still don't have the taps on her relatives' telephones yet. She identified herself and hung up before they talked. Chickened out. Or someone came along. Who knows? Anyway, we're pretty sure she's in Seattle. Find her, and stick with her. I'm pretty sure the daughter sent her that way. She'll lead us to him. You're all we've got now. Don't screw up."

The old man wondered whether he should tell Smith just how important it was. He decided not to.

"One more thing. Ingrid Carlsen's ticket went through to Vancouver. She still has part of the trip left. So we'll have to cover the train station. I want you to do that. And I've got tracers on all the airlines for Sinclair, Carlsen, and Grey. I'm sending you the information on all the relatives. She's got a brother and sister-in-law, and a couple of cousins. We're also working on any old friends. You know, high school girls sometimes have these lifelong friendships. And of course we're doing what we can with the hotels and motels."

They talked some more. Chandler sounded exhausted. That wasn't good. And they were terribly shorthanded. It was tough to flood Seattle, Washington, with a lot of CIA men. The FBI had pledged their cooperation, but the old man was pretty sure they didn't buy his story on the Sinclair woman. He hoped to God they didn't pick her up. They were such zealous bastards.

Back at the bridge table, his wife looked up at him with her adorable blue eyes. She was a soft, plump, pretty woman. He smiled. He knew what that look meant. She'd gone down and badly.

"Don't worry, darling," he said. "There isn't any money on this game."

Margaret's farm was on Maury Island. It wasn't really an island all by itself. It had been connected by a small isthmus to Vashon Island, a half-hour ferry ride away from Seattle. The area was very rural, and it was startling to see a glittery piece of Seattle skyline over the soft swells of green woods—a second-growth forest of tall Douglas firs black against the evening sky, mixed with maples and alder.

Margaret and Mildred had five acres. Margaret jumped

out of the pickup to open a metal gate, and they drove up a winding gravel drive to an open meadow. At the edge of the meadow against a bank of trees was the house, an old-fashioned farmhouse, painted a classic barn red with white trim. There was a long porch running the length of the house, with an old-fashioned swing on it, and a series of outbuildings farther from the house by a green pond.

The sky above was lavender, streaked with clouds edged in pink and gold in fanciful shapes. It looked foreign and Nordic to Sunny now, after years of unrelieved blue skies, and almost ominous, like something in a painting by Munch. But it was undeniably beautiful.

The trip by bumpy pickup, and later a green and white Washington State ferry, and another long leg in the pickup, seemed to take forever. Sunny was tired and relieved that they'd finally arrived. She wanted a hot bath and a good dinner and lots of sleep.

She was sure she hadn't been followed this time. She spared Margaret the details; the labyrinth of storerooms with boxes and fire doors at Frederick's after she'd slipped out of her cot in the infirmary, and then the hasty shopping trip at Woolworth's down the block for a peculiar-looking knit hat and some flat canvas shoes with straps. Sunny knew that tailing meant memorizing a gait, a back, a shape. By switching from heels to flats she changed her walk, and the hat changed her silhouette further.

Thankfully, Margaret asked few questions. Perhaps having had to hide a major fact of her own life made her less intrusive about other people's. She seemed determined to cheer Sunny up, telling her about the benefits of country air and Mildred's delightful home cooking. Margaret looked healthy and happy. She was still large, with a tall bulky frame and handsome square hands. Her hair, cut bluntly at the chin, was the same color as Sunny's, blond, streaked with gray, and she had the same high cheekbones and blue-gray eyes.

Mildred was waiting for them, a small partridge of a woman, with soft brown eyes and fluffy gray hair. They ate chicken in a cream sauce with mushrooms and a salad made of fresh greens from the garden. "Since we've retired," said Mildred, "we've been able to do so much more." After dinner, in the long dusk of a Northwest summer, they took a tour of the vegetable garden, the spice garden, and the chickens.

"Oh, Margaret," said Sunny apologetically, "you must think I'm a complete idiot, panicking like that. If you knew what I've been through . . ."

"You'll be safe here," said Margaret indignantly. Sunny had begun to picture the imaginary cad who'd terrorized her. He had a small dark mustache and a gaudy diamond on his little finger. "Stay as long as you like."

"A few days would be marvelous," said Sunny. She only needed to stay until Marina's phone call. And she pledged to use the time thinking about the consequences of her actions. Should she continue to search for Alex? She hadn't been able to elude followers, and perhaps it was more dangerous to warn Alex than not to. After all, Marina was surely letting her father know about any pursuers.

Chandler Smith watched the Coast Starlight pull out for Vancouver. He threw his cigarette on the platform and turned away. There had to be a better way to find her. For all they knew she'd only booked her ticket to Vancouver to muddy the trail. He walked across the parking lot to F. X. McRory's. He'd made it a habit to eat here every evening after the Coast Starlight left Seattle without Sonia Sinclair. It was a New York-style bar, full of frosted glass and dark wood, with a mammoth collection of bottles and a sea of little marble tables. The place always seemed packed, which was fine with him. He always had a couple of drinks and some oysters before dinner. The oysters were really very good, and Chandler enjoyed watching the people. There was a kind of too-intense gaiety about the people, amplified by the acoustics, which sent scraps of conversation and raucous laughter bouncing off every surface.

A good-looking redhead, probably a secretary masquerading in a female executive suit, for her makeup was too vivid and the material in her suit too cheap, eyed him seductively. He smiled back, but turned slightly in his chair so as not to have to see her. He was thinking more and more about Sonia Sinclair lately. At first, he'd been obsessed with Alex Markoff. He'd imagined him in a thousand different scenarios. But now he was becoming more interested in the woman. After all, Alex Markoff had led a colorful life. A colorful coda would only be in character. But Mrs. Sinclair. Everything he'd read about her made her seem terribly ordinary. Why would a respectable attractive matron from Tucson, Arizona, suddenly racket around using false passports, fight off thugs in an abandoned warehouse, and have a brush with murder in the middle of the night? He thought about the smoky portrait of her, taken when she was twenty. Maybe the answer lay there. Maybe a need for danger that Alex Markoff—and Chandler Smith himself—had been fulfilling for years was lying dormant, till now, in the respectable widow.

The message, when it came, was strangely anticlimactic. Sunny had stood at the desk of the art department in the main branch of the Seattle Public Library, and when the phone rang she'd smiled and said to the young man at the desk, "That's for me, I think. Mrs. Carlsen."

He looked startled, picked up the receiver, nodded, and handed her the phone. "Hello," she said. It was Marina's voice.

"Go to Vancouver. Vancouver, B.C. Check into the Hotel Vancouver." Then a click as the receiver was replaced.

It was simple enough. Even simpler because she had her

train ticket still. It made as much sense to use it as anything else. She could walk from the library, and the train left shortly. She shifted her flight bag onto her shoulder.

She was sure now she wasn't being followed. She hadn't seen anyone questionable since Frederick and Nelson's several days ago. And on Maury Island and the ferry she would have noticed any followers. But this didn't mean she could let her guard down.

12

THE OLD MAN rubbed his hands together gleefully. Chandler had her. He was with her. They were getting closer. Goddammit, they were going to find Markoff and ask him one little question. The question that would answer the question they'd had for so long. Who was he? Who was with you in that cabin? Of course, things could still sour. The old man didn't think they would, though. But if they did . . .

He rose from his desk and strolled around his office for a moment. If the plan went sour, or if he himself were run over by a cab tonight . . . He flipped a button on his desk and barked into the microphone. "Get me a meeting with the White House. Top level. As soon as possible." He had to cover himself, and the agency. With glory, he hoped. But if not, he had to cover his ass.

Sunny really shouldn't have come into the dining car, but she was hungry and also wanted a drink. She sat alone and looked out the window at the familiar terrain of her childhood, fir trees standing blue in the dusk, farms with a blowsy look to them, Holstein cows. She ordered a martini.

Presently a young man came and sat with her. She looked at him carefully. He seemed harmless enough. Actually, he was quite attractive. Early forties, probably. Strong jaw, even white teeth, greenish eyes, and springy, sandy hair. He had the kind of Smilin' Jack looks that had been popular in her youth.

She supposed she'd have to talk to him. It would seem very peculiar for two Americans to share a drink and a meal and not converse.

"He's not in. If you'd like to request an appointment . . ."

Madge turned away from the desk. Should she leave a message? She didn't really know the old man. Well, she had once, when he was more junior, but he seemed to have forgotten. He'd looked at her blankly at one of the Christmas parties when she'd smiled at him and said hello.

As she was leaving the office she heard the secretary answer a phone. "Yes. At the White House. I'll tell him, sir."

The secretary came after her. "Did you want to request an appointment?" She frowned at Madge, looking definitely nervous. For a horrible moment, Madge saw herself through this young woman's eyes. She looked like a crazy old lady, with eyes red from crying. They'd think she was a risk now, wandering up and asking to see the old man himself.

But who else *was* there? She didn't know who else to tell. And she had to tell now. Billy's last requests were so frightening. Instead of asking her for information that crossed her desk, he'd got her to go out of her way to find out about something very big. A search was underway, and Billy was monitoring it, every step of the way. His whole manner had changed. She knew now that it was very important, all the little scraps. She didn't understand all of it, but she knew from his manner, from his urgency, that she had done something very, very scary.

Back in her own department her supervisor looked skeptical when she said she was ill and had to go home. "What's the matter, Madge? Let's have someone from medical take a look.''

''Cramps,'' blurted out Madge, then she realized that she looked too old for cramps, that the supervisor wouldn't believe her. ''Well . . .''

She put her hand to her face in embarrassment.

Her supervisor's brows rose questioningly, but she said, ''Well, go ahead and take the afternoon off. Can we expect you tomorrow?''

''I don't know,'' said Madge.

Later, at home, Madge thought very hard. She knew what would happen if she were convicted of passing secrets. Alderston, the women's federal penitentiary. She'd driven past it a million times. But maybe she was being silly. She put her dinner plate in the sink and sat in the living room of her apartment. Maybe if she told them everything, they'd just pension her off. Maybe she could get another job. Not in Washington, though. Not if anyone knew.

It would be the end.

She went into the bathroom and turned her attention to the roots of her hair. She wrapped herself in a robe and put on the plastic gloves, daubing the gray roots with the dark inky solution that would make them red again. Then she washed her hair and dried it, admiring the job. It really looked quite nice. From the medicine chest she took a bottle of pills. She washed them down with water from the toothbrush glass, one after another. When she'd finished the bottle, she started again, with another bottle. Soon both of them were completely empty.

Madge said good-bye to her image in the mirror and went to lie down on the sofa.

Chandler Smith felt like a fifteen-year-old on his first date. He was sitting across from her, right across from her. He smiled and actually felt himself blushing.

She looked exactly as he'd imagined she would in person,

except for the short haircut. There was something appealing about the short hair. It was sleek and silvery, like a seal's fur, and made her features, especially the smoky blue eyes, stand out startlingly. The smoky eyes stared back at him. Were they wary? Or just curious? She smiled a little sideways smile, as if she noticed he was blushing and was amused by it.

The waiter came, practically falling onto the table as the train lurched. He bobbed back into position like one of those dolls that can't be knocked down. His tray, bearing a martini for her, never changed position and he hadn't spilled a drop. He placed the silvery drink in front of her.

"I'll have one of those, too," Chandler said.

"I've always wondered," he blurted out rather suddenly, "why in old books and movies, characters always talk about whether they prefer to ride with their backs to the engine or the other way around."

She scanned the menu. He noticed she held it out farther than a younger person would. "I think it had something to do with cinders from the smokestack," she said.

"I guess facing the engine you'd get smoke and cinders in your eyes. But what would you get the other way?"

"I hate to disappoint you," she said dryly, replacing the menu on the table and sipping her martini, "but the age of steam was before my time."

She was decisive. She hadn't looked at the menu more than a second. An attractive quality. She must think he was a complete fool, babbling on about cinders and ashes. But that's what people talked about on trains. Trains.

"Oh, I can see that," he said. "I didn't mean . . ."

She laughed. It was a nice, honest, throaty laugh. "Perhaps it's more a psychological thing," she said now, in a tone that was apparently meant to put him at ease. She was gracious. Well brought up. A quality younger women could use a little more of. "Perhaps it depends on whether you're interested in where you're going or where you came from."

"And you're sitting facing the engine, and you sat here first, so you're looking forward to where you're going." He smiled.

"I think I'd always prefer to sit facing the direction I'm bound, whether I think I'll like it or not. It's the only reasonable attitude, don't you think?"

"Very reasonable. Also brave."

"Brave?"

"Most people who don't like the future are frightened of what they don't know, don't you think?" Now he was getting too philosophical. He sounded to himself like a college sophomore.

She shrugged. "I suppose."

"Have you been to Vancouver before?"

She nodded and turned to look out at the dusk through the window. He was interested to see her profile. All her photographs had been full-face. She had a very straight nose and a neat decisive chin.

"I haven't. I'm going to write about it. What-to-do-in-a-weekend sort of thing. Where should I start?"

"You're a writer?"

"A travel writer."

"For anyone in particular?"

"*Sunset.*"

"How interesting."

"But I can't just write travel for them. I have to write about closet space and hot tubs, too."

"Sounds like you prefer travel."

"Well, that's how I started out. But you can't make any money. All you get is free trips from the airlines and the tourist bureaus of countries off the beaten track. I did that for a while and raced through a trust fund, hoping I'd be good enough to get paid, too, later. Never happened."

This was true. He'd been recruited in Bangkok, at first thinking he could support his traveling habit doing the odd bit of work for the CIA. Then he got hooked.

She looked at him rather fondly, tilting her head to one side. He guessed she liked him for barreling through a trust fund. People always liked that idea. Maybe because they think they would do it themselves.

"Do you do the pictures, too?" she said. "The photographs?"

"Not for *Sunset*."

"Where's your photographer?"

He smiled easily. Was she suspicious? He realized now that when he told her about his embryonic career as a travel writer, he hadn't been thinking about his cover at all. He'd simply been telling her the truth.

"We have a stringer in Vancouver."

Chandler's martini arrived, and they ordered. He also ordered them a bottle of wine. "Well, you should see Stanley Park, I suppose," she said vaguely. "I don't know really. I haven't been there in some time."

It was clear she wasn't going to Vancouver as a tourist. A tourist would have firm ideas on what to do and see. She had to be on business, not that there was much doubt anyway.

"Tell me," she said now, leaning forward so he could catch a little of her perfume, a clean floral scent, "who are those people *Sunset* uses in their photographs? You know, the ones sitting around tasting the Cabernets or putting together bird-feeders. They all look so wholesome."

He laughed. "Real people. Not models. People who live in the houses we cover, or people who work in our Menlo Park office. You look like you could be one of them yourself," he said.

"Wholesome?" She raised her eyebrows and looked amused.

"No. Tan. Healthy. Well groomed. Kind of . . . sparkly." He leaned forward confidentially. "We edit out the unattractive people sometimes. We take their picture standing next to the deck or garden or whatever, then we use the shots without them."

"Nice to know I wouldn't end up on the cutting room floor," she said.

"On second thought, you might anyway."

"Why?" Mock indignation.

"You might be a little too interesting-looking. Too much character in your face. And too . . . well, attractive. It could distract from the story."

She touched her throat with her long fingers, a slow movement that Chandler Smith found seductive, smiled, and tilted her head back slightly as if she were appraising him beneath lowered lashes. It was a fascinating gesture, he thought; curious, confident, and rather elegant.

Sunny sat at the dressing table in her rather old-fashioned hotel room. God, I look like hell, she thought to herself, and this damn hair makes me look like Saint Joan.

She attacked the small silver waves with a brush, but whatever she did, her hair looked the same. It occurred to her that she'd gone temporarily insane with her nail scissors in the Oslo airport. She could have left her hair a little longer.

Thank God, though, that the passport had worked so well. Gray-haired women probably all looked alike anyway. She rummaged in her makeup bag and came up with a small compact of blusher. She added some to her face. Her eyes sparkled more, but she wondered if she looked like an over-rouged old lady. She flung the compact back in the bag and went to lie down on the bed.

What would happen now? Would Alex appear at the hotel? Would some mysterious stranger take her off to Pago Pago in a private plane? Anything could happen, including nothing. This last possibility struck her with an emotion almost akin to fear. What if she couldn't find him, if she'd traveled all over the world for nothing, if she'd been slapped around in a deserted warehouse and seen a crumpled young man dead in a train compartment, all for nothing?

Suddenly she began to shake. What if she had caused that

death, by some bungling of her own? She was out of her league, dangerously out of her league. And now she was waiting, alone, in a strange hotel room, waiting for something she knew nothing about.

She'd planned to think hard on the train trip to Vancouver. She'd been so busy moving, eluding surveillance, she hadn't had proper time to think. Instead she'd spent a cozy couple of hours with that good-looking young man from *Sunset Magazine*. It was rather appropriate, really, his being from *Sunset* and distracting her so. *Sunset Magazine*, full of cool adobe houses and simple but elegant dinner parties, was her real world. She didn't belong in a grubby frightening world full of spies. Really she belonged right now back at Rancho Salubre. Suddenly she thought of Marjorie and a flood of regret over her lie to Marjorie came over here. Regret over springing the switch on her when it was too late to go back, knowing in the back of her mind about Marjorie owing her a favor, knowing a secret of Marjorie's and using it.

She found herself crying softly now and hating herself for it. They were tears of anger at herself, for becoming involved in something so absurd and potentially violent. And tears of frustration at being so near her ultimate goal, Alex Markoff, and still not having a clue as to where he was, who wanted to find him, and why. And she'd told the cruelest lie of all to him. Telling him he had a son. Well, was it really such a terrible lie? It could have been true. They could have had a son. And Alex would never have known because he'd disappeared to go off spying, without saying good-bye. She decided her lie was justified, if any lie was. If only she could stop sobbing.

In a steel room near Washington the old man sat, with five other men. They were a carefully selected group. One man was the chief of counterintelligence. Another was the director himself. One was the man who'd worked with Gerhard Mannheim, debriefing him over many months, checking and rechecking every story, every scrap of information. The other was the chief of the Canadian bureau. The fifth man was a special liaison with the President. Others could have been included, but the old man just wasn't sure. He had to be prepared for repercussions if anything went wrong at this late stage.

"Gentlemen," he began solemnly, "for years we've been looking, wondering, about the possibility of a deeply penetrated Soviet agent, a long-term agent close to the center of our operations, an American Philby.

"Over the years, we've received a fair share of defectors. It's been the judgment of the agency that many of them were sent to us simply to cover for this deeply penetrated agent, providing us with disinformation that led to small catches but protected the big fish.

"For many months we've been debriefing an East German defector, a high-ranking officer, of the same generation as Philby and presumably of the long-term Soviet man in the CIA. Gerhard had a scrap, a piece of information that fit the pattern. We had to compare his information with all the information we've received from other defectors in the past. We think he's square.

"In Norway in 1944 Mannheim picked up the first information from this man. A précis of the Anglo-American plans for counterintelligence gathering in the Soviet Union, to be put into operation after the war. Mannheim didn't know then what he'd picked up, but he learned later, and the knowledge stuck. It amused him to hear about that first drop, because he realized he had been the Communist agent who started the ball rolling. He made the pickup in a cabin in Norway—occupied Norway. He met two men in a cabin. One of them was Alex Markoff. The other man he never saw. Mannheim also learned something even more important. The man with Markoff was the agent. Markoff, as far as he knew, was innocent, unaware of the nature of the mission.

"Markoff, as you may recall, was an agent inside Russia in

the late forties. And, unlike the rest of our guys there then, he got out. That made us suspicious of Markoff years ago, and it still looks bad. Unless our American Philby kept him alive for protection. We think that's what happened. Markoff was insurance if years later that drop at the cabin was traced. Markoff alive could divert suspicion. Markoff dead could do it, too, but not as well if the Russian agent was still active.

"We don't know who was in that cabin with Markoff. We've never found him. We think he's our man. That means OSS. Which fits with everything else we've gleaned over the years.

"Markoff disappeared ten years ago. He disappeared then for a good reason, having to do with his service in Southeast Asia. It was important then, it's not important now." The old man grinned.

"The story he felt was too hot for anyone, including his own agency, has since been picked up by the global intelligence community, thanks to a reporter for the New York *Times*. It's an old, dirty story. Markoff doesn't know he can come home. And from what we can tell, he doesn't want to come home.

"He's snapped. We only hope he's got his wits together enough to tell us the answer to one question: Who was the other man with him in Norway in 1945?"

The old man turned now to the Canadian bureau chief. "And you're here, Tom, because the end of the story is taking place in your territory. There's a woman in Canada now who's pretty close to finding Markoff. She's a free agent, a wild card, operating apparently without control. Although she could be working for the KGB to silence Markoff. If she is, we don't think she knows it. I've got a man with her. A good man. He's going to find Markoff through her. He's going to ask the question.

"And then, gentlemen, the chase will be over. Unless, of course, it's all a trap. In which case we mop up and begin again. But this time, I think we've got him cornered. He'd be an old man now, but could be still useful. In any case, finding him would mean rewriting the true history of the agency for the last thirty-five years. The ramifications will be enormous. We have to begin now to prepare for a complete reanalysis of everything over the years, every defection, every recruitment, every operation, successful or not.''

"But you haven't found him yet?" said the White House liaison. "Markoff, I mean.''

"As good as,'' said the old man confidently. He wished he could be sure.

"And if he won't cooperate?'' The chief of counterintelligence knocked his briar pipe smartly on a large ashtray.

"He will have to,'' said the old man simply.

"It better be clean,'' said Tom, the Canadian bureau chief. "I don't want a mess in my territory. I'll have to tell the Canucks something, just in case.''

"No,'' said the old man. "We'll explain later if we have to. You'll be fully briefed. We're working out a cover story now.''

"I hope it's damned good,'' muttered Tom.

The director cracked his knuckles. "Haven't we been through all this before? Getting close to the long-term Soviet agent? Hasn't that been a theme running through this agency for years?''

The old man nodded. "That's right. But it's never been so simple before. That's why I'm betting on it this time.''

"Too simple,'' said the counterintelligence chief, frowning. Then he smiled. "They never do it this simple.''

Sunny's sobs were stifled quickly with the sharp, untelephonelike ring of the bell on her nightstand. It was almost a hoot, not a proper ring at all. She watched the instrument and listened to two more hoots before she sniffed, wiped her eyes, and took the receiver.

"Hello," said a pleasant male voice. It was slightly familiar. "This is Chandler Smith. The man from *Sunset*."

Sunny stiffened. Was he the contact? Or was he someone else? Damnit, she didn't want to guess or wonder. If he knew the code—*sporløs*—then she'd talk to him. But otherwise, he was either dangerous or getting in the way.

"Yes," she said frostily.

He didn't seem to notice the frigidity in her tone.

"I've just run afoul of Canadian liquor laws," he began. "It being a Sunday, I can only have a drink in the hotel. And the bar here is pretty grim. I noticed you checking in right before I did, and I wondered if we could have a nightcap together. I think you'd cheer up the bar beautifully."

She didn't reply.

"Am I being too pushy?" he said now.

"No, no. I'm tired, I guess." She sighed. A nice drink with an attractive man would have been pleasant. "But thank you."

He sighed elaborately. "Well, I've just used up my only phone number in town," he said.

She hung up and smiled. A little gallantry from a man practically young enough to be her son was cheering. As a matter of fact, his voice had been a warm welcome note of reality. She almost wished she'd joined him.

Now she felt restless, and wide awake.

The phone rang again. She almost expected it to be Chandler Smith. She smiled. He couldn't be a spy. He'd never call himself Smith.

A strange male voice with a very slight accent that clipped the syllables said, "Welcome. Come downstairs and stand next to the very large potted palm next to the newspaper stand."

She hurried down to the lobby, her heart beating strongly. Would Alex be standing there?

No one was standing there. She feigned interest in the headlines in the Vancouver *Sun*. Next to her a telephone rang. She looked up, startled. She was standing next to a booth. She walked in, picked up the phone.

The same voice said now: "Dad is looking forward to seeing you and his son. Can you be ready tomorrow morning at six? We'll come up to the room. Dress warmly." It almost sounded like a recording. She said frantically, "But my son isn't here yet . . ." She ran her fingertips over her mouth. "I want to prepare his father first."

"We haven't time for such niceties, I'm afraid. You must bring your son. You have until six tomorrow morning to get him with you. Otherwise I'm afraid the outing is out of the question." The line went dead.

Sunny went back to her room. The elevator ride up seemed so much shorter than the one down. She let herself in the room. It looked bleak and abandoned.

"Damn, damn, damn."

She slammed her suitcase lid shut. She wasn't going to stop now. She'd have to tell them in the morning that if she couldn't see Alex she at least wanted to get a message to him. If only she could produce a son, a son in his thirties, in one night.

Her eyes narrowed. It was dangerous. Very dangerous. But she thought she could handle it without Smith being the wiser. And even if he were, well, Alex could take care of it. She wouldn't be alone much longer, not if she found a son for Alex. Even if she were bringing a viper into his lair, she could warn him in time.

She went to the mirror and redid her makeup. It looked as though she'd been crying, but she repaired the damage as best she could and hoped the bar would be dim. Then she went downstairs.

She was terribly annoyed, once she reached the bar, to see Chandler Smith in animated conversation with a pretty young woman on the adjacent barstool. What a fool she was, an old woman taking his invitation seriously. She stood for a moment, deciding whether or not to leave, when he spotted her. It was as if he'd sensed her with some radar, because he turned around, stared at her, and smiled. She smiled back shyly, and he excused himself from his companion who looked curiously, and with undisguised annoyance, at Sunny.

"I'm sorry," said Sunny. "I should have realized you wouldn't be lonely long."

"I'm glad you changed your mind." He led her, not to the bar where she'd envisioned a grim threesome, but to a secluded table.

"I couldn't sleep," she said.

"Good. Martinis?"

"Sure."

When the drinks came he twiddled with the stem of the glass. "Do you travel a lot?"

"A fair amount."

"Then you probably get propositioned by lots of lonely route salesmen in hotel bars," he said cheerfully. "When I called your room I was afraid you thought I was one of them."

She bit into her olive. "Not at all. For one thing, my age is a pretty good defense. With you, anyway."

"Not necessarily. We're both over twenty-one, aren't we?"

"You just told me you weren't one of those lonely route salesmen."

"I'm more charming," he said.

She didn't answer.

"Come on, you're supposed to say I am."

"You're too charming for your own good. Besides, someone as young as you are shouldn't know they're charming. It spoils them. Makes them affected."

"What are you doing in Vancouver?"

She took a deep breath. She may as well get on with it. If he was an agent of some kind, she wouldn't find out chatting over martinis. It was a risk she was prepared to take. "I'm here doing some government work," she said.

"Government work? And they let you stay at a hotel like this? Must be important."

"It is important. Tell me, were you ever in the service?"

"Yes." He looked startled. "Navy. Don't tell me you're here looking for Vietnam-era draft dodgers." He smiled.

"No. I can't tell you what I'm doing."

He frowned. "Then you shouldn't have started telling me what you're doing. Let's forget it, shall we?"

She liked that. And of course he was right. Maybe he'd think she was completely crazy. Well, it was either this story or one about some romantic problem, and while cousin Margaret had lapped that up, she didn't think this fairly reasonable young man wanted to get involved in some stranger's domestic squabbles.

"I'm telling you because I need your help," she said simply. She tried to remember Billy's pitch, the first time. She heard herself say very calmly, "How would you like to do something for your country?"

Chandler Smith looked absolutely amazed.

"You're not kidding, are you?"

"No, I'm not," she said simply. "I've run into a snag, and all you have to do is say you're my son. Just for a half hour or so." She had decided she'd display Chandler, then arrange to meet Alex herself. If he was coming to the hotel in person, which she doubted, it wouldn't matter; she could explain and get rid of Smith. If she was going somewhere else, she'd have a better chance if she had a son back in Vancouver. And if she had to take Chandler with her . . . well, she couldn't do that, but she would manage somehow when the time came. All she needed was a presentable son at six o'clock tomorrow morning.

A waiter came to their table and told Chandler he had a phone call. Sunny didn't like that at all. Now he'd have a chance to tell someone; dangerous if he wasn't what he seemed to be. He'd also have a chance to think about it. If he was who he said he was, he might have time to decide she was crazy.

"Don't take the call," she said, her hand on his.

"I've got to. It's my editor. He said he'd call."

"At this hour?"

Chandler grinned. "He's a cheap sonofabitch. Always calls after nine. I'll be right back." He slid out of the seat and patted her hand.

The old man replaced the receiver incredulously. Across from him sat the chief of counterintelligence, wreathed in bluish pipe smoke.

"Jesus," said the old man softly. "She's recruiting him."

"What?"

"I told him to go along with it. It's perfect."

"Too perfect. He better watch himself."

"Sorry. Believe me, I didn't welcome that interruption any more than you did. Please go on."

"There's not much more to say," she said wearily. "I just need someone to say he's my son tomorrow morning at six o'clock."

"Why?"

"I can't tell you."

"I'm afraid you'll have to."

"I don't know much about it myself," she began. "Except I'm supposed to meet someone tomorrow, and I have to have a son along. After I make the meeting, you can fade out of the picture."

"I'm too old to be your son."

"Just a little. This son was born in 1946. He was put up for adoption and he's just resurfaced. He wants to meet his father, but, and this is very important, he has ambivalent feelings and wants me to smooth the way first. I'm his mother. I'm going to talk to the father."

Smith stroked his jaw. "Why?"

"I've told you all you need to know. Other than that it's all in a good cause. I know it sounds absurd."

Chandler looked around the bar.

"Let's talk about this somewhere else," he said. "Come up to my room."

Sunny liked that. He couldn't talk on the phone anymore. She could make sure he didn't talk to anyone.

Billy Sinclair sat hunched over the bar at a noisy restaurant in suburban Maryland. Next to him sat Lewis Strickland. Billy had recruited Lewis years ago. Now he worked in Ottawa, as the assistant to the Canadian bureau chief, a colorful and volatile man known in the agency as Tommy Gun.

"So how is it working for old Tommy?" began Billy.

"Not bad, not bad." Lewis had begun to speak with careful determination, pronouncing each syllable carefully. He was only on his third. Billy remembered that careful cadence usually after Strickland's fifth drink. This might take less time than he thought. Real nervous, though. Always worried about blowing something and the goddamned Canadians getting all hot and bothered. "Understand you and he came down for a pretty top-level meeting. Big doings, huh?"

"Oh, yeah. And Tommy's sure it'll blow sky-high. Seems like we spend more time trying to hide out than anything else. The last thing he wants is a big mess on Canadian soil. Guess he'll be sending a man out to Vancouver to pick up the pieces if this thing blows. Strictly internal problem in the agency and they have to sort it out on Canadian soil. Boy, is he mad. He was mad after the briefing and madder still when they called him back and told him tomorrow morning at six things might be coming down."

"Six our time?" Billy laughed. "Great. He'll have to get out of bed, too."

"No. Vancouver time. He told me he's so nervous he's

not going to eat breakfast. He's afraid he'll throw up or something. When he gets nervous like that he always thinks he's going to throw up. But he doesn't. He just yells and writes memos and then tears them up again and calls me in and yells some more. What a life!''

''It's a rotten life,'' said Billy. ''Let's have another drink.''

Chandler Smith had poured out two drinks in toothbrush glasses. Now he stepped into the bathroom and turned on the shower. ''That's what they do in the movies so that no one will overhear,'' he said, shrugging. ''Now, tell me who you are and who you work for.''

''I've told you my name. Ingrid Carlsen. And I work for the American government. All I want you to do is pretend you're my son for half an hour. Please don't ask me any more questions.''

She slumped into a chair.

''You've been through the mill, haven't you?'' he said softly.

''I'm afraid so. Just tell me if you'll do it. If you won't, then, well . . . you won't. But don't ask me any more questions.''

He looked thoughtful. ''I've done a bit of this kind of thing in my time. Really. In the Navy. How do I know you're who you say you are?''

She put her head back and closed her eyes. ''You don't. And I don't know who you are. But I'm in a spot and I need help. And you're a fine patriotic young man with a taste for adventure, and you'll be cool and keep your head. Okay?''

She felt his hand on her brow and opened her eyes. ''Okay,'' he said. ''I'll do it.''

''You're sweet,'' she said, smiling with new animation.

''But is it dangerous?''

''Of course not. You don't think they'd send me on anything dangerous, do you?''

He sat on the arm of her chair. "Why not? You might like that sort of thing. Some people do."

She looked at him, startled, her eyes widening. She saw a look of recognition in his face. Then he kissed her on the mouth.

"If it's dangerous you should stay here with me until tomorrow."

"Don't be silly," she said. "It's not dangerous. And turn off that shower. It's a very simple, routine thing." She wanted to kiss him again.

"You don't know anything about me," he said. "Don't you think you should keep an eye on me until tomorrow morning?"

"Probably. But I don't want to stay and listen to the shower all night."

"If I turn it off," he said, "we can't talk anymore. That's what happens in the movies." He went into the bathroom and turned off the shower.

"We're not in the movies."

"Sure we are." He kissed her eyes and brushed back her silver waves. She put her hands lightly on his shoulders.

"We can't . . ." she began.

"Why can't we? Anyway, we're not allowed to talk anymore, remember?"

"But . . ."

"Don't talk," he whispered, placing a finger on her lips, and then kissed her again, slowly and delicately.

Billy St. Clair sat waiting at an all-night restaurant. He looked around at the unappealing decor. All these fast-food places seemed to be orange. Probably to get the customers all wired up and energetic so the tables would turn around faster. He looked at the menu and sighed. "Don't you have anything but hamburgers?" he said plaintively to the waitress.

She was a young girl with drooping bleached hair and bad

skin. "There's breakfast, but it's too early for breakfast," she said. "We start breakfast at five."

"I'll take the Tahiti burger and a coffee."

He was proud of the job he'd done. He knew now exactly what was happening. The old man had sent Chandler Smith to Seattle to find Sunny. Now Billy had to find her, too. The easiest way was to keep monitoring the old man's activities. Thank God for Madge, and the others who had helped. Somehow he liked Madge and the other frightened ones the best. He had other informants in the agency who told him things not because they were frightened, but because he'd recruited them long ago. Idealistic young men, most of them. Easy to turn around without their even knowing it. The idealistic ones thought Billy was working to keep the agency on the right track. He told them just enough to let them think they were the righteous ones. They were dangerous. And he didn't have something to hold over them to frighten them. Well, of course he did now. Because now they were working for him. But he couldn't use that until the very end, and it was dangerous.

A tall, square-looking man came into the restaurant and joined Billy. Billy regarded him with a measure of contempt. No matter how long he'd worked in the West, the man he knew as Luke still looked like he was fresh off the boat. He wore an open-neck sports shirt in a garish pattern, and his hair looked like his wife cut it for him, all brushy and sticking out at angles.

Luke ordered a Coke.

Billy smiled. "I think you'll agree we're on top of things," he began, rushing the words a little too much. "We'll find him. The woman is meeting him tomorrow at six A.M., local time, in Vancouver, Canada. Of course, Vancouver's a big place, but . . ."

Luke stirred his Coke, his coarse features showing no emotion. Suddenly Billy hated him. He was so bland looking, with a fat nose, like a peasant. Billy hated the bluish cast to his poorly shaven beard and his damned passive expression.

"We will find them and trace them to Markoff," said Luke. "You will do nothing. Center has made it clear you are no longer to run agents."

"All right, all right. I don't. I've phased out my network, and you know it."

Luke looked angry. "Oh. And who killed the CIA agent following the woman on the train?"

Billy shrugged. "And who ordered that rough stuff in the warehouse? Stupid, clumsy."

"The situation is grave, and you know it," said Luke. "Your situation. We should have brought you home as soon as Mannheim defected."

Billy was shocked. He'd never heard an admission of failure before. He didn't agree, though. There had been plenty of defectors. Real ones and loyal KGB or GRU men, too.

"I took proper measures to discredit Mannheim," said Billy. "You didn't even know what he had on me until I found out for you. And all he has is a fragment, a fragment that depends on Markoff. Everyone knows how unreliable Markoff is. If he's alive."

Luke glared at him, and the two men fell silent as the waitress approached. She set a Tahiti burger, festooned with canned pineapple, in front of Billy.

"But he knows who the other man was in that cabin. All they need is to ask Alex Markoff one simple question: Who was with you?"

Billy shrugged. "Markoff is unreliable. He might not say."

"You made your first mistake when you took him with you to deliver that information to us years ago," said Luke.

"You weren't even born then."

"Center wants to bring you home now. We think it's wisest."

"But my work here . . ."

"Your work here is finished," said Luke. "All we want to do now is protect our investment. We're wasting time. The arrangements are being made. Please do not discuss this with your wife. She will be told at the appropriate time."

"Let me prepare her . . ." began Billy.

"No."

Luke looked at him sternly. Billy was frightened. He mustn't ruin it now. If they thought he was unreliable, they might kill him, they really might.

"I'll await my orders," he said stiffly.

"Very good," said Luke.

Billy licked his lips and looked down at the chunks of pineapple, its thick syrup mingling with the meat juices. He felt nauseated all of a sudden. He jerked his head back and looked directly at Luke. "When I am . . . home . . . I will be very useful," he said. "There's much more I can do for you."

Luke smiled. Billy had never seen him smile before. "Yes, you can be. And a good thing, too. For both of us. Be ready tomorrow. Plan to take nothing with you. Stay close to home. And remember, if you interfere with any operations in Vancouver, it will go very hard with you."

Billy made a very early flight to the West Coast. He couldn't go home. Very carefully, over a Bloody Mary, he thought about all the possibilities. They could kill him, although that would be pretty wretched after all he'd done. And it wouldn't make it very easy to recruit anyone else like him in the future. It would be bad publicity all around for Mother Russia if the story came out. They wouldn't dare. Still, he hadn't gone home last night.

They could keep him in place. If Markoff died before he talked, Billy could stay in place. Palm Springs, he thought, optimistically. It would be nice to really retire. He hadn't wanted to before, but now Palm Springs sounded divine.

Kikuko would like it there. And if she didn't, well, too damn bad.

If Markoff talked, then they'd bring him home.

All in all, Billy preferred Palm Springs.

The more he thought about it, the more he realized that's what he deserved. They hadn't been able to find Alex. Only Sunny had. And Sunny was his agent. So he'd really saved the day. He should get whatever he wanted. He was the one who'd saved them.

He drank again and thought fondly of Sunny and Alex. He'd loved the old OSS days. They were gallant days. Sunny and Alex were gallant. He wanted to work something out, something so that he could retire quietly to Palm Springs, and so that Alex and Sunny would be able to end their days pleasantly, too. It could be managed. There had to be a way. Something with finesse.

Yes, there was a gentleman's end to it all. He couldn't forget his old comrades. He'd managed before, and he could do it again.

The plane was circling now. If only he knew what that bastard Luke was planning. It was impertinent not to let him in on it. Damned impertinence all around. Well, Billy would show them all. This was his last bow, and it would be elegant, classic, refined. Nothing crude and messy.

When she woke, Sunny was confused for a moment. Where was she? Then she smelled his scent on the pillow and smiled. She put her hand out to the other side of the bed, but it was empty. Shifting quietly to her side, she pretended to be asleep, and opened her eyes just a crack. He stood there naked, tall and tan with golden hairs on his body. He was snapping a small black pistol closed and placing it in a black leather shaving kit.

A few minutes later he was dressed and kissing her. "Ingrid. Wake up. It's almost six o'clock."

13

THE MAN WHO knocked on Sunny's door at six o'clock was a large Indian, with shiny black hair and rather old-fashioned black plastic glasses. He wore a plaid wool shirt and jeans. The Indian took a small notebook from his shirt pocket and wrote in it, tore out the page and handed it to Sunny. He had written "*sporløs*." He took the page back.

After a quick look at Sunny and then at Chandler Smith, he said, "Okay, all ready to check out?" The last word was pronounced in the Canadian way, almost Scottish.

They nodded. Sunny wore jeans and a sweater, with her Burberry on her arm. Smith wore jeans and a down jacket over a flannel shirt.

Sunny was restless and excited. "Where are we going?" she asked the Indian.

He gave her a look of surprise and didn't answer.

"Well, my son has to know. You see, he can't really go with us. He's got to be in Vancouver on business."

"Mother's worried about my meeting my father," said Chandler gently. "She wants to prepare him, but I'm ready. I don't see any point in putting this off any longer. I want to come, too."

"You'll have to or we forget the whole thing," said the Indian. She recognized his voice. It was he who had called her, arranging the meeting.

Sunny glared at Smith. This wasn't the plan. But then, she'd seen him opening that pistol this morning, and closing it with a professional ease. It was clear he was after Alex, too, and she'd have to keep an eye on him. Mostly she wanted to get his pistol. She couldn't let him kill Alex. Should she try and tell the Indian? No, she couldn't. She'd never be allowed to see Alex. She'd have to wait till they got to Alex. And then she'd warn him. She had one thing on her side. Chandler didn't know she knew. She'd watch him every second. It was too bad he wasn't what he seemed. She liked him. She would have liked him even if they hadn't made love last night, a development—surprising and rather delightful—that she couldn't sort out right now. Maybe she shouldn't try and sort it out, although she certainly couldn't forget it.

She hitched up her flight bag, her old companion, full now of the remains of Billy's cash, Ingrid Carlsen's passport, her own wallet, now without Harriet Grey's credit cards (her own identification was slipped behind the lining of Marjorie's suitcase back at Rancho Salubre), a collection of simple clothes she'd bought in England, her makeup pouch, and her purse, folded flat. Chandler had a suitcase, and his shaving kit was presumably inside the leather flight bag, similar to hers, that he carried on his shoulder.

It seemed to take forever to check out. There were some phone calls on Chandler's bill, and some room service charges. And then, when she paid in American funds, it took time to make the currency exchange. The clerk, a pleasant pink and white lady with an English accent, proceeded in leisurely fashion. A bellman gathered up all their baggage, which had been arranged in a clump next to them, and the Indian retrieved it all in a rather surly way. The English lady looked up, surprised, as it was all handed back over to the Indian.

Finally they all loaded up into a pickup truck with British Columbia plates and bounced off through the streets of downtown Vancouver. Sunny wondered if they'd end up somewhere in the interior of British Columbia. Maybe at an airstrip to take them farther. Anything could happen.

The Indian didn't speak, but he turned on the radio and hummed along to vague Muzak-like tunes. Sunny thought that maybe she and her supposed son should be talking, but she remembered they didn't know each other well, either, and they were probably nervous about the forthcoming meeting. Silence seemed appropriate, and it gave Sunny time to think. She had to get that gun somehow and disarm Smith before he and Alex met. She remembered Billy's warning, although she couldn't imagine Chandler being an assassin. She sneaked a look at him on the seat next to her. His hair was rather tousled and his eyes looked sleepy. He'd shaved, though. His jaw was smooth and she could even smell a lime-scented shave cream. He caught her looking at him, smiled, and took her hand, running his thumb lightly against her palm.

She pulled it back in horror. He was supposed to be her son. What if the Indian saw? Although she supposed a son might hold his mother's hand. But she couldn't react to his touch like a mother. And he might be a cold-blooded killer. His mouth tilted slightly in amusement, and she looked back at him sternly, then smiled herself, overcome by nerves as well as by the more ludicrous aspects of the situation.

They rattled across the Lions' Gate Bridge, flanked by stone British lions, across the deep water, to the North Shore. An hour later, after they had driven west and then north for some time, they pulled up to a small marina. The Indian unloaded their things, said "I'll be right back," and drove the pickup back onto the road. Sunny and Chandler watched him pull into a gas station and talk to the attendant.

"Probably arranging for some work. He should have something done about the suspension," said Chandler. "Listen, sweetheart, I'm glad we can talk for a moment. What's my name? And yours? I'm afraid we didn't get a story together last night. We got distracted."

Sunny sighed. "You're what was referred to in my day as a fast worker."

"Don't be coy," he said. "It doesn't suit you. Is that Indian looking at us? I want to kiss you. Well, maybe a filial kiss." He kissed her forehead. "Now, what are our names?"

"I'm Sonia Sinclair. My maiden name was Isdahl." She spelled it. "Your name can be anything. Smith might be too pat but you're used to it, so better stick with it. I'm your natural mother and you were adopted at birth. The man we're seeing is your natural father. Alex Markoff. You were conceived in London at the end of the war. You've traced me and now you're meeting him for the first time. He didn't know you existed."

"I'm half-Russian?"

"And half-Norwegian."

He scanned the area. "Looks like we're taking a sea cruise. Our friend's coming back."

"You weren't supposed to come this far," she said.

"I wasn't going to leave you," he said simply.

"You might screw everything up."

"I won't."

The man known as Luke ran a gnarled, red-knuckled hand through his spiky hair. He had coded the message himself. He handed the series of numbers to the clerk and went back to his office to think.

If he could only keep the situation in careful perspective, think it through like a tough chess problem . . . Instead, he felt anger rising within him. But that damned St. Clair! Now he'd taken off. He'd never trusted him. Of course, he never trusted anyone, but St. Clair was worse than devious. He was unreliable.

Anything could happen now. St. Clair could turn, if he hadn't done so already. He could ruin everything. It was his own stupid fault. Luke felt he should have eliminated St.

Clair immediately. Whatever he was doing could ruin Luke forever.

For a second, in his anger and his fear, Luke even thought about going to the Americans. Maybe it would be his only chance. But he suppressed the dangerous, unworthy thought immediately. He would have to do his best, and if he failed, he'd have to prepare for the consequences. He figured he had another few hours at most to do something about St. Clair.

One thing had been made very clear to him. If Alex Markoff were alive, Moscow would do whatever was necessary to eliminate him and anyone who knew where he was and what he knew. His secret would put the whole history of Cold War espionage in a new perspective. His secret formed the basis of many secrets.

Marjorie Devine admired herself in the full-length mirror in her room at Rancho Salubre. She really did think her thighs looked trimmer. They felt trimmer. She pounded them with satisfaction. She must look better. The staff certainly seemed to think so. They were so flattering lately, and at first they'd treated her like a naughty child. Two more days. She wondered if she could lose another pound in two more days. She really hadn't lost much. They kept telling her you had to lose slowly. And that inches counted as much as pounds. That was true. She looked better than she usually did at a hundred and thirty-six. It sure had been nice to get under one-forty, her old plateau.

As soon as she got back she'd have to find out what had happened to Sunny. She'd managed the deception very nicely. It was fun being someone else. It was almost as if it gave her a chance to get Sunny's body, too, as if the name change had helped with her transformation.

She sat down thoughtfully on the bed and looked at her yogurt flip nightcap, decorated with a sprig of mint. She'd wait till she was all tucked in to drink it.

All at once she knew what Sunny had done. It was so

simple really, why hadn't she thought of it before? Sunny Sinclair was so secretive. Plastic surgery. Maybe a little work around the eyes. She'd heard Sunny complain about her Scandinavian eyes. She'd explained that they turned down at the corners. An outer-epicanthal eyefold. And that it got more pronounced with age.

Sunny was the type who would be secretive about plastic surgery. To her, it would have seemed like cheating.

Marjorie wondered if Sunny was vain. She'd always kept in shape, of course, but was that vanity? After two weeks at Rancho Salubre, Marjorie had begun to understand it was something else. A kind of control. Sunny liked to be in control of herself. Marjorie was beginning to like it, too.

She could hardly wait to show Sunny how much better she looked. And to look at Sunny. She'd look carefully for any signs. Little tiny scars around the eyes. And behind the ears. They always ended up pulling things behind your ears. Marjorie could hardly wait to inspect her friend when they met again.

Around them the water was a choppy gray-green, and now whitecaps were beginning to appear. It was getting rougher. "Prepare for a long voyage," the Indian had said. They had been on the boat for hours and hours now, and it must be late afternoon. Sunny now wondered if they were going to Alaska. They were certainly heading north, although with the many islands and rocky coves it was hard to say. Still, there were bluish mountains to her right, and had been most of the day. Vancouver Island must be on her left. It was a distant line of land on the horizon, but now that the weather was grayer, it was little more than a smudge.

She drank tea from a tin cup and leaned on the rail. It was a fishing vessel, an older purse seiner, well cared for and well appointed. It was funny how after all these years she remembered so much about Papa's business.

She glanced over at Chandler Smith. He'd been silent

most of the day, as had the two Indians, the man who'd come to fetch them and another who'd been waiting for them aboard when they'd come to the marina.

Sunny still hadn't managed to get Smith's gun, or to figure out a way to get her hands on it. He looked tired now, hardly like a cold-blooded assassin. He also looked pale and generally unhappy.

"What's the matter?" she said, her voice full of concern. "Seasick? I thought you'd been in the Navy." Sunny knew how much the power of suggestion could affect seasickness. "You look terrible. You'd better go below."

The Indians, one at the wheel, the other at his side, turned and stared at them, which seemed to irritate Chandler even more.

"I'm fine, I really am."

"You look green," said Sunny.

"Shut up, will you," he mumbled. "Anyway, Lord Nelson got seasick."

"Let me help you." She took his arm and began to lead him down to the cabin, a neat little space with four bunks and a table that folded down from the wall.

She noticed that he clung to his flight bag, even as she eased him into a lower bunk. She slipped it off his shoulder and onto the floor, and pulled up a light blanket.

"Will I live?" said Smith, bravely trying out a smile. He groaned from the effort and rolled over on his stomach.

She looked down at his head, his face buried in his arms, his hair engagingly disheveled, and kissed him right next to his ear, smoothing down his hair. With her other hand, she opened the flight bag and felt for the shaving kit. When her fingers found it, she sat up and asked Smith if he wanted anything.

"Nothing. I want to die alone. In dignity."

She had the shaving kit open now, and she felt the cold metal of the pistol. She managed to get it inside the deep pocket of her Burberry.

Many hours later, after a night and part of a day, the

fishing vessel set anchor in a small, rocky cove on a tiny island.

The two Indians lowered a small boat, and the larger man—the man who'd come to fetch them—rowed them to shore. The island was softly lit now, at early evening, although this far north it could be later than she thought. A grove of trees, Douglas firs, loomed before them, inky dark against the pale sky. The terrain at the water's edge was rocky; large, smooth gray rocks, with green water lapping into the cracks between them, and patches of barnacles. The rhythmic lapping was a sound from her childhood, and a comforting sound. The island looked startlingly like the island where Sunny had spent childhood summers at camp.

As they clambered out of the boat and onto the rocks, Sunny heard the fishing vessel's engine start up again. They were stranded on this island. She felt a sudden stab of fear and lost her footing for an instant on the rocks. Her raincoat swung out at an awkward angle, thanks to the weight of the pistol. She gained her balance and felt the pistol, still, thankfully, in the pocket, slap against her thigh.

Past the rocks was a small, pebbly beach, with bands of water-smoothed-and-bleached driftwood: twigs and branches of pale, twisting wood. The pebbles made crunching noises under their feet as Chandler and Sunny followed the Indian up the beach to the mouth of a creek, and then some yards up the creek—a rust-colored stream shaded by firs, alders, and madronas—to a clearing.

At the back of the clearing sat a huge house. It looked like a lodge really, a long, low structure, made of heavy logs. It was softened with moss, which gave it a bright green, fuzzy, rather festive roof, but the overall impression was grim. Sunny decided that must be because the windows were very small and shuttered tight.

Sunny found herself running across the clearing, through yellow wispy, wild grass that came up to her calves. Alex was in that house, he had to be.

At once she felt a hand on her shoulder. It was the Indian. "Not so fast," he said. "Don't want to startle him. Let's just walk in nice and slowly."

She stopped and peered into the Indian's face. It was rather a kind face. "Is he . . . all right?"

The Indian smiled. "Yes. He's all right. Just cautious."

Over his shoulder Chandler Smith raised a questioning eyebrow at Sunny. She turned away and walked slowly to the steps.

They were wide, shallow steps, leading to a covered porch that wrapped all around the building. Some old-fashioned lawn furniture made of flat boards in a simple, squat shape, and painted green, sat, looking as if they had been there for fifty years.

Slowly the central door, a massive door of thick planks, swung open. Framed in the doorway, half-obscured by darkness, was a tall figure, watching them as they made their way toward him.

"Alex?" she cried out.

He stepped into the light. It was Alex.

He walked slowly onto the porch. She stood at the bottom step, frozen, looking up at him. He looked like Alex, the Alex she knew, but he was craggier, browner, wider somehow in the chest and shoulders. There was less gray in his hair than in hers; it was still half dark. His eyes, dark and Slavic—shaped under level brows—were alert.

"Is this . . . ?" he looked at Chandler Smith, then back at Sunny. Smith came forward and shook his hand shyly. Alex seized him by the shoulders and stared into his face. Suddenly he started to laugh. There was little amusement in it. It was a laugh of joy.

He put an arm around Smith and around Sunny on the other side and started into the house. "I like the look of the kid," he said. "He's got a damned nice face."

Inside the house was a collection of old, rustic-looking furniture, arranged with no apparent plan around a large fireplace of sea-washed stone. On the mantel were a few odds and ends from the sea: Japanese fishing floats, pale green bubbles of glass, and some shells. The house had clearly been someone's old summer place, it had that kind of shabby grace as well as a slight smell of mildew. A rangy yellow dog with a pointed nose slept on a braided rug in front of the hearth.

Alex arranged them rather fussily on some rattan cushioned furniture and went over to a bar. "Let's have drinks," he said. "How was the trip? MacNab here take care of you?"

Sunny and Chandler turned to the Indian. Now that he had a name he seemed altogether a different person.

"Still drink Scotch, Sunny? With a little water?" Festive sounds of glass and ice filled the cavernous room. "How about you, Chandler? I suppose I should say 'son.' It'll take some getting used to for both of us, I imagine."

Sunny closed her eyes and pressed her lids over them with her fingertips. "Alex, Chandler Smith is not your son," she said firmly.

She looked back at him. He turned around quickly and faced them both. He was pointing a large black gun at them. "Well, then, who the hell is he?"

Billy St. Clair stood in front of the mirror while the tailor knelt before him, wielding chalk and tape measure. Things had been so depressing lately, and a new suit or two could always cheer Billy up. And, if you couldn't go to London and have an English tailor do it, why, you could always find an English tailor in Canada. He thought the herringbone and Glen plaid, though he hoped the latter in black and white wouldn't be too flashy. Maybe charcoal and white would be more appropriate.

So far, his trip had been rather a washout. He'd talked with his man here, the one who'd been following Sunny since Tucson. Of course, he'd lost her when she gave them the slip in London, but he was back on the track again. All he'd been able to tell Billy was that the Canadians didn't seem to know what was going on, but that Lewis Strickland, Tommy Gun's assistant, was in town. Good.

Billy wondered if he dared to make contact with the local Russians as well. They might know more. But they might also know he'd disobeyed Luke and left the Washington area. Unless, of course, Luke was too embarrassed to reveal it. It was all very distressing. Still, Billy felt basically cheerful. He thought he'd be able to find Sunny and Alex. He had to, he just had to.

The tailor asked Billy where the suits should be delivered. "I'll pick them up myself," said Billy smiling. "Not sure where I'll be."

When she saw the gun, Sunny pressed herself backward into the rattan cushions of the sofa. Above the black metal gun, Alex looked calm enough.

Alex nodded to MacNab, who came over to Chandler, motioned him to stand, and patted him down. When MacNab silently questioned Alex about frisking Sunny, Alex shook his head in the negative, then seemed to change his mind. She stood and felt MacNab's apparently professional touch as he skimmed along the outline of her body in an impersonal way. She tried not to eye the Burberry trenchcoat. It lay draped over the back of another chair.

"You still haven't answered my question," said Alex.

She sighed. "I don't know who he is exactly. I'm sorry, Alex, I had to reach you and I didn't know how else . . ."

"I'm a reporter for *Sunset Magazine*," said Chandler Smith, interrupting her.

"Is that so?" said Alex, smiling. "What the hell are you doing impersonating some strange man's son?"

"Alex, I had to bring someone, he's just someone I met on the train . . ." She realized she was protecting Smith. She hadn't mentioned his gun. That was foolish. "Your message said I had to have the son with me or I couldn't see you.''

"Why do you want to see me?" he said.

"Can I talk to you alone?" she said plaintively.

"You can speak freely in front of our son," said Alex bitterly.

"Alex, it's important. A lot of people want to know where you are."

"I'm well aware of that."

"Not from . . . whatever happened before. It's something else."

"Okay, we can talk alone. But first I want MacNab to take a look at your luggage. I trust you won't mind."

"Not when you're pointing a gun at us," said Smith.

Alex looked vaguely down at the gun in his hand, set it down for a moment, and handed everybody drinks. MacNab turned his attention to their bags.

"So Sunny here is in this to tell me something. Why are you here, Smith?"

Smith swallowed hard. Sunny imagined he expected MacNab would find his gun momentarily. "I'm here to ask you a question, sir. From the old man. Maybe you called him something else."

Alex lifted up his gun again and took a sip of Scotch.

"No, we called him that even when he was young, younger than you are now. Didn't we, Sunny?"

A vague memory of a rumpled, earnest, prematurely balding young man came back to her. "Of course, Harry . . ." She stopped herself.

"What's on his mind?"

"Can we talk alone?"

"That's what she said. I think we can all talk together. I get so little company I hate to have you wandering off when you just got here."

"Fine," said Sunny, suddenly exasperated. "Let's all talk. I don't care anymore. I'm tired and I've been traveling for two weeks, and I've lied and even stolen, and I've been abducted and slapped and I've hurt some people very badly. I'm not sure why, either.

"Except Billy came to me two weeks ago and said I should find you and tell you the CIA wanted to kill you."

"Who's Billy?" said Smith sharply.

"Let her finish," said Alex.

"I thought he was drunk or crazy, but then he disappeared, and a nice young man came and asked me if I'd find you for the CIA. I couldn't understand why they asked me. But later, in San Francisco, I learned you'd been spotted in Tucson. Alex, did you spend the night in my guesthouse?"

Alex looked startled. "What? Do you live in Tucson?"

"I guess so." She sighed. "I mean, of course. It seems like part of another life. Anyway, seeing as Billy had said they wanted to kill you, and then they appeared, well, I thought there might be something in it. But I didn't trust Billy. He was drinking. I didn't trust the CIA, either. So I looked for you on my own. At first it started out as kind of a lark, and then I realized that lots of people wanted to find you. I realized that something dangerous was going on. So I kept looking for you. To warn you. I thought if I gave you all the pieces you could figure them out yourself."

"I see. And where exactly does he fit into the picture?" Alex gestured at Smith with his Scotch.

"I think he was following me. I needed someone to play the son. So I recruited him."

"Convenient for you, Smith. Seeing as you had a message for me."

"She was the only one who was able to find you," said Smith. "I was lucky."

"And I was a failure," said Sunny, "unable to avoid surveillance. How did you find me?"

Alex waved his hand impatiently. "Never mind all that spy stuff. We can talk about that another time. What's your question, Smith?"

Smith took a deep breath and exhaled slowly. "In 1945 you were in Norway to pass a message to a man on skis. The rendezvous point was a mountain cabin somewhere in the Oslofjord area. You were with another man. A man whom you said hurt his ankle. The old man wants to know who was with you."

"Why?"

"That man, if he's still alive, is a long-term Soviet agent," said Smith. "And that's the absolute truth."

"The absolute truth, eh?" Alex startled Sunny by laughing. "Let's have dinner. You hungry?"

"Aren't you going to answer?"

"I'll think about it."

Chandler Smith looked angry. He said firmly, "I wish we could discuss this right away. It's important. To your country, to everything you ever worked for." Sitting next to him, Sunny observed a tightening of a muscle in his jaw.

"Relax," said Alex. "I got the message. I want some time to think. I want to sleep on it. Tomorrow morning we can talk business."

MacNab was certainly doing a thorough job. He was poking holes in a jar of Sunny's cold cream with a pencil.

"You know," said Alex, his dark serious face looking suddenly amused, "all of a sudden, this whole thing strikes me as so absurd. Comic. You know what I mean?"

Sunny took an icy sip of Scotch. "Alex, it isn't one damn bit funny. There was a man on the train from San Francisco. The CIA man who was trying to recruit me in Tucson. Alex, he was killed."

Alex leaned forward. "Killed? San Francisco? After you saw Marina?

"MacNab," he gestured with his Scotch. "Get on the radio, will you? Check on Marina. Thanks."

MacNab reluctantly left his excavations in the cold cream, screwing the lid back on the jar and leaving the room.

"There's a radio here?" Chandler looked excited.

"That's right. But I'd just as soon you don't use it until I say you can."

"Marina's a nice young woman, Alex," said Sunny. "She's got a nice baby, too. And she misses you."

"I had to leave. I had reason."

"Billy said you were afraid of getting killed."

"I was for a while. Now I wonder if anyone cares. And I didn't want to testify." He looked into his drink. "I hate lying. Sounds funny coming from an old spy. I guess, but goddammit, I hate to lie. I guess I got sick of it. And I didn't want my little girl to know what I'd done. And then I wanted to be alone, far from everything."

"Sounds lonely," said Sunny.

"You can come back, you know." Smith leaned forward eagerly.

Alex smiled at him. "I'll take your word for it." He stretched his arms out along the top of the sofa, an overstuffed relic from the forties covered with a faded tropical print of the era. "After I got away, and thought about it for a while, I think I also began to enjoy the idea that I'd managed to retire, really retire. You know, you can't ever really get out of this business. Have you thought about that, Smith?"

"That what Billy said," said Sunny. She looked at her empty glass. "You won't shoot me if I get up and get a refill, will you?"

Alex laughed, a nice warm laugh that Sunny recognized from the past. She'd always loved it when he laughed, because he always sounded so genuinely and absolutely delighted, and he never laughed enough. He got up and made her a drink. "I wouldn't shoot you." He stood in front of her, handing her the drink, looking down at her from beneath his dark lashes. "For old time's sake." He smiled. "Son or no son."

She looked back up at him. "It was a cheap trick," she said. "The son. I apologize."

He shrugged. "Nature of the business. Didn't Billy say you couldn't retire?"

"And I told him I had."

Alex took Smith's glass and went back to the bar. "You didn't," said Alex. "You were just on hold for a while. But at the first opportunity you were back in the thick of it. Weren't you?"

"Kind of ridiculous, at my age, and after such a respectable ordinary life," said Sunny.

"There are lots of reasons to get out of this business, I suppose, but that's not one of them," Chandler said to her. She imagined he was annoyed at all this philosophical chitchat from his elders about spying.

MacNab came back into the living room. She'd heard the front door slam, so she supposed the transmitter was somewhere else on the island, perhaps on higher ground. "Checks out okay," he said, settling down to searching their luggage.

"Does Marina know you can check up on her like that?" said Sunny.

"Marina knows very little. For her own protection."

"Alex, she's scared to death. She's worried about her own safety and the baby's. People watch her all the time, especially now that they want to find you again. And she's frightened. If you came back you could end that for her."

Alex looked startled. He stared at Sunny, wide-eyed.

Sunny even pushed further than she'd intended. "And she hates it that you left her. You're her only relative left. You should go see that baby." She'd said too much, perhaps, but it was clear Alex had no idea how unhappy he had made his daughter. Men, decided Sunny, were often cruel out of sheer stupidity.

MacNab gave a long low whistle. "Take a look at this, Alex." He handed something very small to Alex.

"Oh, great," said Alex. He held a small black disk in the palm of his hand. "This belong to you, Smith?"

"No. I wouldn't have risked it," said Chandler.

"What is it?" said Sunny.

"I've been out of the business a while. I don't know this model," said Alex. "But I'm pretty sure it's an electronic tracking device. What can you tell us about it, Smith, other than that you didn't pack it in your luggage?" Alex looked dubiously at Smith.

"It was in her bag," said MacNab. "Slipped into the strap."

Alex turned to Sunny and raised his eyebrows.

"You mean someone can hear what we're saying?" said Sunny incredulously, staring at the tiny plastic disk.

"No," said Chandler. "But they can tell where we are. It's a transmitter. Gives out a steady signal. It's American made, but that doesn't mean anything. You can practically buy this equipment in department stores. The Russians prefer our stuff, and so does everyone else."

"The Russians? A damn sight more likely the CIA wants to find out where I am. So they send a nice kid like you, and this, too, just in case."

"At the hotel," said Chandler, turning to Sunny. "Remember? Did you notice how surprised the woman at the desk was when the bellman came to collect our luggage? I thought there was something odd about that. I thought she was surprised at MacNab here taking all our stuff back. But maybe she was surprised because she'd never seen the guy before."

Alex dropped the device to the ground and crushed it beneath his heel. He turned to Sunny. "I've always been a sentimental jerk, I guess. I'm going for a walk. MacNab will stay here with you. I want to batten down the hatches in case we have any more visitors."

Aboard a Russian trawler, just outside the two-hundred-mile limit, off the coast of British Columbia, Yevgeny Denisov stood, scanning the horizon. He heard the helicopter before he saw it. Although it was still evening, and fairly light, it was misty over the ocean. For the year he'd been assigned to the trawler, he had been prepared for this day. He had never believed it would really come. Inside the helicopter, he knew, were six other men, men with whom he had trained, men assigned to other trawlers plying these waters. He'd been disappointed when he'd pulled this duty, although it was better than the Chinese border. He'd thought it was safer. Now he wasn't so sure.

When the helicopter had landed on its pontoons and sat bobbing crazily in the choppy waves, and as Yevgeny was being rowed toward it, he said, very quickly, a little prayer his grandmother had taught him. He didn't really believe it would make any difference, but then, neither would it do any harm. Unless, of course, it became known that he said one of the childish little prayers from time to time.

After Alex left, MacNab produced a tray of sandwiches, thickly cut slices of dark rye bread with ham and roast beef and cheddar cheese. Sunny ate four. She and Chandler didn't talk much, because of the Indian's presence. She was relieved at that. She felt if she talked to Chandler about Alex, she'd be disloyal. And vice versa. Besides, she was tired and sleepy. She felt a strange peacefulness, an anticlimax that wasn't really unpleasant. She had found Alex, she had told him what she had to tell him, and her job was done.

"Where do I sleep?" she said to Alex after he'd returned. She looked from Alex to Chandler and back again, and realized for the first time that she was in the somehow slightly embarrassing position of being under the same roof with two men with whom she'd slept. At least, she thought she should be embarrassed. But it was all so silly, really, and she was so tired.

"There are three bedrooms upstairs," he said. "You can take your pick."

She looked at the dark stairs that curved into darkness. It

looked cold up there. Besides, she didn't want to hear either of them breathing through the walls. "You take those rooms. How about if I take one of those sofas here?" she said. "Then I can be by the fire. It's cold."

"That's right. You live in Arizona. I'll get you some blankets." He left, and MacNab left for some more firewood. She was alone with Chandler for the first time.

"Where the hell's my gun?" he hissed. "The Indian never found it."

Billy had said the CIA wanted Alex dead. Chandler was CIA. "I took it and I threw it overboard," she said. "It scared me."

"Well, its absence scares me. And so does Markoff. Don't you think he's a little paranoid?"

She sighed. "I don't know what to think. I just want to sleep. I did what I set out to do. I found Alex and I told him everything I know."

When she did sleep, after staring into the dying fire after the others had gone upstairs, it was heavy and dreamless.

14

THE WIND MOVED through the boughs of the firs and cedars, the water lapped into the cracks between the rocks along the shore. Far enough outside the rocky cove that served as the tiny island's natural harbor to be unheard, the helicopter on its huge pontoons settled into the water. Its engine was cut suddenly, and the smoothness of flight changed to the rolling and pitching of a boat.

In response to a quiet command, the men inside the helicopter launched two inflatable rubber craft. While specially muffled outboard engines were started, equipment, weapons, and radio gear were passed into the boats by men dressed in black, with black paint on their faces. While the head of the mission repeated the rendezvous time to the helicopter pilot, Yevgeny Denisov looked at his fellow commandos. With the black paint, and the black clothing, they looked like some kind of creatures from an old fairy tale, not like human beings. When the helicopter ascended, leaving the two boats bobbing in the water, he felt very, very alone. The boats headed toward the mouth of the cove.

About one hundred fifty yards from shore, after the two vessels had entered the cove, the engines were cut, and the men began to row ashore with silent, practiced strokes, the blades of the aluminum oars entering the inky black water at precisely the right angle.

It had been a very long time since Yevgeny Denisov had been on land, but the large, seaweed-slimy green rocks encrusted with barnacles weren't a welcoming sight. The men clambered out of their boats and over the rocks, hauling the inflatable craft after them. Their leader whispered a last message: "We'll spend twenty minutes on a survey of the island. We believe there are at least four on the island. Who knows how many there are really? Find out who's here and where they are. And I'll shoot the first man who so much as coughs. Remember, if we succeed here, it will reflect well on you and perhaps result in a better assignment next time. We meet back here twenty minutes from"—he glanced at his watch—"now."

The men headed off down the beach in different directions. Yevgeny seriously considered holing up somewhere for twenty minutes and lying low, but he decided he dare not risk it. Instead, he pulled out his Makarov pistol, screwed on the silencer, and set off.

He really had no idea what to expect. He'd rather imagined a tent with a few men sitting around it. Instead that huge *dacha* had loomed up in front of him in the dark. Surely there were more than four people in such a building. He didn't like anything about this. There was nothing military about this place, except that the windows were shuttered tightly. He hadn't seen so much as a chink of light coming from behind them, or any noise. Perhaps they were all asleep. It would be easier if they were. A simple bullet behind the ear and then back to the boats.

A dog with a pointed face came bouncing across the grass toward him. He heard a low growl in its throat. Before the growl could explode into a volley of barking, Yevgeny squinted, took aim, and with arm extended straight down, sent a bullet into the dog's head. Despite the silencer the sound of the shot seemed loud in this absolutely still clearing. The dog flew backward, a tangle of legs and soft, floppy ears, yellow fur, and dark patches of blood. When the animal landed, Yevgeny crept over to the carcass, picked it up by a hind leg, and flung it into some low bushes. He glanced at his watch and headed back toward the beach.

Back in Washington, Luke checked his watch. By now Moscow should have put its plan into effect. It was out of his hands.

Inside the house, in an upstairs bedroom, MacNab's eyes opened. He put on the black plastic glasses that sat on the nightstand. Underneath the light blanket he was fully dressed. He slipped out of bed, put on a pair of boots, and went downstairs and outside, through a rear door. Some distance from the house, he came upon a patch of blood in the grass. He investigated the low bushes at the end of the clearing. The yellow, pointy-nosed dog was still warm, but from the bared teeth and the still, open eyes it was clear he was dead.

Yevgeny Denisov didn't like his orders at all.

"No use a bunch of men clumping around the house," the chief had said. "We'll all be in position around the clearing and one of us, you Denisov, will enter the house and carry out the mission." A commando raid was one thing. Sending him in to kill someone as he slept was different.

As the party of men made their way back to the clearing and to the house, Denisov checked his pistol, replacing the bullet he'd used on the dog.

MacNab crouched in the low bushes near the mouth of the creek and watched the men in black on the beach.

The house was well secured. Denisov revised his opinion. This could well be a military operation, despite the garden furniture on the porch and the rustic look of the place. All the windows were shuttered tight. The front door was fastened with what appeared to be a sophisticated lock. He worked his way around the building, slowly. Let those other bastards wait. There was no need to hurry on their account. He strained against the logs, trying to hear any movement from within. It was all eerily silent. Finally, at the back of the building, he reached a dilapidated old porch. The railing looked rotten, and he didn't trust it. Instead, he walked carefully in the middle of the broad, sagging steps. The whole structure squeaked. He winced and proceeded slowly.

This door was unlocked. He tried the knob. He didn't like that, especially as everything else was firmly locked up. It meant either a trap, or that someone had just left the building. Maybe he and the others had been spotted on the beach. Maybe the people in the house had fled. He hoped so.

He nudged the door with his foot. It swung inward. Inside was a cavernous kitchen. Saying a little prayer once again, he went inside. On the floor was a black and white pattern, like a chess board. The white squares showed up bluish in the dark. Large white shapes around the edge of the room looked bluish and glowing too. His eyes, as they adjusted, told him they were big American appliances.

The kitchen gave onto a narrow dark hall. His face brushed against hanging coats and jackets. They hung on a rack of antlers, the whole thing forming an ominous shape in the dark.

The hall led to a huge room, full of sofas and chairs. At least in this room he could see more than shapes, for there was a pinkish light from the huge fireplace as the last of a fire glowed, small logs trembling with light, covered with a thin covering of powdery white ash.

On one of the sofas a woman was sleeping. She lay on her back and looked very peaceful. She was a good-looking woman, older, with short silvery hair. Denisov stood over her, looking very carefully at the spot behind her ear where he knew the pistol should be placed. He knew he must do it quickly, before she woke, but he stood instead looking at her face.

MacNab had been able to work his way silently through the bushes to the back of the house. He imagined that there were men in back, too, perhaps there was even someone in the house by now, but he sprinted the short distance from the bushes to the rear door that led into the kitchen without any interference.

Actually, the men were stationing themselves at regular distances from each other in a circle, and only one man saw MacNab sprint the short distance from shrubbery to kitchen door. He didn't have time to fire.

MacNab landed on the porch in one bound, burst through the kitchen door, fastened it after him, and dashed into the living room, intent on raising the house. By the light of the dying fire he saw the silhouette of a man with a gun, standing over Sunny. As MacNab burst into the room, the figure turned and raised his gun toward the Indian.

MacNab flattened himself on the ground, the gun discharged.

Sunny's eyes flew open. She saw MacNab splayed out on the ground, and the tall figure in black in front of her. Tangled in a Hudson's Bay blanket, she rolled off the sofa, partly in an offensive move, partly in confusion and fear. She rolled into the stranger's legs, knocking him down. His gun clattered to the ground and went off again, making not a loud, horrible bang, but a small, muffled sound, like a champagne cork. The recoil and the position of Denisov's hand on the floor caused him to let go of the gun. In a second MacNab was at Sunny's side, and the gun was in his hand. She untangled herself from the intruder and stared incredulously at his face. MacNab had him in some kind of grip. The man had a perfectly ordinary face—blond, boyish, a frank, open kind of face. He blinked.

MacNab handed her the gun. "Take that silencer off," he

whispered. She looked at the thing in her hand, swallowed hard, made sure it was pointed away from MacNab and the stranger, and twisted the long metal tube on the barrel. It came off, rather like part of a kitchen faucet. She handed it back to MacNab. He held the gun toward the ceiling and away from them and fired. Now the sound was deafening, making an angry explosion that rang in her ears.

A few seconds later Alex and Smith, both still dressed, came into the room. Alex carried a gun, too.

MacNab said to Alex, "There are more of them out there."

"I need a gun," said Smith.

"How the hell do I know those guys out there aren't your guys?" said Alex.

Smith turned to Sunny. "Did you really throw away my gun?" he demanded.

She went to the Burberry and took it from the pocket.

He held out his hand. Alex watched them both. She shook her head slowly. "I'll keep it," she said. "I know a little bit about these things. From the war."

"Let's all keep down," said Alex. "These shutters and the walls should stop a bullet, but I've never tried them." He worked his way over to MacNab's side and placed his own weapon at the temple of the intruder. "Who the hell are you?" he whispered.

Yevgeny Denisov's eyes closed. Tears sprang from under the lids and coursed down his face. His face was red, almost purple, from the way MacNab had his neck circled with a thick arm. Awkwardly, very slowly, as the four of them hovered over him, waiting for an answer, Alex's gun still held steadily against his temple, Denisov made the sign of the cross. Something about the gesture looked strange. Sunny wondered if he were left-handed.

"My God," said Alex, lowering his gun, "he crosses himself like a Russian." He began shooting questions in Russian.

Denisov opened his eyes and answered in a labored fashion, still purple from MacNab's powerful grip on his throat.

Alex rocked back on his heels. "This man says he's an active member of the Red Army."

"Jesus Christ," said Chandler Smith. "How many guys are out there?"

"I saw six," said MacNab. "Counting this one."

Alex came out with more Russian. Denisov replied. "I don't know if he's lying or not," said Alex, "but he looks pretty scared. He says there are six of them, in two small inflatable boats. And they were sent here to kill everyone."

"Pretty nervy," said Smith. "We're in Canada."

"If they're who they say they are," said Alex.

"The man is a Russian," said Smith. "There's no reason for assassins to pretend they're anyone else. Not when we're isolated like this. For Christ's sake, give me a gun. And let's figure out how to get the hell out of here."

"I wish we knew if we could believe this guy," said Alex. "I want to know how many of them there are and where they are."

MacNab looked down at the Russian in his arms. "I'm tired of holding him," he said. "Let me put him out of commission."

"Okay," said Alex.

Sunny looked away. MacNab twisted the man out of his grip and gave him a resounding blow on the head. Whatever he'd done seemed to work. The Russian went limp. MacNab took a knife from his belt, went to the curtains and cut off a length of cord, and wrapped the man's limp limbs around expertly. Folded into the fetal position, he ran the cord from the bound up ankles and knees to the wrist, and rolled the doll-like form a few feet away like a piece of baggage.

"Is there a way out of here?" said Smith.

"There's a tunnel that takes us into the woods. But we need a boat."

"Haven't you got a boat? We're on a goddamn island," said Smith.

"There's a boat. But they've got boats, too; we could be followed. And the boat's some distance from the tunnel exit."

"It would have been handy," said Smith, "if the boat had been closer."

"I never planned on taking four people out of here," said Alex.

MacNab sighed. "I'll go out and get the boat in position. If it's still there. Those guys might have found it. And I'll sink theirs if I can."

"I'll go," said Alex.

"No," said the Indian. "You're a better shot. And I'm quieter."

Alex looked at him for a second. "Okay. Here, wait a minute, you'll need some help. Just in case." He went to a long, low bench that ran around the room. He opened the lid. By rights it should have contained mildewy swimsuits and croquet paraphernalia. Instead he came up with two light machine guns. He handed one to Smith and kept one himself.

"Thanks," said Smith, examining the weapon. "M-sixteens. Sonsofbitches always jammed."

Alex handed MacNab a grenade. "You know how these things work, don't you?"

"I was in Korea, remember?"

"And here, take my pistol."

The Indian put the pistol in his belt, resheathed the knife, and put the grenade in his shirt. He crawled into the hall.

"Okay," said Alex. "Let's keep these guys busy."

He worked his way to one of the shutters, opened it a crack, and fired. Smith did the same at another window.

Sunny flattened herself against the floor. A second later the shutters broke out in splintery patterns, as fire was returned. The noise was excruciating. "Kalishnakovs!" screamed Smith. "Christ."

In a grove of trees twenty-five feet or so from the house, a door of planks was lifted from the forest floor. MacNab came slowly out, unobserved. Fingering his knife, he crept along a narrow path between the trees, pausing every few feet to look around him.

He took a circuitous path to the shore and emerged from some huckleberry bushes onto a pebbly stretch of beach. Good. The boat was where it should be, wedged between two huge logs above the high-tide line. They could do it, if they weren't pursued.

He dragged himself along the beach toward the cove, keeping close to the ground, using the huge, weathered logs and large smooth rocks as cover whenever he could. From what he could tell, the invaders' boats were unguarded.

He waded into the water of the cove, knife in hand. It was icy and dark, and he scraped his knees on barnacles. His clothes tore. His knee was bleeding and the salt water bit into the opened skin. When he reached his goal, he raised his arm and plunged the knife into the canvas, making long, neat strokes, disabling both vessels.

At the house, Sunny was now firing Chandler's pistol from another window. She'd worn a sidearm as part of her uniform during the demobilization of Norway. She'd never drawn it, except to threaten an amorous British officer early one morning who tried to get into her room in the house where they were both billeted. But she remembered her training.

"Don't expect to hit anything," Alex had said. "We're just trying to buy time and create the impression that we can hold out for longer than we can."

The sound of all the fire was painful. Even more painful were the occasional lulls. The quiet seconds seemed to last minutes.

During one pause Smith said, "Why the hell didn't we get out of here last night, right after we spotted that tracking device?"

"All we've got is a small boat, not really designed for four people. And these coastal waters are treacherous. I thought dawn would be soon enough. And frankly, I didn't expect the Red Army. I thought your guys were just keeping track of you."

"I wish they did know where I was," said Smith. "Where's that transmitter of yours?"

"Forget it," said Alex. "Let's get off the island first."

"What if you don't make it?" said Chandler.

"What do you mean, 'you'?" interrupted Sunny. "You're coming with us, aren't you?"

"I'd rather transmit the answer to my question first," he said. "The question you've never answered. About the man with you in Norway in 1945."

"They're being too quiet out there," said Alex. He turned to Smith. "The answer's easy. It's the same guy that tipped me off before I disappeared and came up here. I thought he was doing me a favor at the time. Billy St. Clair."

"God, St. Clair. That old rummy. Interesting. And where's the transmitter?"

"Highest point on the island. A little rise, right in the center. And then you climb up into an arbutus tree. But you'll never make it."

"I figured I'd wait in your tunnel," said Smith. "Will that work?"

"I suppose." Alex looked dubious. "How long are you prepared to wait?"

From outside, on Sunny's side of the building, they heard a tremendous explosion.

"Sounds like an incendiary grenade," said Alex.

The wall where Sunny was leaning suddenly became hot. "They're burning the place down," she said.

Alex scooped up a handful of grenades. "Time to leave,"

he said, taking a second to look around him. "Come on, hall closet. Smith, you'd better come with us. You haven't a chance on this island."

Automatically, Sunny scooped up her flight bag. She put her Burberry on over her nightgown and quickly pulled on her shoes. Alex put an arm around her shoulder and led her into the hall. "If you're going to stick around, Chandler, help yourself to a few clips from the bench there. The rest of it will make a spectacular blaze."

In the hall he opened a closet, lifted up a floor of wooden planks. He turned toward the fireplace and heaved a couple of grenades into it. Then he pushed Sunny down through the opening in the closet floor. She fell down several steps into darkness. From above there was some light, but ahead there was a complete void. There was a clammy feel to the air here, and a musty, earthy smell.

Behind her she felt Alex, pushing her down the narrow passageway, and then she heard Chandler following Alex. She touched the sides of the tunnel as she felt her way along. The cool dirt walls were braced every few feet with rough timber. After a few seconds he pushed her to the muddy ground and threw himself on top of her. A violent explosion had sent a shudder through the tunnel and she heard the soft sound of dirt falling in little streams around her.

Alex pulled her back up. "You okay?" he whispered. "I didn't want one of these timbers to knock you down."

"I'm okay." She put her hand on his chest to steady herself.

"How about you, Smith?"

"I'm okay. I think we lost some of the tunnel in back of me. I hope everything's clear in front."

Sunny plunged forward now, almost recklessly. She was now more frightened of the tunnel collapsing than she was of walking into darkness, which had seemed unnatural just seconds ago.

Once, when the tunnel seemed to curve, Sunny almost

burst into tears. She had a horrible image of never emerging from the tunnel at all, spending her whole life plunging ahead into the dark, surrounded by clammy air.

Finally they reached a blank wall. Alex pushed her aside and reached up. She heard the sound of wood against wood, and saw a crack of night sky as he moved a square of boards slightly to one side. The sky above her, even a simple crack, looked absolutely lovely. He pushed it the rest of the way open, and starlight shone in on them. Alex pulled himself up and disappeared through the hole.

She could see now, inside the tunnel. She turned to Chandler Smith. "Are you coming with us?"

He shook his head. "Can't."

"You're being a fool," she said sharply.

"I guess you're right," he said. He took her around the waist, kissed her hard on the mouth, and passed her up above his head to the opening. Alex reached down and pulled her to the surface. She lay face down in wet, sweet-smelling grass for a second as Alex replaced the lid and pushed loose dirt and branches over it.

MacNab was waiting some yards away, crouched on the beach with the boat. Sunny was shocked to see what a simple little boat it was, nothing more than the kind of rowboat a life guard might sit in at a child's bathing beach.

Alex gave MacNab a bearlike hug, and the three of them carried the boat to the water's edge. Sunny was relieved to see a small outboard motor, but they began their journey with oars, to maintain silence. MacNab pulled at them in a regular rhythm, and while at first the boat seemed to be practically scraping bottom, they made steady progress out from the island into the rolling misty sea.

Alex's house made a huge blaze, and the night sky glowed a smoky gray-rose. When they'd pulled far enough away from the island to see the blaze itself above the silhouettes of the tall firs, they heard a series of explosions within the fire. Alex's arsenal, she imagined.

It was only then that she remembered the young Russian who lay unconscious and bound with cord inside the flames.

The *Sandy Lou* was a very large cabin cruiser. She was anchored quietly off a small island on the British Columbia coast. Her skipper, Leonard Lundquist of Eureka, California, stood at the rail with his wife Sandy and his children, Tammy and Craig. They were wrapped in down jackets over their pajamas, and they watched in awe as a column of smoke moved up into the sky, backlit by an eerie glow across the sky.

"Probably just a forest fire," said Leonard, but Sandy said, "Still, we should tell someone. There might be someone on that island. Besides, how could a fire start by itself? There hasn't been any lightning."

Leonard wasn't sure how to raise a local fire department. As far as he could tell there wasn't any civilization around for miles and miles. So he decided to radio the Coast Guard, and they could tell anyone else they wanted to.

Some time later, after the children had gone back to bed, a red and white Canadian Coast Guard cutter came and circled the island. It was clear there was a fire on the island, and they alerted their station, who notified the local volunteer fire department. While the cutter was circling back, they picked up three people in a small boat without lights. The captain of the cutter didn't ask them many questions; they were an odd trio, a white man and woman, all streaked with dirt, and an Indian. Their small boat was taken aboard, too, and contained an automatic weapon. The captain arranged for the boat to be met at the dock by the Royal Canadian Mounted Police.

Glenn Larchmont was excited and pleased. It was just what he'd been waiting for: a really big drug landing off the British Columbia coast, in his territory. Of course, there were lots of gaps to fill in. There wasn't any actual contraband. But there was the next best thing. The woman had been carrying a flight bag with a lot of cash in it. In American funds. And there was the M-16.

The four of them sat around a battered old oak table. Glenn smiled at them. "Perhaps we could begin very simply. Tell us about the fire."

The white man held up a hand. "I'm sorry, I won't make any statements at all. Until I talk to one man."

Larchmont's eyebrows rose. He had a pink and white, rather childish face, and the arched eyebrows gave him a little more character. "Who?"

"Sir Raymond Phillips. He's one of you."

Larchmont smiled. "I'm sorry, that's impossible. Sir Raymond Phillips is . . ."

"I know," said Alex. "He's also an old friend of mine. From the war. You want your little mystery cleared up, don't you? I won't help until you call Ray. Tell him it's about Alexander Markoff. Of the Office of Strategic Services. He'll remember."

Larchmont thought the man was crazy, but he supposed it wouldn't hurt. Sir Raymond's office would simply refuse to accept the call.

Larchmont shrugged. "Fine. We'll see what his office says. Meanwhile, I'll send a couple of men to that island and find out what you've left behind. I can't imagine you destroyed every shred of evidence, you know."

"You'd better take more than a few men," said the woman sweetly. "There are half a dozen men on that island with machine guns."

Larchmont looked at her. Now that she was cleaned up, she looked quite nice. He couldn't imagine what a nice gray-haired lady like this was doing mixed up with drug smugglers. "What else can you tell me?" he said.

Sunny sighed. "Nothing. I just wanted to warn you about the men. But I'd rather not say anything, either. Until I can talk to the American consulate. Isn't that what you're supposed to do when you're in trouble in a foreign country?''

"That's right, madam. If you're an American. But you're carrying a Norwegian passport.''

"Nevertheless,'' she said, "I'm an American citizen, and I'd like to call the consul in Vancouver. That's the nearest one, I suppose.''

Larchmont turned to MacNab. "And whom do you want to call?'' he said.

"No one in particular,'' said MacNab.

Larchmont decided this Indian would be most helpful. After all, he was probably just the local guide, in way over his head. The Indian, however, was as silent as the other two.

Well, he'd know more when they'd been to the island. Meanwhile, he felt he had enough to hold them. As they were led off to separate cells he asked the woman, "Those guys on the island, with automatic weapons. Are they your friends? Or did you have a falling out with them?''

"They're Russians,'' she said.

Larchmont's eyes grew larger, and the expressive brows shot up again. It occurred to him he was dealing with a group of crazies.

"How about those phone calls?'' said the white man.

"Sure, sure,'' said Glenn. "I'll arrange it right away. And you can call the Prime Minister and the President, too.'' He shrugged. He'd let them call anyone they wanted. He was still going to take his time and find out what these people were up to. The Indian had a pistol and a grenade on him. These drug smugglers were getting rougher.

Billy was whistling as he got out of the elevator on the fifth floor. He wasn't sure quite what he was going to do, but that was fine. Some of his best work had been completely off the top of his head. Just some vague talk about having to find an old friend, a government employee. With some vital information. He hoped he'd somehow manage to make contact with whoever was in charge of the local station. Enough suitable noises about helping to troubleshoot the little problem that might just erupt here any day now.

He stood at the counter in the consulate, amazed as he was so often these days, at the number of young people who seemed to be running things. These people all looked so young, he doubted whether they knew enough to put him in touch with the right people. All Billy knew was that he had to find out, somehow, where Alex Markoff was. And if the CIA knew, Billy intended to find out from them.

A bored-looking brunette acknowledged his presence at the counter, but went on with other tasks for a moment. Doors opened and closed, and a man in his shirtsleeves trailed out of one room into another, carrying a glass coffeepot. From within another office raucous laughter could be heard. Really, the atmosphere here was rather un-businesslike. Billy frowned.

A blond girl rushed past the brunette, who now sauntered over to the counter toward Billy. The brunette turned to her and said, "Did you tell him about line three, still holding? It's long distance, from Port Elizabeth. A Mrs. Sinclair." The brunette lowered her voice. "She sounded really too old and respectable to be in a jam. I think he better talk to her."

The young woman now turned back to Billy. "Can I help you?" she said.

"I don't think so," said Billy. "I'm afraid I've made a mistake. Um, that is, I had an appointment, but now it occurs to me it wasn't really for today. But thank you so much, my dear."

The girl shrugged as Billy walked away from the counter, and went back to her filing.

Sir Raymond Phillips laughed into the phone. "Sounds like you got yourself in quite a mess, Markoff. By the way, I'm amazed to discover you're among the living. Well, maybe not *too* amazed."

"They've charged me with arson," exclaimed Alex. "It's ridiculous. A flimsy charge."

"Fortunately," observed Sir Raymond dryly, "our police have a little more leeway than yours do. It's much easier to hold people."

"Well, can't you do something about it? There's more than I've told you. It's a national security issue."

"Whose? The U.S.? Canada?"

"Ray, I wish you'd send someone out here. Or come yourself. Your man doesn't know it, but you've just been invaded by the Russians."

A flicker of doubt passed over Sir Raymond's genial face with its rigid silver mustache. Was Markoff crazy? He tried to remember the old CIA gossip about him now. What had it been? Was he mad before he vanished?

"Well, hang on, Markoff. I'll check this out and get back to you."

Sir Raymond took a Players out of the ebony box on his desk and lit it thoughtfully. This was more than just an old friend in a jam, asking for help.

An intercom on his desk buzzed. A disembodied female voice said, "A call from Mr. Thomas Gunderson." Sir Raymond looked startled and brushed back his silver hair. He'd just been thinking of calling old Tommy Gun and asking him about Markoff.

"Ray? Tommy here. I understand you just heard from Alex Markoff."

"How the hell do you know that?" said Sir Raymond.

"Oh, come on, Ray. Cut it out. Listen, we've got to know where he is. This is awfully important to both of us."

"I'm sure he'll call you," said Sir Raymond soothingly. "That is, if he wants to. What's the story on Markoff anyway? Why are you so anxious to find him?"

"You mean you won't help us?" said Tommy Gun, exasperated.

"I didn't say that." Sir Raymond blew a perfect blue smoke ring toward the ceiling and admired its symmetry.

"I'm checking out the situation personally, and I'll brief you as soon as I know what's going on. This is a Canadian matter, unless, of course, Mr. Markoff, whom I presume is still a U.S. citizen, cares to call you or the nearest consul. Can't talk anymore, Tommy. Got to dash."

He hung up before Tommy could get in another word, and ground out his cigarette in a large glass ashtray. He flicked the intercom button. "Alison, dearest, I want to go out to B.C. Right away. Arrange it, will you? I don't think I want to fly commercial. Oh, and tell our chap at Port Elizabeth, B.C., that I'm coming. I think Markoff said his name was Larchmuir. My destination's absolutely classified."

He frowned at the thought of the leak that had tipped Tommy about Markoff's call. Of course, the whole switchboard had been alerted and apparently Markoff's call had been routed all over the building before it actually got to his office. And of course, if he plugged up Tommy's leak, Tommy would plug up his own and they'd both have to start all over again. Damned nuisance, all of it.

Sunny stretched out on the old-fashioned blue and white striped mattress. It was actually rather comfortable, firm and not lumpy. She couldn't imagine it had been used much. From what she could see, Port Elizabeth consisted of the RCMP station, a concrete block building with a small office bearing a picture of the Queen, and two file cabinets, another room with an oak table, and three cells; an Anglican church; a general store; and the Canadian Legion post.

She actually welcomed the solitude and quiet of the cell. True, there were some dead spiders in the corner, but they simply gave the impression of a seldom-used room. The area had a nice, neutral feeling. And ever since Alex had called his old friend in Ottawa, Sergeant Larchmont couldn't have been nicer, bringing cups of coffee and an uninspired but satisfactory lunch of melted cheddar cheese sandwiches and canned tomato soup.

She was sure they'd all be sent home soon, and she was eager to get home. All of a sudden her adventure seemed oppressive, depressing, draining. She had barely the energy to worry about Chandler Smith. She assumed he could stay hidden. After all, the Russians would assume everyone died in the fire. Still, the idea of remaining underneath the ground, in the dark and the damp, sent such fear and almost disgust through her that she suppressed the thought.

Sergeant Larchmont had been enthusiastic about going to the unnamed island and finding out what had happened and who was left. He'd discarded the woman's remarks about Russians as some sort of lunacy, but the idea couldn't help but be intriguing. Since the man had made the call to Sir Ray, though, he'd changed his plans. And the call about ten minutes later, advising him to prepare for a secret visit from Sir Raymond, well, that clinched it. He'd arrange to keep the island under surveillance from the water, but he wouldn't land. It wouldn't do to act rashly. He was able to recruit a few civilians for this duty. They assured him no one could leave the island and escape their notice. It was a wise precaution, in case the woman's story about the men on the island being without boats was a lie. The civilians deployed, Larchmont began to make more important preparations for Sir Raymond. Always reasonably fastidious about his small station, Larchmont viewed his surroundings with a new critical eye and set to work with a mop and a bucket of soapy water.

Billy had originally thought the pilot might be the way out, but after the ride up, he decided he'd have to think of something else. When the pontoons of the little seaplane landed at the dock of Port Elizabeth, Billy stuffed a few bills into the man's hand and frowned. All his hints about making a good deal extra for the return trip if the man was willing to be discreet had been fended off curtly by the raw-boned, red-haired man. Billy stopped trying and ignored the man's withering looks as he pulled occasionally at his whiskey flask. Who cares what this hick thought anyway? After all, Billy had a very unpleasant job ahead, he hadn't slept properly for quite a while and he was generally depressed. Besides, back home, a few time zones away, the sun was nearly over the yard-arm.

He clambered from the plane and onto the wet dock. Everything in this part of the world was wet and gleaming and shining with moss. Billy hated it. Oh, to be in Palm Springs. Well, if all went well, he might still manage it. One thing was the same, though, all over the world. A knot of little brown children, Indians, stood on the dock and stared at him as he emerged from the seaplane. All his life, it seemed, Billy had been surrounded by curious groups of little brown children. At least, these kids didn't have their hands out. He pushed them aside and strolled down the dock.

Billy had been surprised when he'd learned the little settlement was accessible only by water. Walking along the dock he could see that the town was built that way. All the buildings faced the small bay, and they were lined not with streets, but with wooden sidewalks that gave the small cluster of buildings a vaguely resortlike appearance.

Along the dock Billy noticed a collection of craft. One of them, a powerful but small inboard, looked suitable. He only hoped that there were charts aboard. He assumed there were. In any case, the tiny size of the town made it all possible. The people here wouldn't expect a thing, and he'd have some kind of lead time.

He frowned. It was true, he hadn't much of a plan, but dammit, there wasn't time for any. Besides, hadn't some of his best work been done off the top of his head?

It wasn't hard to find the RCMP station. There wasn't much else around. He eyed the Canadian Legion hall. He knew that in rural Canada this was often the only place to get a drink. It would be lovely to have a nice drink there, a Scotch on the rocks, in a real glass. But there was no time, and, besides, the place was probably closed at this hour. It looked less than clean anyway.

He took the flask from his inside pocket, a very attractive silver flask that had been his older brother Edgar's, and drank. God knows, what he was about to do was going to be rough. He looked down at the flask, thought of dear innocent Edgar at a Harvard-Yale game with this flask in the pocket of a raccoon coat, treating himself to a few nips.

If only Edgar knew what things had come to. And really, it was Edgar's fault, wasn't it? Edgar had started it all, back at Cambridge. Billy had been so excited when Edgar let Billy meet his new friends. They'd been full of exciting, fresh ideas. Billy had wished he were old enough to go to Spain and fight fascism. He could have, he supposed. No one kept track of anybody's age. But Mother would have fallen apart without him. She was ready enough to let Edgar go, but not her baby Billy.

Billy had never cried when his brother died. He'd waited over thirty-five years for the tears, but they had never come. Now, unaccountably, Billy felt the warmth of tears in his eyes. He repocketed the flask. Was he crying for Edgar? He wasn't sure. He chided himself for being a sentimental fool and pushed open the door of the RCMP station.

The place was apparently empty, except for a baby-faced young sergeant attacking a nest of cobwebs in a corner of the ceiling with a broom. He turned to face Billy.

"Hello," said Billy cheerfully. "Charles Crawford. From the American consulate. We've had a call from Mrs. Sinclair. I'd like to see her. And the other prisoner, too, of course. He's an American as well, you know." Billy waved a hand airily, as if the matter were a minor annoyance and all in a day's work.

"I suppose so," said Sergeant Larchmont, looking slightly confused. "We've arrested the odd American," he said, banishing the uncertainty from his voice, "but no one from the consulate has ever showed up before."

"Rather important business," said Billy. "I wonder if I might have a word with the prisoners alone. Do you have a private room somewhere?"

"Yes, of course," said Sergeant Larchmont. "Wait here, please." He fetched Sunny and Alex, who both seemed curious and pleased to see the man from Vancouver.

In the short corridor, leading to a small room with the oak table and chairs, Sunny asked Alex, "Do you think we're getting out of here?"

"Beats me. I was kind of counting on Ray. He isn't due for hours."

"Maybe this American will bail us out."

"We haven't been before a magistrate yet. There isn't an amount of bail set. Besides, they don't really have us on any charge, they're just curious."

Larchmont remained silent and led them into the little room, locking them in. A minute later he returned with Mr. Crawford, who, in the hallway outside the door, admonished him that the following interview was to be confidential.

"If you wish," said Larchmont, obviously irritated. Billy could see he resented this high-handed approach. He wondered why he was cooperating. Perhaps he suspected the prisoners might be someone important.

The door closed behind Billy and Larchmont turned the key. He stood for a moment near the door as if planning to eavesdrop, then frowned and left the hall.

Inside the little room Billy stared at Alex and Sunny. They stared back.

"My God," said Alex softly. "Billy."

Sunny seemed to be scrutinizing him with curiosity. Something about her look told Billy that she knew. And Alex's face had whitened. They knew. Damn.

"I'm sorry," Billy began, fighting a tremor in his hand.

He reached into his inside pocket and came up with his Browning. He pointed it at Alex, then at Sunny. A horrible wobble had come over his hand. The gun seemed to be waving back and forth. He felt the beginning of a sob in his throat and watched their faces—frozen, startled, rather pleasant middle-aged faces.

"You can't," breathed Sunny.

"But I must," he said. "You know I must. It has to be done."

Sunny closed her eyes. The horrible finality of the gesture frightened him. He'd done this sort of thing before, but never directly. He was sure he'd have had the stomach. Slowly the wobbling gun turned in his hand. He placed the cold tip of the barrel on his own temple. She opened her eyes, and both their faces relaxed. Billy thought to himself: Why? Why not them? Instead of me.

He turned the gun back at them. This time it was easier. The damn gun didn't weave back and forth by itself like it had before. He took careful aim.

Before he had time to pull the trigger, Sergeant Larchmont's arm had encircled his throat, and another arm had expertly swung to the gun hand and disarmed him. The Browning clattered to the floor. Larchmont looked up at Sunny and Alex. "I'm sorry," he said. "I just realized how weird it was. They would have telephoned first. The consulate, I mean. Any idea who he is?"

Sunny collapsed into a straight-backed chair. "His name's Billy St. Clair," she said.

"Sinclair?" Larchmont looked alert. "Any relation?"

"No, no," she said patiently, enunciating clearly. "*Saint* Clair." Then she looked up at Alex. "The man in the train. The man who died, the young man in seersucker, I thought he said Sinclair. But I bet he was warning me. Saying 'St. Clair.'" She turned angrily to Billy. "Did you kill that young man on the train?"

Billy was weeping now. He wasn't listening properly.

"Train?" he said vaguely. "Oh. That. Not on my orders. Fellow went too far. Just wanted my man to be the only one to be following you. He got a bit heavy-handed with the competition."

"Heavy-handed?" said Sunny, furious now. "He killed that young man. And you were ready to kill us. It's horrible. You're crazy."

Alex put an arm around her shoulder as Larchmont maneuvered a pair of handcuffs around Billy's wrists. "No, not crazy. Just a spy."

Billy stood a little straighter now and faced them directly.

"Billy," said Alex sternly, "you didn't have to kill us. You could have let us live and you could've gone to Russia. Didn't you ever consider it?"

Billy shuddered. "Not for a minute," he said.

"Right," said Sir Raymond Phillips with a crisp military inflection. He stood in the little RCMP headquarters with his hands behind his back, his posture erect, surveying Sunny and Alex, Larchmont, and MacNab. Billy had remained in a cell by himself while they talked. Phillips hadn't been too keen on having Larchmont hear the whole setup, but he could tell the young man was keen on a career with the service. He felt he could count on his loyal silence. A nice promotion would guarantee it. And all in all the fellow seemed capable.

"Larchmont, I hope you'll agree there's no purpose in holding Mr. MacNab here. He's a local, simply acting as an, er, assistant to Mr. Markoff here.

"As for Mrs. Sinclair, I can't think of any reason to hold her, either."

"She did enter Canada with a false passport," said Larchmont primly.

"For Christ's sake, how do you know that?" said Sir Raymond. "Where is the damned thing anyway?"

Larchmont produced the document.

"I'm embarrassed about that," said Sunny. "It belongs to my cousin. She doesn't know I have it."

Sir Raymond riffled through the pages. "Hmm. Well, let me worry about it, will you? We'll send the thing over to Oslo and have someone find it on the street or something. Get it back to her. How's that sound?"

Sunny beamed. Sir Raymond really was a gallant old gentleman of the old school, and very handsome with his silver hair and well-tailored portliness. Of course, he was about her age, she assumed, but he had an old-fashioned avuncular quality that made him seem from another generation.

"Now, Larchmont," continued Sir Raymond, "seems to me the best thing to do is to round up the damned Russians Markoff here says are on that island. That'll corroborate his rather fantastic story. And, mind you, it'll also present us with a ticklish diplomatic situation, requiring complete discretion." Sir Raymond seemed to hiss the last word, and Larchmont looked nervous.

"Yes, sir."

"How's your Russian, Larchmont?"

Larchmont made a gargling sound. "Russian?" he said after a pause.

"Thought so. We'll have to take Markoff here. If he was able to talk to the one fellow they captured, I imagine his Russian's pretty good. Now I propose you round up a party of men to go out there with us. Meanwhile, I'll have to talk to Ottawa. Russians landing on a Canadian beach." He shook his head. "It's fantastic." He leaned to Larchmont. "Naturally, the conversation will have to be scrambled. I can't go through your regular local switchboard." Larchmont looked suitably impressed. "I'll take you down to the telephone office," he said. "We'll have the operator clear out and hold all local calls while you get through."

"Fine. And as for Mr. St. Clair," said Sir Raymond, "he'll have plenty to answer for, it sounds like. I don't see any reason to pursue the assault with intent to kill business. I think he'd be more useful back in Washington, answering a few questions. I can't imagine these two will want to press charges.''

"One more thing, sir," said Larchmont hesitantly. "Douglas Fairbairn's outside. He's the editor for a local paper. He says he hears there's plenty going on here. Shall I get rid of him?"

"Hell, no. Won't work. We'll think of something."

Alex had chosen the largest teddy bear at the Vancouver airport. Helping him choose from among the collection of expensive stuffed animals had rather depressed Sunny. It was so obvious that guilty traveling fathers who neglected their children bought gifts like this in desperation at the airport. And seeing Alex carrying the giant animal with its snub-nosed face, she couldn't help but think that an extravagant present for his grandson wouldn't begin to rebuild his relationship with Marina. Still, it was some kind of a start.

They settled into their seats on the San Francisco-bound flight. Alex would get off there. Sunny would transfer to a Tucson flight. The bear was awkward, but finally Alex stowed it above them and settled into the aisle seat with his Vancouver *Sun* and *Time* magazine.

She welcomed the few moments of the ascent, where the *whoosh* of the engine made conversation impossible. She leaned back in the seat, closed her eyes, and imagined herself back at home. She missed, all of a sudden, the hot sun, the pool, the familiar clunk of her refrigerator, the sound of the newspaper hitting her porch every morning, all the funny little things that made up the day.

When the seat belt signs went off and a blue haze drifted up from the smoking section, she turned to Alex. "I'm so glad to be going home," she said. "It seems like years."

"For me, it has been." He smiled. He was handsome when he smiled, but there was always something sad about the eyes. There always had been. Sunny decided that the melancholy she'd found attractive when she was younger was now simply painful to observe.

"I wish to God Chandler Smith were going home," she said, turning away.

"Who knows?" said Alex. "I told you. We searched every inch of that island. Including the tunnel. Either the Russians killed him and hid the body somewhere very clever, or he swam away. Or floated off on a log. It *is* physically possible."

"I'll always remember him at the bottom of that damn tunnel, looking up at us from underground. While we went up into the fresh air."

"It was his choice, Sunny. There was a time I would have made a choice like that." He looked at her thoughtfully. "As a matter of fact, I did make a choice like that. When I left London in 1945."

"Wasn't much of a life, was it?"

He shrugged. "For a long time I thought it was exciting. That stimulation kept me going."

She understood only too well the kind of excitement he meant. She suppressed the guilty knowledge. "You're all crazy," she said, leaning back into the cushions of her seat, adjusting the button on the arm rest so she could lean back even further. "You. Chandler, if he's alive. And Billy."

"You know, I never knew Billy was such a sentimental old guy."

"Sentimental? He was ready to kill us so he wouldn't have to share a bathroom with six families in Moscow." Sunny was genuinely angry again, thinking of Billy.

"But Sunny, he could have killed me years ago. It wouldn't have been hard. He must have realized years ago that I knew about his first mission for the Soviets. Instead of killing me he lured me into self-exile.

"Of course, I was easy to lure. I was fed up and jumpy."

"Paranoid," said Sunny, thinking of Chandler Smith's

remark, "I would say, from your escape tunnel. Really, Alex, what made you think you'd ever need it?"

He laughed. "But I did," he said simply.

She laughed, too, and turned her head to look at him. "So you did." After a pause she said, "Alex, were you in Tucson a month or so ago? That's what the men in the crystal warehouse said."

He nodded. "As a matter of fact I was. I was doing a little banking south of Mexico. Came back through Tucson."

"I guess you were spotted. You didn't . . . hole up anywhere, did you?"

"Seems to me I drove on to Phoenix and stayed at a motel," he said. "Why do you ask?"

She told him about the guesthouse, about the scrawled soap message on her mirror. "Who would have done that?"

Alex smiled. "Did it make you more anxious to find me?"

"I think so. It all seemed to tie in, made it less ridiculous for me to keep looking."

"Then it was a good idea," said Alex. "Of Billy's. Just the theatrical touch he might add. He probably planned to tell you later I'd been spotted in town, but you disappeared before he could."

"He was rather remarkable," she said. "I wonder what will become of him." She closed her eyes again and listened to the rustle of Alex's newspaper.

"It won't be pleasant." Suddenly he shook her arm. "Sunny, take a look at this?"

She opened her eyes and looked at the newspaper. She pushed it away so she could see better. The headline read: "Russ Fishermen Rescued." There, in a smudgy photograph, stood six barely discernible figures in dark clothing. Several of them wore watch caps.

"It's our Russians," she whispered. The story, little more than a caption, really, said: "Six members of a Russian fishing crew were escorted back to the Russian fishing fleet by the Canadian Coast Guard after they were rescued off a small island near Port Elizabeth yesterday. Their fishing boat sank two days ago, and they had been camped on the deserted island, according to Sergeant Glenn Larchmont, RCMP, Port Elizabeth.''

''Notice anything wrong with this picture?'' said Alex.

She turned to him. ''There were six of them,'' she said. ''And one of them burned to death in your house. So there should be five.''

''That's right.''

He handed her his reading glasses and she used one lens as a magnifying glass. Beneath a watch cap, his face turned slightly from the camera, she made out the distinctive features of Billy St. Clair.

''But why?'' she demanded.

Alex shrugged. ''Could be a lot of reasons.'' He flipped the paper back to page one and tapped the lead story, about an important Soviet-Canadian wheat deal. ''Or maybe it's an exchange. We'll never know.''

''Funny it made the papers,'' said Sunny, frowning.

''That local reporter doesn't know it, but he just missed the biggest scoop in Canada,'' said Alex. '' 'Russ Invade.' Not to mention 'CIA Shootout.' The Canadians are pretty touchy about that sort of thing. I guess Ray patched everything up as well as he could. Still, I can't imagine what the old man will say when he hears Billy slipped through the net.''

The stewardess came by with a tray. Sunny opted for a cup of coffee. Alex took tea.

''I hate the whole business,'' said Sunny, surprised at her own remark. ''I guess it took this last jaunt to make me realize it.''

''I'm glad you went out one more time,'' he said. ''I think you saved me. From Billy, who would have found me eventually. And from myself.''

She was worried he was going to be sentimental. Thank

God it was just tea he was drinking; he couldn't toast her with some sentimental Norwegian-style toast. She realized how much she'd had to since she'd got back into the life of a spy, starting with Billy's dinner at the Arizona Inn.

"Sunny, after a while in San Francisco I'd like to come out to Tucson and see you. Would that be all right?"

She looked at him carefully. He looked like a stranger, really, but underneath there was someone more familiar, an old friend. She smiled. "That would be lovely," she said.

Epilogue

THE OLD MAN favored Chandler Smith with a beatific smile. "You did a great job, Smith. You know that, don't you?"

Smith grinned, relaxed into the chair, and said, "Thank you."

"Message came through loud and clear. Not a breath of CIA about the whole thing with the Canadians. You got in, did the job, and got out clean." The old man neglected to mention that after he'd received Smith's message he'd sent a car out to Billy's house only to find the bird had flown. Why dwell on failure? And as for the Canadians turning him over to the Russians, that was well outside Smith's purview. No, now was the time to tell the boy what a splendid job he'd done.

"As a matter of fact, Smith, you got out so clean we've got a new assignment for you. Now, you can refuse this, of course, but with the fire and all, and a body in it, and the fact that you're single, no close relatives—well, we'd like to list you as deceased. It'll give us the opportunity to create a new identity for you. You can do some important things for us, unencumbered by your own identity. We're fixing it all up for you now. What do you think?"

Smith's grin faded, and there was a flicker in his eye that lasted merely a second, before he smiled again and said, "Of course." That little flicker could have been fear or it could have been loneliness. The old man noticed it, but he smiled a jolly smile. "It will be," he said, "pretty exciting stuff, I imagine."